COUNTER POINT

Book 1

HEATH'S POINT

Suspense

Marji Laine

(Clembine)
Eph. 3:20-21

Marji Laine

Write Integrity Press
Counter Point
© 2016 Marji Laine

ISBN-13: 978-1-944120-11-5
ISBN-10: 1-944120-11-4
Ebook ISBN: 978-1-944120-12-2

This book is a work of fiction. Names, characters, places, and incidents are either products of the author's imagination or used fictitiously. Any similarity to actual people and/or events is purely coincidental.

Scripture quotations marked "NIV" are taken from The New International Version ®NIV ®. Copyright © 1973, 1978, 1984, 2011 by Biblica, Inc. ™ Used by permission of Zondervan. All rights reserved worldwide. www.zondervan.com.

Scriptures marked "ESV" are from The Holy Bible, English Standard Version ® (ESV ®), copyright © 2001 by Crossway, a publishing ministry of Good News Publishers. Used by permission. All rights reserved.

Scriptures marked "KJV" are from The Holy Bible, the Authorized (King James) Version.

Scriptures marked "NASB" are from The Holy Bible, New American Standard Bible. Copyright © 1960, 1962, 1963, 1968, 1971, 1972, 1973, 1975, 1977, 1995 by The Lockman Foundation.

Published by Write Integrity Press, PO Box 702852, Dallas, TX 75370.

Find out more about the author: Marji Laine
Or email her at: AuthorMarjiLaine@gmail.com
www.WriteIntegrity.com

Printed in the United States of America.

Dedication

I dedicate this, my first published novel,
to my mom, Sharon Starks.
Without her challenge almost six years ago,
I might never have committed to this
wonderful writing career.
I love you, Mama.

Marji Laine

Some trust in chariots and some in horses,
but we trust in the name of the Lord our God. ~ Psalm 20:3 NIV

Chapter 1

Villa Montes, Chiapas, Mexico

"A boy." Sevilla clapped his hands. The smack echoed against the bare adobe dome. "He will be a fine boy." He beat his boot heels on the marble floor. His black beard bounced against his white tunic. "Ha. Go upstairs, wife. Lie down. Rest."

"I have plans for the afternoon." Oleta took a step backward, putting the leather sofa between them. Her large eyes wary. But her middle already showed evidence of his child.

"You will do as I say." He snapped in her direction and put his back to her. His child would be the heir to his business. His kingdom. He must be strong and healthy. "Go now and take care of my son."

"He is my son, too." The woman's voice cracked. She pressed her back against the wall.

She tested his good humor. His eyes hardened as he shot her a glare. His hands fisted at his side, prepared to take action on her

5

insolence.

But this was supposed to be a joyful time. He relaxed his muscles and applied a measured smile under his black whiskers. "Be careful, Oleta. I cannot guarantee that my gratitude will last too far beyond my son's birth."

She stiffened. Good. She should be scared. She'd seen enough to know her fortunate circumstances and to be thankful for them.

Sidestepping out of his study, she scurried up the stairs. Her heels clicking like the little mouse she was. Popping in a hollow manner. The sounds grew louder. She gasped as glass broke, echoing in the entrance of his villa.

"Oleta?" He stepped toward the great hall.

"*Señor* Sevilla." Two from his security. Good. He needed answers.

"Go, check on Oleta. Make sure my son is all right."

Captain Ortega gestured to the other man. "We must get you to safety."

"Another drill? These are getting tiresome."

"They prepare your security team to keep you safe, sir." Ortega ushered him through the thick hallway to his helicopter hangar.

The other man had seen to Oleta. "Make sure my wife comes."

The captain touched his earpiece and issued the order.

Sevilla climbed aboard the revving bird and looked back.

Ortega grew pale. "We must go." He climbed aboard.

"Not until Oleta arrives. She is carrying my son. My heir." His humor returned. A young prince to carry on his legacy.

The angled roof sections lifted.

"Stop. I will not leave without her."

"We have to go, Señor." Ortega strapped a belt around Sevilla and shouted at the pilot.

"I will have your head." Sevilla kicked at the man, willing him to fall out of the gaping side of the transport. No such luck.

Ortega pulled the sliding door closed as they cleared the roof. Pings hit the heavy metal siding.

"What is that? Is something wrong with the rotor?"

The copter lurched forward and accelerated.

"Gunfire, Señor."

"You idiot. You left Oleta back there."

"I am sorry, sir. Fernandez reported that she was dead when he reached her. Shot on the stairs."

No. Bile gathered in his mouth. "She carried my son. The coming leader of the Montes Cartel."

"There is no more Montes Cartel, sir." Ortega shouted over the pounding of the blades. "There is only you, me, and our pilot."

"What are you saying?" What about his soldiers? His loyal followers? His faithful ones who would die before injury befell him? "The cartel lives."

"All of your property is under siege except for the bunker near Asmirandu." Ortega wiped sweat from his eyes with the back of his hand. "A few men there. And the *federales* know nothing about the compound."

"Asmirandu." Sevilla growled the village name. "His home."

"The missionary?"

"He did all of this. His noble report in the face of fear." The man would pay. "He has no idea what fear looks like."

"I will kill him myself, Señor."

"No." Sevilla tapped his fingertips together. "I want him to worry. And then see everything that he loves destroyed. As he has destroyed everything that is mine."

"Most of what he loves is in America."

"Then I will go to America." He spat out the hated word. "By the time I am finished with Raymond Johnson, he will understand true terror."

Heath's Point, Texas

"We've lost contact."

The shout, spurred on by a January gust, flew past Cat McPherson without fully engaging her brain. "You did what?"

Violet Alexander rarely came to the diner at sunset, but Cat's focus was on the needy people who waited in the treacherous cold for dinner. She stepped off the stoop of Mac's Diner, handing a boxed meal to a dirty-faced man dressed in clothes much too large for him. "Do you have shelter for tonight?"

He nodded.

"Got him a spot near mine, Miss Cat." Dash, a regular for as long as Cat could remember, put his hand on the younger man's shoulder. "I'll take care of 'em."

She smiled and handed Dash a meal. The man's wide smile showed his gratitude. "You such a blessing, Miss Cat. Can't tell ya how thankful I was to know you'd keep serving meals after your daddy passed."

Cat's mouth twitched. She wished Dad were there. Talking about Jesus. Praying over the meal. How could she ever fill his shoes? "Sunset dinners are way too important to let them go." And she'd do everything in her power to keep the diner profitable, as long as Dad's silent partner didn't get in the way, if only to keep serving these dinners.

Rubbing her hands on her blue jeans, she hoped to ignite heat and restore feeling to her fingers. Vi came closer.

Cat paused. Her hand steadied the rolling cart just inside the door. The chilling gale rested a moment. A warm breath from the heater inside caressed Cat's frigid cheeks. "I'm so sorry, Vi. I couldn't hear you over the wind."

She caught a glimpse of Violet's face. The woman's puffy, red eyes, a contradiction to her usually flawless makeup, shook Cat from her routine. The rare sight of a not-having-it-all-together Vi shoved the words back through Cat's brain, this time engaging it. *We've lost contact.*

The nerve endings along Cat's spine filled with ice. The wind picked up, whipping her curly ponytail into a knotted frizzle. She grasped the edge of her red wool coat as the gale snatched at the hem. Trying to shout over the force of the blast used all her energy, and she struggled to form the single syllable that came out as a broken whisper.

"Ray?" Her heart lurched at the name she hadn't uttered in months.

Vi bit her bottom lip.

Cat's breath came in sharp gasps as her eyes locked onto Ray's mom. "Is he all right?" Surely the message contained more information. Some hope. He had to come back.

But the woman stood silent as tears pooled against the bottom rim of her eyes.

No.

Dash laid a hand on her shoulder. "I can finish handing out these here dinners if you need some time."

She stared at him for a full second, her thoughts whirling to some wilderness where Ray was trapped, unable to return, or maybe … Shutting her eyes against her worst fears, she nodded. "Thank you."

"Come inside." Vi pulled Cat out of the frigid air and into the

9

diner, warmed from hours of grilling. Aromas of stale frying oil mixed with freshly baked chocolate cake failed to offer Cat their usual familiar comfort. Her mind refused to settle on one thought. Like when the doctors told her they could do nothing more for her father.

This couldn't be happening. Even with Ray's silence when he left for his mission field, she still dreamed of a future together, the ministry they had spent hours talking about. Was that dream gone forever? Lifting her eyes, she hoped to ask more questions.

Vi lowered into the nearest chair. Her hands folded in her lap. Her gaze somewhere between the edges of the red laminate table.

Oh God, comfort Violet right now.

Cat couldn't imagine losing Ray, but when Vi looked at him, she saw her baby. Unwilling to allow her angst freedom, she hurried into the kitchen. She had to get control of her emotions. Before she caused Violet even more pain.

Cat grabbed a pair of sodas from the fridge and rejoined Vi. The hollow clomps of her boots on the black and white checkerboard linoleum reverberated in her chest. Empty. Alone.

She pushed the ache aside and set the Dr Pepper in front of Vi. "Have some. You'll feel better. Or can I get you some of Grady's leftover cookies?"

"No, no. I'll be fine." She tugged a napkin out of the table canister and folded it. Resetting her can on the makeshift coaster, she popped it open.

Cat opened her Diet Pepsi and observed the woman, her eyes still rimmed in red, though wiped dry. Petite with short, highlighted hair and the same chocolate eyes as Ray. If anyone had a right to crumble it was his mother, but Vi stood strong. Coming to offer comfort to Cat instead.

"What is the board doing about it?" Cat wrapped her hands around the can and took a sip, forcing the bubbles down with a loud gulp.

Vi stared at her soda. "They've contacted Ray's ministry partners, but those missionaries live over a hundred miles from his village."

"Wherever *that* is." Cat chided herself immediately for letting her frustration have voice. Especially around Vi.

But the fact that Ray had told her nothing, advancing no trust whatsoever, cut as deeply as his leaving her behind. Almost as deeply. Taking the future they expected to share for himself and leaving without her was a betrayal she could never forget.

But she'd always expected him to return.

"Ray's journal noted an appointment to preach last Sunday at the little church he helped to build, but he logged in nothing further."

"Haven't they contacted the US Embassy? Called the police? Anything?" Surely there were ways to find him. She bounced her right leg.

"Things are different in other countries, Cat. You know that." She sniffed.

Cat laid her hand across Vi's. "We'll find out this is just a mistake. I bet you hear from him tomorrow. He'll be fine and have a good laugh at the worrywarts back home."

Sad eyes lifted. "I have learned that some of the surrounding villages have been contacted." She pulled another napkin from the canister and rubbed her nose.

"So, maybe he went someplace else. Maybe he tried a new place and has yet to update his journal." Cat could believe that. And Vi needed other options to think about besides …

"Someone from one of the communities responded to the contact."

Cat glanced at Vi's reflection in the darkened glass of the storefront. The woman opened her mouth and shut it again. Beyond that virtual mirror, the small group that had huddled outside dispersed with their dinner packages.

"What did they say?" Despite the warmth of the diner, she shivered and jumped as Dash opened the door.

He shoved the cart through, staying well outside the doorframe. "You all right in here?"

She waved at him. "We're okay. Thank you for your help."

The old man whose girth didn't match his nickname stepped back a few steps and waved at Cat through the window.

"Probably as close to being inside a building as Dash has been for some time."

Vi's jaw muscle twitched briefly. The corner of her mouth angled downward.

Cat's attempt to lighten the air failed. "Oh, Vi, you know God is with Ray. You told me yourself how He led him to the mission. Don't give into fear now."

Brave words. And she tried to believe them.

Tears brimmed Vi's lashes again. "There's word that the mission fell under attack."

Outside Asmirandu, Chiapas, Mexico

"*¡Pégalos!*" Get them.

Voices of the hooded attackers chasing Ray Alexander echoed under the canopy of trees. He stumbled over briars and weaved between gnarled trunks. Branches slapped his face as he followed the man who pulled him from a chaos of shouts and gunfire at the small church he helped to build.

Dodging the vine tentacles, he pushed aside the fronds of

invading plants along an invisible path. His lungs burned. His shoulder screamed pain. Dislocated? *Keep moving.* He focused on the man, Miguel, a recent transfer to his mission team. He dared not lose sight of him.

Not here. Especially not now.

Voices somewhere behind him called out again. His own crashing boot steps far overwhelmed the sounds of his pursuers. Had he widened the gap?

Miguel halted then folded his frame into the fronds of a large fern. Huffing, Ray tucked himself behind a giant elephant ear leaf nearby. He struggled to listen over his heaving chest. His blood-stained shirt clung to his limp left arm.

Shouts began again. Farther away, he felt sure this time.

"Are you okay?" Miguel's hoarse whisper blended with the jungle noises.

Ray nodded. He yanked the leather belt from his waistband. Lassoing his middle, he lashed his useless arm to his torso.

Miguel bobbed his head. Time to move on.

A steep ditch lay on his right, and Miguel dropped over the edge. Ray slipped from his cover. Without hesitation, he scooted down the ridge. Angular trees provided regular braces on the way. He practically fell against the first, catching himself with his good arm. The same technique worked for the second descent. Reaching for the next trunk, he stepped into a rotted log. The misstep propelled him into the rough and broken bark, left-shoulder first. He gritted his teeth against a choked cry. Pain blinded him. Miguel glanced back and changed course, but Ray waved him on. Breathing deep, he pushed off the tree and forged ahead.

His rescuer hesitated while Ray closed the gap. At the bottom, a gully with a trickling stream provided them with secretive travel. Downed trees and boulders made the path look like something out of a video game.

But the men searching for them weren't playing.

"Not sure how many are dead at the mission." A man's low voice in sharp Spanish staccato floated down from behind the heavy undergrowth on the ridge above them. Obviously he'd been involved with the attack.

Ahead, Miguel paused and held up his hand. Ray halted.

"The missionary got away, but we're looking for him."

Ray went cold. He'd received threats from the drug cartel when he helped to shut down their traffic within his area. His actions had even flushed out the powerful leader of the cartel, Sevilla. But that placed Ray in a precarious position. The *policía* hadn't arrested the drug lord yet, but Ray was hopeful. Could Sevilla have arranged for the attack on Ray's mission? Was he really that powerful?

After a pause, the one-sided conversation above him continued. "We believe he headed to Dumaus, and when we find him, we will bring him to the compound as instructed."

Ray recognized the village name. He hoped Miguel had a different destination planned.

"Say again? The signal here is not so good." The man's voice rose. His footstep tramped closer in the undergrowth on the plateau.

Miguel motioned for Ray to crawl beneath the overhang created by a massive Montezuma Cypress on the edge of the eroded ravine. Soundlessly, Ray darted for cover, hunkered under a cascade of exposed roots.

"I've passed on the explicit instructions. Raymond Johnson will be taken alive."

A sliver of fear danced around the back of Ray's neck. Using a fake, utterly common, last name struck him as overkill at the onset of his mission. Now he thanked God that this powerful man couldn't trace him or his family. Good thing there weren't any other Johnsons in Heath's Point. But then, no one knew his hometown either.

The man's voice faded, but his intent had been clear. People—friends and brothers in Christ—had just given their lives so some insane man could prove his power to Ray. Sevilla gave little thought to the people of the church. He only wanted to destroy the pastor.

Guilt added more weight on his already heaving chest.

They waited for the silence to deepen. The music of birds and animals marked the absence of the phone-using marauder. Ray worried their delay allowed the hunters to get ahead of them. What if he and Miguel caught up to them while trying to escape?

Finally, Miguel stepped out and climbed up the roots.

He shimmied back down, rejoining Ray underneath. "I see no one."

"I must thank you. I owe you my life."

"You owe me nothing, my friend. I am happy I came to Asmirandu when I did."

Only a few days before the raid, Miguel had arrived from a village to the north. He'd brought with him some supplies for the mission and a letter of introduction from a missionary Ray had met a few times.

Miguel wiped the back of his hand across his forehead. "I saw the men heading for the mission, but I could not run fast enough to warn you."

"I'm still in your debt. I don't want to think of what might have happened if you had not pulled me out the back door." In truth, Ray didn't want to think about the raid at all, but he expected the scene to revisit him again and again.

Miguel took the lead again. They broke through the forest cover far too quickly to suit Ray. Miguel dashed across a large field of head-high grasses. Ray accelerated, but his guide disappeared into bobbing reeds. He hoped his steps remained straight. An accidental circle to return the way he came promised disaster.

Shots rang out behind him. The assassins had caught up. At least gunfire confirmed he ran in the right direction.

He climbed a hill. More shots went off. Running in a dark brown shirt through the waving tan stalks, he stood out like a cockroach on a wall. Ducking low, he veered right. Twelve paces. Then peeled to the left for seven. The soft *pffft* of bullets finding ground nearby made him dart right again.

Reaching the crest, Ray escaped into the shelter of thick forest.

Miguel waited for him inside the dark shadows. "Do you need to rest? We could stop."

"No!" His burning lungs couldn't waste air on words. And the crack of a shot hitting a nearby tree propelled him on.

Miguel led him through the outer edges of the Montes Azules Reserve that lay in Chiapas. The shouts from behind them faded, finally stopping altogether. Ray followed his guide's breakneck pace, desperate to reach safety before the dimness of jungle became the blackness of night.

They slowed to a jog when the growth thickened. Several times Miguel stopped to help Ray push through walls of vegetation. His shoulder ached and his cheek stung with every drop of sweat that found its way to a cut he'd received during the attack. Thankfully it stopped bleeding.

Thoughts of Cathy filled his head—the way she looked running through the hayfield, her bright red hair standing out among the stalks. Leaving her behind tore him apart but, at least, his lone departure kept her safe. What would he have done had she been at the mission with him? He shuddered.

With God's help, he hoped to see her again, though he knew things would never be the same between them.

Ray lost sight of Miguel in the filtering light. He'd ducked into a low arch in a mass of vines. Ray saw no other way around the layers of underbrush. Like the *Going on a Bear Hunt* book his mom used to read to him, the living barrier allowed no access around, over, or through the bushes. He had to follow Miguel and crawl under heavy branches. He thanked the Lord that he had tied up his arm to keep the lifeless thing out of the way.

He hit all fours—well, threes—hopping like a lame dog. He struggled through the labyrinth, army-crawling for the last few yards. Working his way out, Ray left the great wall of jungle. A western road that led to San Salbitaso lay under his knees.

At least the path didn't go near Dumaus, though the hunters might have changed course.

Ray's memories of the vicious surge, led by the four hooded men, hurt worse than the throbbing of his shoulder and his cheek put together. He had no idea who or how many, but people died in that little stucco building. His people. They had depended on him. He let them down. He didn't know how deeply the assassin's knife had slashed his cheek, but nothing cut as deeply as the consequences of his failure.

All of his failure.

Miguel stopped to look at his cheek before the setting sun removed all chances of seeing anything. "Your cut looks bad, amigo. Better stop and clean it."

"The airfield's close, right? Wait 'til we get there." Ray didn't pause. Let Miguel catch up with him for a change.

Hesitations caused this problem in the first place. Ray received threats but didn't take them seriously. Well, he believed them now. With people he cared for at risk, he dare not let his guard down.

He jogged to the rise above San Salbitaso. The valley spread below him like a panoramic photograph. The last rays of the sun illuminated the tiny village of thatched roofs cradled between two rocky hills. Though he likely viewed the beauty for the last time, he dared not pause to create a mental picture, as the camouflage of the jungle no longer protected them. The little-used road gave direction, but if Miguel found this washed-out, two-rutted track, those hunting them would have no problem. The remaining light faded. Dusk worked in their favor. He picked up the pace.

Safety neared, but uncertainty threatened to blast a hole in the net.

Though I walk through the valley of the shadow of death,
I will fear no evil,
for You are with me. ~ Psalm 23:4 NASB

Chapter 2

Cat turned her new Civic onto the two-lane highway toward Sunrise Inn. The new-car smell failed to enchant her. Funny how the vehicle lost its luster the day its purchaser died. Dad had been saving up to surprise her on her birthday last November. And he had. Standing there with cheeks puffed out in a big grin.

"I'd be a pedestrian the rest of my life if I could just have Daddy back, Lord." She tapped her foot against the mat. But Cat would never wish for her father to leave the Lord's presence. "I just miss him."

And please take care of Ray.

Lost. In the technological world around her, the whole concept seemed impossible. Surely, if she opened a weather satellite page and examined it closely enough, she'd find him.

She thought of Ray's senior picture safely tucked into her wallet. She'd had to work behind the photographer's back to coax that smile from him. Straight white teeth peeked between his curved lips. Such a tender look. Long lashes ringed his warm chocolate eyes. Dark hair, short on the sides with controlled waves on top.

He'd penned a short note on the back of it that she didn't have to see to remember. *For my Cathy, your Ray.*

He alone called her by the name. Like her mom had, but Momma's voice had been silenced long ago. "Oh God, please let me hear Ray's voice again."

She shook her head. *Stop torturing yourself.* He'd written the sweet message before they graduated. Before he left for college and the opportunities he found there. Before he'd forgotten they shared the dream to go into the mission field.

Together.

Dwelling on him did nothing but deepen the hole he'd left behind. First when he abandoned her and now, with this news.

Speeding was common on these backroads, but she took a curve faster than normal. Still, with the police chief as her godfather, she didn't need to worry about getting ticketed.

A loud explosion rocked the car. The wheel jerked out of her hand. The right side reeled. With an adrenaline shot, she slammed both feet on the brakes. Screeching tires silenced when the car shot over the edge of a steep embankment. Another loud pop. The world went white. She lost her breath as the airbag pressed her against the seat. She became weightless for a second. Her knees banged against the steering column. The car contacted solid mass and the glass beside her shattered.

Then, as though the earth bent its knees to receive her, she landed upright on a trampoline of some sort. The airbag drained with puffs of white powder and she found herself in the upper branches of a cottonwood tree overlooking Lake Grayson.

A branch gave, pitching her forward an inch. Shallow water below her. She still stood on the brake and braced her arms against the steering wheel. She didn't want to calculate the height.

Help me, Lord.

Her purse lay tangled at her feet and she lifted the strap with her foot to draw it closer. With the heavy leather bag to protect her hands, she punched through leftover shards of glass from the missing driver's side window. Then she hurled the bag as far up the bank as she could swing it. She hoped it didn't get caught in the tree or land in the water.

Another branch broke and the car leaned forward. Cat's stomach flipped. No airbag this time. A final limb gave way, tilting the car crazily to the right. She didn't know how far she fell, but the crash into the lake jarred her against her seat belt. Icy water splashed inside. She unlatched her restraint and anchored herself on the edge of the passenger seat as she attempted to climb through her open window. The car lurched, straightening in the water. She banged her head against the doorframe and lost her hold. Things spun for a second until she choked on a mouth full of water.

The interior filled up fast. She gasped and went under, feeling her way back to the window opening. Remaining glass shards pierced her hands. Her heavy coat weighed her down. She kicked it off and pushed against the steering column to break the water surface. Bubbles accompanied her as the black roof disappeared under the surface.

She couldn't stay there. She'd freeze, though the air wasn't much better. At least the wind had died somewhat with the sunset. Turning to shore, polar bear divers drifted through her mind. *Crazy people.*

One stroke. Two. Her arms felt like cement and her chin wouldn't stop wiggling. Another stroke. She'd be able to stand in a second. Just another couple of feet.

Her face went under and she jerked it back up. She could do this. She had to. Taking a deep breath, she let herself drift to the lake bottom. Only a short distance. Using all her strength, she pushed off, propelling toward shore. Again, she went under, bent her knees and kicked hard.

That was enough. Her hand scraped a large, rock outcrop. She paused for a moment, but visions of Jack's ending in *Titanic* crossed her mind. She might freeze to death, but she wasn't going to drown. She crawled onto the stone and rolled onto her back. "You g-g-got me this far, Lord." *Please, help me get warm.*

Pushing to her knees, she crawled further onto the shore and looked up at the mangled tree. Her purse should be somewhere close. The shadows created tar pits on the moonless landscape. She scanned the tree again. Easy to see where she'd been caught. Half the cottonwood had been torn away. She followed an invisible line from the missing half. The bag had to be within a few yards.

Searching with her hands, she huddled near ground, as much to avoid the frigid breeze as to find her bag. She finally touched leather instead of dry grass, rocks, and debris. She had a better arm than she thought. Pulling out her phone, she prayed for a signal and dialed 9-1-1.

Ray didn't breathe easily until the 747 rose from the tarmac, making Mexico City a sprawling Google map below. Had it only been a week since his escape to San Salbitaso?

Miguel had brought him that far then returned north to his previous village for the last week of his tour before he went home to San Diego. Ray didn't know how he could ever repay the man for his kindness, but he meant to try.

With his arm in a sling at his side and bandages covering half his face, he felt a little like a monster. The kid across the aisle must've thought so, too, peeking around his mom's ample middle with wide eyes. At least until Ray glanced his direction. Then he darted out of sight. An innocent diversion until the boy's mom looked up and caught Ray. The woman probably thought he had intellectual issues.

She winked, offering a flirtatious gleam.

Game over.

A bounce of turbulence made him reach for the armrest. Mom would've white-knuckled. Again the pain in her voice constricted his heart. He'd called his parents first thing this morning from Mexico City, his first opportunity. Mom cried. Shame on him for causing her such worry.

Leaning his head against the cushion, he thought of home. It had been so long. Even in his little town, things changed.

Like Mac's death. That was a shocker that hadn't even fully hit him yet. Cathy must've been devastated. He hadn't laid eyes on his precious redhead in four long years. Hadn't spoken to her since before he left for the field. He might be going home, but not to her. Their relationship had disappeared. By his own hand.

Who was she seeking comfort from during this difficult time?

Ray tugged his backpack out from under the seat. His wallet and passport alone came with him as he fled. He pulled out the folded cowhide and flipped open to the empty holder where Cathy's picture should have been. He'd kept it there all through college and three years on the mission field, even after his decision to leave her destroyed all hope for their life together.

He knew he hadn't removed it. Like some type of sign from above, every connection to her faded. If God willed for them to stay apart, why hadn't He removed Ray's desires?

Cat continued to shiver even after Dell Tate, Heath Point's

police chief, parked his cruiser in front of the Inn. Her skin stung as puffs of heat began to thaw her cheeks.

"Are you sure you don't want me to take you to the emergency room?"

"No. I'm f-fine." A trip to the regional hospital was the last thing she wanted. "A few bruises." She glanced at her hands in the dim light. "I could probably use a couple of bandages." Small trickles of blood remained, but the cuts, though not too deep, were jagged. "Myra can help me."

He supported her up the steps. "I called Ellis to let them know what happened."

"I hope you didn't worry them." Ellis and Myra Stone had been such a blessing when they asked her to move out to the inn after Dad's funeral. Probably so she wouldn't have to face the house in town alone, though they went on about how much they needed her help at the inn.

The door opened before she got to it.

"Cat, honey, are you all right?" Myra held out a large mug. Steam danced upward, laced with the rich fragrance of dark chocolate.

"Let's get her inside first, Sugar." Ellis walked her into the cozy sitting room and plopped onto the seat next to the fire. Dell followed.

"There now." Myra set the cup in Cat's hands.

She stifled the cry of pain as the mug handle grazed a cut but didn't hesitate to take a sip. The thick creamy flavor and the warm rush through to her stomach were worth the slight ache from her injury.

"Take care of those cuts." Dell took off, back to the crash site, though Cat couldn't fathom why he found her soggy car so interesting.

"Cuts?" Myra's eyebrows twisted.

Cat showed her hands to the couple. Ellis hurried from the room.

Myra surveyed the damage. "Dell said you had an accident. He didn't say you were injured. Do you need stitches?"

Ellis returned with a white First Aid box. "Don't fuss, sugar. He woulda taken her to the ER if he thought they needed stitches."

"They're just scratches really." Not exactly, but close enough to settle their minds.

"You're soaked through." Myra tucked the blanket tighter around her as Cat took another sip of chocolate.

Ellis doctored one of her hands. "How in the world did you end up in the lake?"

She shook her head. "Crazy story. I was driving here. Then the wheel just jerked."

"Blown tire?" Ellis swabbed a scratch across her palm.

She winced.

"On that brand new car?" Myra peeled back the paper of a Band-Aid.

Cat shrugged. "I guess." She took another sip. "I got lost in the airbag at that point. Then a big old cottonwood caught me."

"A tree?" Ellis set her cup on the table and began working on the next hand.

"I don't know what would have happened if it hadn't been there. Gave me time to throw out my purse." She didn't know why she even thought to. "I guess it was a reflex." And a blessing. Halfway between the inn and town, she'd have been in a bad way without her phone.

"Oh my gracious." Myra opened another bandage package. Tears glistened in the corners of her eyes. "You're lucky you weren't killed in the top of that brittle thing."

Ellis patted her knee and took the plastic strip. "Luck had

nothing to do with this."

Cat sipped her cocoa. He was right.

"Vi called. I suppose I should call her back." Myra hopped up and made for the kitchen.

"Morning is soon enough. She's already so worried about Ray." Cat had to raise her voice to be heard across the echoing foyer.

"I doubt she's the only one." Myra returned with a plate of shortbread cookies. "I don't want to pry, but I'm concerned about you."

"You're not prying. I'm fine. Really." If only Ray would be fine.

Myra set the plate down near Cat. She narrowed her eyes. "You're not fooling me. I know you still have feelings for Ray no matter how you deny it."

So much for not prying. Cat took a bite of the cookie, but the rich buttery flavor stuck in her throat. A drink of the warm chocolate washed the dry mass downward. "I'll always care about Ray." Tears stung her eyes. Her throat contracted before she finished her thought. She was divided over her anger at his betrayal and the feelings she still had for him.

She focused on her cocoa. "But I have to live my own life … here, helping you and Ellis with the inn and taking care of Dad's diner. I don't have time to think about might-bes when Ray returns."

If he ever returned. No, she couldn't fathom that. She took another bite of cookie, though her gut twisted so that the morsel threatened to cement itself to the back of her tongue.

"I think you consider the possibilities more than you say. You must know that Ray had his reasons for leaving." Ellis wrapped gauze across her palm.

She swallowed hard. Reasons he hadn't bothered to explain. A twinge shifted across her shoulders. If only he had spoken to her.

They could have worked things out. But none of that mattered now. Not if Vi's reports were true.

"I'm sure you're right. He just never shared them. But I don't want to rehash the past. Ray made his choice, and he didn't choose me. Simple as that." Not that simple, but assuring the couple of her contentment alleviated their concerns and got her out of twenty questions.

"Well, this place wouldn't run at all without you." He tucked the end of the second strip of gauze into her wrapped palm. Cat felt partially mummified.

And she knew better than to believe his claim. It ran fine for years with only the two of them and a cleaning service. Cat had helped out over the past several months, but only with projects when she wasn't working at the diner. Using both hands to pick up her mug, she took another sip of the chocolate, forcing the anchored blob of cookie to release its hold.

"And you are welcome here as long as you like. That won't change. I promise." Myra rose.

Cat stood and wrapped the dear lady in a hug. "I can't thank you and Ellis enough for all you've done." She duplicated the bear hug for Myra's husband.

"Oh poo." Myra collected her mug and plate. "Get some sleep, sweet girl. Things will feel better in the morning." She shuffled through the kitchen with Ellis in her wake.

Only after the two left did the futility of the woman's promise hit her. She could stay here. In someone else's home. In a solitary room with nothing more to show for herself than cheerleading trophies from high school.

Oh Lord, please have more in Your plan for me than that.

After arriving home well past midnight, Ray slept in the next morning. He met his mom in the kitchen and gave her cheek a quick kiss as he helped himself to a mug of coffee.

"You're up earlier than I expected." She sorted through a stack of mail on the desk built between massive shelving units. "You sure you caught up on your sleep?"

He nodded. She didn't need to know about his aches and pains, or his nightmares.

"A letter for you came this morning."

"Did you steam it open first?" He chuckled. If the mayor so much as sneezed, Mom, as chief operator of the Heath's Point grapevine, would be the first one to say, "God bless you."

"I guess from some of your friends down in Mexico?" She handed him the envelope. "It went to Philip at the church first, but of course he knew you'd taken that fake last name."

He glanced at the envelope. *Raymond Johnson* was printed in a bold slant above the national mission board's address. His mom kept up the chatter while he ripped open the empty edge of the envelope.

"Are you going over to visit Cat?"

"I thought I would." Thought? Try to keep him away. She'd been almost the only thing in his thoughts since his flight through the jungle.

"She'll be shocked to see you." A worry line appeared above his mother's brows. "I wish I had delayed telling her you were missing. But I felt she'd want to know as soon as possible."

Ray hated that he'd been unable to call until safely in the embassy in Mexico City. "How did she take Mac's death?"

"Hard." His mom wiped the lipstick off her mug and took another drink. "And I think the news of you hurt even more because of the loss she already felt."

The muscle on the side of his neck tensed. She had every

reason to hate him. He should avoid her and let her live her life. "You haven't told her I'm back?"

"When would I have done that?"

He sure couldn't just barge into Mac's without warning. "Maybe you should call her." He set the mug down and traced his finger around the wet rim, coaxing a tiny squeal from the pottery. "I don't want to scare her."

And he did have to see her. Had to do his best to make amends. Even if only to salvage their friendship. That relationship alone could be enough for him.

Returning his attention to his letter, he noted the Mexican stamps. Maybe this was a note about the attack? He pulled out the single sheet. Something small drifted out and fluttered to the ground, but Ray didn't reach for it. The signature caught his eye.

Sevilla.

Mom reached down and came up with a picture. "Ray, isn't this the photo you had of Cat?"

He glanced at the picture he'd been carrying in his wallet. Until it disappeared. The face had been torn off, leaving only her orange-blond hair tumbling over her cream-colored blouse. He flipped it and found part of the note she had written on the back. *Your Cathy.*

Flattening the letter on the table, he lowered himself onto a cushioned chair. His mother came close behind him, her hands on his shoulder.

I warned you to leave Chiapas. The dead you left behind are on your head. I am not a man to be played with. As you destroyed my life and my family, I have destroyed your life in my country. And I will destroy all that you love. Even in your country. Beginning with "your Cathy."

"Omigosh, Ray. You need to show this to Dell. He'll want to

put Cat in protection or something."

Something. Cathy needed security. The kind that Ray should have given to his mission. But that was before the attack. Before he witnessed Sevilla's power.

She peered at him from under troubled eyebrows. "What are we going to do? You know how independent Cat is. Worse with Mac's illness. But I'm worried."

"Good reason to be." He pointed to the bottom of Cathy's picture. *Heath's Point High School* stood out in gold letters against a shaded background. "I never told anyone where I was from."

O LORD, in the morning You hear my voice;
in the morning I prepare
a sacrifice for You and watch. ~ Psalm 5:3 ESV

Chapter 3

Cat felt like she lifted a cement truck. Aside from the scratches on her face, both knees looked painted in a dull gray, and a long purple line cut from her shoulder, across her chest, and disappeared under her right arm. At least her hands hadn't swelled. Shallow cuts like she'd hoped.

Ignoring the pain of every movement, she wrapped her letter jacket tighter around her, wondering if they'd salvaged her wool coat.

Dell had promised last night to come get her. Not much of a morning person, he'd groaned when she called to remind him. She wondered how long he and his officers stayed at the lake. But he probably got more sleep than she had. Besides her discomfort, thoughts of Ray haunted her all night. His disappearance on top of the loss of Dad and the accident—no wonder ugly dreams tormented.

She straightened her shoulders and breathed in crisp, invigorating air. Both actions hurt her chest, but she ignored the pain. She'd have to do a lot more than stand and breathe at the diner today.

Working up her internal Pollyanna, she descended the seven

31

wooden planks as normally as possible. This day needed every ounce of optimism she could muster. Especially with all the questions about last night.

She was alive. That thought should have thrilled her. "But really, my car? How much more can I lose, Lord?" She repented of her ungrateful attitude. God caught her in that tree as surely as the catcher on the Rangers baseball team caught a curve ball. And then He eased her into the lake and led her right back out of it again.

She didn't want to think what might've been if the tree hadn't been there.

She hiked out to the edge of the lot that faced the all-but-abandoned freeway. Her steps on the gravel resounded like orchestrated crashes in an otherwise unearthly silence. She paused and strained for echoing sounds. Had there been other footsteps hiding within the noise of her own?

The yellowish light from the Sunrise Inn sign cast an eerie glow on the dead grass and the white fence. She unlatched the gate and hauled it open for Dell's cruiser. Then she faced the dark edges of the lot again.

Why such a creepy feeling? She'd lived in this area all her life. And on a cold morning like this, she'd hardly see any mangy coyotes. The darkness surrounding the lot revealed nothing. Wait. Had she heard something? A shuffle. A click?

A tiny light flared.

Cat gasped. Had she really …?

Soundless red and blue flashed across the landscape down the farm-to-market road from town.

She released her breath. Dell's cruiser lights. That had to be what she'd seen.

The chief turned into the black asphalt lane that bordered the freeway and led to the inn's lot. "Too early in the morning for this nonsense." He unfolded himself from the sedan and pressed his straw-colored cowboy hat on his graying hair. "You feeling better?"

"You're late. Think you coulda hurried a bit more? Maybe turned on the siren to get here faster?"

"I turned on the lights for you. But it's not likely that my rushing over here with the singer blaring is gonna make the people who keep normal time very happy." He pulled out a paper mug. "I visited the truck stop for some cocoa."

Her chin sank. Ungrateful again. "I'm sorry I snapped."

"Gracious, Kitten. If that's the worse chewing I get today, I'll call it Christmas." He slapped a smug look on his pinkish, jowled face.

She climbed into his passenger seat. Dell's sweet thought moistened her eyes, though she was desperately weary of tears. She had little time for them anyway, with the sky graying toward the east.

An hour later, she still dealt with delay that the cuts on her hands caused, impeding her work. The grill, not fully warmed, caused issues when gruff Mr. Havesheim came in for his morning biscuits and gravy. Grady, her cook, nuked some of the leftovers from yesterday morning. If Havesheim knew the difference, he didn't say anything. Luckily he hadn't wanted bacon.

"You're my hero," she whispered through the order window to the burly, middle-aged man on the other side. The grill finally started to sizzle with the aroma of pancakes and sausage.

He grinned. "Dun learned my skill from the most famous kitchens in Heath's Point, Texas."

She chuckled, determined to turn her rough start around. She poured her charm on the customers of her breakfast rush. Not always so easy with some of the town's prominent citizens."

Mrs. Williora Heath and her daughter Lila fell into that category. The self-appointed matriarch and her family had long avoided Mac's Diner. Probably stemming from the animosity between Dad and Mr. Heath. Long-time hard feelings of the way Dad ran Mac's. Especially since Dad's majority interest in the diner forced Heath to collect his profits with no say in the day-to-day business.

This morning, they marched in. Two of them anyway. Mrs. Heath eyed the glass door while her daughter rubbed her finger along the vinyl. They finally settled into chairs and waved away Cat's menus.

"I'd like one of Grady's cinnamon rolls, only could you have him butter the top instead of ice it?" More of a demand than a request.

"It's already got white icing on it. But he can butter it as well." Cat loved Grady's rolls with a thin layer of butter across the glaze.

"Just have him scrape the icing off, then."

Really? Scrape off the icing?

The highlighted head tilted to the ceiling as she seemed to consider more. "I'd like hot water and Lady Gray tea bags, several."

Cat layered on her best smile. "And for you, Lila?"

The Goth-dressing girl was actually a year older than Cat, and twice her size, but she looked more like a rebellious teenager. "Just coffee. Black."

"You should eat something." Her mother's quiet tone didn't hide the directive. Mrs. Heath definitely ran things in her circles.

"Fine." Lila huffed and snatched a menu from Cat.

The other one slipped out of her hand and fell to the floor. Cat reached for it. "No worries." Not like the girl had apologized.

The diamond in the side of Lila's nose winked at Cat as the overhead lights caught it. "Gimme some bacon, and one blueberry pancake. One egg, over easy. And don't bother bringing it if the yolk breaks. I won't pay for it." She laid the menu on the table and shoved it toward Cat. "And I want one a' them sweet rolls, only pick the raisins out of it."

"Of course." Like mother, like daughter. Cat picked up the menu and scooted away before either of them added, or subtracted, any other details.

After they received and devoured their food, they scowled at Cat across the register counter. "I can't leave you any tip in good conscience. Lila found a raisin in her sweet roll and there were still several chips of icing left on mine." Mrs. Heath handed over the exact change of the tab. Her lips pursed.

Was she kidding? Cat shouldn't have been surprised. Though one of the wealthiest families in town, the Heaths always made excuses for not donating to any fund. And from what she'd heard, they never left tips. Only complaints.

Cat stared at the retreating backs of the irritating women. Their foul-mood germs seeped under her skin. She straightened and prayed for grace. "Have a nice day, Mrs. Heath, Lila."

They pushed through the door without a backward glance. Just as well. Her voice sounded pleasant, but her face refused to join the charade.

Father, help my attitude. Help me glorify You. Even today.

"I'm impressed. I'd have spat in Lila's eggs." Daisy Sanderson set down her tray and adjusted her apron.

"You wouldn't dare." Despite herself, the look she imagined on Lila's face made Cat giggle.

"Oh, you know I'd never. Fun to think about, though." She picked up a coffeepot and filed through the tables, refilling mugs.

Daisy had a way to pick her up at just the right moment.

"Order up." Cat ripped a sheet from her pad and slipped the note into the order wheel with a half dozen others, she turned the metal ring, so Grady could see the message as she announced it. "Turkey Supreme—mayo."

"For breakfast?" The cook flipped several pancakes as he

raised his eyebrows.

Cat shrugged. "Turkey Supreme—mayo."

"Humph." He filled and folded one of his signature omelets. "Well I'll tell him you said so."

"Tell who? Huh?" Cat paused at the window, but when she took in Grady's face, she realized she'd bit into a joke of some sort.

His ivory grin contrasted the deep chocolate tones in his face. "I dun heard you call the mayor a supreme turkey with my own ears."

Cat smirked before turning to the register where yet another customer scowled at her from the other side of the counter. Not a bad looking guy, though older than Cat. He had an air of sophistication with his fitted suit and overcoat. Mac's Diner didn't get too many business types. Maybe he'd been stood up for a breakfast date? After the man collected his change, he stalked away.

She shrugged, grabbed an empty tray, and carried it to his recently vacated table. Collecting the drained coffee mug and crumb-filled plate where a blueberry muffin used to be, she figured it wasn't the food that annoyed the guy. She took the tray to the kitchen and snatched up a clean cup towel and cleanser. Spraying the flat surfaces, she wondered when she might get the chance to repair the chips in the turquoise blue wall above the booth. She shined up the chrome and left it ready for the next diner.

Giggles erupted, drawing Cat's attention to the other side of the room where Daisy held the interest of several men. That woman had a way about her. Tall and talkative. Tagged as *Stilts* on the basketball court in high school, she loved attention in any form.

She tossed her bleached hair, making the tinted pink ends flip outward over her collar. Cat had heard the comments of others. *A paint job like that just looks silly on a woman about to celebrate three decades.* But Cat disagreed. Daisy was a free spirit in every detail. Luckily, Cat's friendship with her, as diverse as they were, kept the blonde employed and even in an old-fashioned uniform. Wonder of wonders.

"Order up." Grady's baritone shout accompanied the whack of a spatula. The *ting* of a metal bell snapped Cat back to reality.

That free spirit needed to get her tail in gear and start helping.

Plates filled the window as the front door sleigh bells jingled, announcing new customers. Cat had replaced the cowbell that had always hung above the door with a multi-belled harness for the Christmas season. Thinking they sounded merry, she left them up. After a second month of the Jingle Bells, she was beginning to regret that decision.

She snatched up a couple of menus, and slipped out from behind the counter. Tugging on her friend's skirt, she seated some new arrivers.

"Oops. Gotta go, fellows." None of Daisy's flirting bothered Cat. Especially when the woman peeled herself away from her admirers long enough to actually wait on tables. Sometimes that act took a crowbar. Thankfully, not this morning.

The abrupt jingle of the bells on the front door made Cat glance at the entrance. Donna Culver, from Betty's Beauty Barn, pushed through the opening. "Omigosh, Cat, are you all right? I just heard."

"Just heard what?" Daisy refilled a soda at the machine.

She echoed Cat's silent query. Which catastrophe from last night had Donna heard about?

"I talked to Mrs. Hawkins on my way over. She told me you were in an accident last night."

"Oh no. Not your new car." Daisy set the glass on the counter. "Is that why you've got those wraps on your palms?"

Cat nodded. At least she didn't have to talk about Ray. "We've got people to serve." A lot of them since the sun had finally come out again.

Daisy collected a platter from the window and reclaimed the soda. "I thought you were going for a different look. Sort of scroungy fighter type."

Donna snorted. Cat couldn't help but chuckle. She could see herself dancing around a boxing ring, up against some massive bruiser. She cashed out a table full of workers.

"At least you don't have to worry about Ray anymore."

Cat flinched. Had more news come out? Was he ...? She pressed her wrapped palms against her stomach.

Daisy rejoined them and wiped down the counter. "What's wrong with him?"

"Nothing. He's fine." She turned to Cat. "I can't believe you didn't tell me he was back."

Back? Fine? *Thank you, God.*

"Wait, you mean you didn't know?" Donna laid a hand on Cat's shoulder.

She winced and shook her head. "How do you know he's back in town?"

"I saw him. He was crossing the street when I pulled into the parking lot."

Quick-stepping around the bar, she leaned over the front booth to stare out the window. Only a couple of people outside, going into the post office. She returned to the register and checked out another patron.

Donna smacked her lips. "Sun-bleached highlights in his hair and a hot-looking tan. Mmm." She winked at Daisy. "Definitely Ray Alexander."

The blonde shook her head. "Too short. And too committed to God and Cat."

Cat reeled. Committed? Not to her. An ache filled her chest

that had nothing to do with bruising.

Thank you for bringing him home. Even if it's not to me.

Ray kneaded the steering wheel as he trudged through what passed for traffic in downtown Heath's Point.

Mrs. Hawkins, dispatcher for the Heath's Point Police Department, directed Ray to a section of Highway Seven, some miles north of town. "Chief Tate is working an accident up there."

No trouble finding the spot. Two police cruisers and a large tow truck. Ray hadn't adjusted yet to the cold, but welcomed the sting of the chill on his cheeks when he stepped down from his pickup. Especially accompanied with the bright sunshine. The air had the nostalgic smell of fish. His favorite spot was just down from here, under the bridge.

The chief wrapped Ray in a tight hug. "Mrs. Hawkins said you were headed this way. Can't tell you how glad I am to see you, boy." He stepped back, his gaze roaming from the stitches along Ray's cheek to his shoulder wrapped with a sling. "Looks like you had a bit of trouble."

He nodded. Memories of the people he left behind weighted his chest. "I'm all right." He couldn't muster more. Stuffing his good hand in his pocket, he swallowed and glanced at the backend of a submerged car. "Looks like you've had some fun with joyriders."

Dell's eyes drifted over the lake. "No joyriding. Blown tire." He turned back to Ray. "Cat's."

Ray whipped his hand free. The weight became viselike. "She wasn't in there, was she?" He took a step down the incline.

"Hold up. She's okay. Half-froze last night, but she's fine now. Bruised some. Up at the diner working. Not like anything could keep her from that."

Air refilled his lungs. Once. Twice. He let the words settle on him. *She's okay.* But a blown tire? And just at this particularly tight turn in the highway? He didn't like the foreboding that filled him. "You sure it was a blown tire?"

"Now where in the world did that question come from?" Dell tilted his chin up, like he examined the overcast sky. He settled on Ray's face. "Care to tell me why you asked that?"

Shutting his eyes and dropping his chin, Ray fished the envelope from his back pocket. He'd have to tell the story. Most, if not all of it. Had to expose his stupidity.

Dell read the letter in silence. His Adam's apple bobbed and the muscle under his rough jaw tightened. "You wanna tell me why this lunatic is after my goddaughter?"

"I was at the wrong place at the wrong time." He sighed. "And I lived to tell about it. I'm thankful to the authorities who went after Sevilla. Though not successfully." He massaged the back of his neck. "We tried to keep my hometown a secret."

The older man held out the picture. "Also unsuccessful."

"Yeah."

"And I'm guessing this guy has the rest of this picture."

"Good bet. Or somebody who works for him." And Cathy was in danger because of it. The blown tire couldn't have been an accident.

The chief must've thought along the same lines. He whistled through his teeth and called, "Danvers."

A taller guy, about Ray's age with sandy hair broke from the group of cops and strolled over.

Dell pointed toward town. "Git over to the diner and hang around. Keep Cat in sight at all times until I tell you differently. Got that?"

Danvers was new. Good-looking cowboy type. Why hadn't

Dell sent Officer Phelps, the squarish father of five?

"So you think this tire was rigged to blow?" Dell shook his head. "Farfetched."

"I think you oughta look at it real close."

His task done, Ray should have felt settled. Satisfied. Cathy had security. He remounted his truck and turned the key. "She'll be fine." He tried to convince himself.

But he knew a lie when he spoke one.

Cat glanced at the black and white cat clock above the order window for the hundredth time since Donna told her about Ray's return. Once again, she resigned herself again to the truth of his actions.

He didn't care about her.

Lieutenant Danvers slipped through the door as Donna moved to leave. His arrival at the diner wasn't unusual. Except that he was late for breakfast and early for lunch. And he didn't claim a seat.

Cat exchanged a look with Donna. The woman had been curious about Jason Danvers since he arrived almost two years before, but he didn't open up to anyone. Especially women.

Well, Go on? Surely her friend would at least talk to him?

Donna shook her head, eyes wide. She edged past him and darted out. Coward.

He stood stoically beside the door, refusing Cat's offered menu. The man had the charisma of a soggy sponge. "This a new duty, Lieutenant? Random downtown guard?"

"Chief sent me to keep an eye on you."

What? "Why me? Am I a suspect for something?" She summoned a chuckle, but the motion hurt the bruises on her chest.

"I couldn't say."

Somewhere under that concrete mask, Danvers had to have a heart. A personality. Cat didn't care to work hard enough to find it. "Could you at least sit down then? So the customers don't start thinking you're on a stakeout?"

He sighed. Face tense, he stepped around the side of a chair and lowered into it.

"There now. Isn't that more comfortable?"

Silence. What would it take to get a little friendly banter from this guy?

"Can I get you a soda? On the house, since you're sort of our personal security team."

He shook his head and scanned the room.

Cat followed his gaze. Most of the breakfast crowd had subsided. She sat in the seat next to him and focused on her customers. "So what are you looking for?"

"Have to ask the chief about that one."

"You mean you don't know?"

He turned his head a bit. "*I* know why I'm here. But the chief'll have to share the data with *you*."

The faint Midwestern accent came through, probably because those were the most words he'd ever threaded together around her. His bright blue eyes scanned the few remaining patrons again.

Dismissed, Cat returned to her kitchen.

Donna could have the guy.

"Scoffer" is the name of the arrogant, haughty man
who acts with arrogant pride. ~ Proverbs 21:24 ESV

Chapter 4

Ray shifted as the salesman droned on about the various phone models. His discussion with the chief should have eased his mind, but Cathy's immersed car intensified his foreboding.

He drummed his fingertips, waiting for the clerk to complete the setup of his new cell. He had to have a phone. And now was the best time to get one. But procrastinating on his talk with Cathy knotted his insides.

Especially if she was in danger. Already. At least Dell had someone keeping an eye on her. Even a single guy like Danvers was better than no one. Finally released by the salesman, Ray parked his truck across from the diner. He shed his coat and climbed out as Dell strolled down the sidewalk from the direction of the PD.

"Talk to your girl yet?"

Ray matched his stride, though the taller man stretched it out. "Cathy is hardly my girl after I left her three years ago."

"Yeah, I probably owe you a busted lip for breaking her heart like that."

"You'd have rather she went with me into that treacherous place?"

Dell rubbed the stubble on his chin. "That bad, huh?"

"Look at me." Ray pointed to his left side, stitched up cheek and wrapped arm and shoulder. But Dell's words revisited with a sting. "I broke her heart?"

"First you and now her dad. That little girl's got a lot of pain she's stuffing down deep." He stopped at the diner's door.

Ray paused. He caught a glimpse of Cathy's bright orange ponytail bouncing near the window. His chest gave a lurch. He didn't know what he would say, or how she would take it, but he'd been longing to settle things between them for some time.

She sat at a table. That was odd during working hours. The profile of Danvers sitting next to her cleared up his confusion. Yep. She had a broken heart all right.

He ground his heel into the sidewalk and turned back to his truck.

"You coming in?" Dell opened the door.

"I have a few things to do." He glanced over his shoulder and waved.

Dell called something after him, but he kept moving. If he drove far enough and fast enough, maybe he could erase the image of Cathy cozying up to the cop. Either way, his conversation with her would wait.

Cat stood and shrugged off her apron. "Looks like your boss finally made it."

Dell hollered to someone down the street. "Just don't take any action without my say-so." The door shut with a clamor of jingles.

"Might as well stick a twig in a fire ant mound."

"Not the season for fire ants." Cat smirked and hung the cloth on the kitchen wall.

"He's gonna git burned. Him or somebody else."

The man made as much sense as peppermint lemonade. "Who are you talking about?" She limped into her office to find an Aleve. Her right knee hurt more with each step.

"That boy of yours. Ray's got to get it in his head that he either works with me or not at all."

Ray? A cop? Her mouth fell open, and she dragged her purse to the doorway. "He's working for you?"

"Not like that." Dell pinked. "He has a … project. But he keeps going off on his own instead of following directions."

"You've talked to Ray?" She dug through her purse. Had he visited with everyone in town already?

"He met me at the lake. We were pulling your car out." He leaned against the kitchen doorway. "Oh, and I dropped your coat by the cleaners. It's a mess. Not sure they can save it."

She struggled with the bottle. Had Ray even asked about her? Thoughts swirled, but she had to get them under control.

"And Mrs. Stone dropped this by. Said you should probably have it as soon as possible." He held out an envelope.

Norton-Hughes Attorneys at Law in the return address. "I didn't expect this until next month."

"They're usually pretty quick with the probate. Two weeks tops. Unless there's an issue."

She grabbed a clean glass off the shelf. "Not likely any trouble with this one." She poured water into the glass, popped her tablet, and took a swig. "Dad wasn't all that organized, but there's not so much left to guess work. House, diner. He'd even sold his car."

Dell caught her hand as she moved to slip the mail into her

apron pocket. "I think you should look at this, Cat."

Something about his face ... "I take it you already have your copy?"

He nodded and led the way to the booth near the front door. The picture that hung next to the entrance caught her eye. Her parents, young and newly married, grinned at her from in front of the diner's freshly painted glass door. They looked so grand in the ornate wooden frame.

This place was their legacy. She resisted the urge to touch the frame as she often did at the end of the day. Instead, she sat facing the portrait and tugged the letter from her pocket.

Ripping open the shorter end, she slipped several pages from the envelope. The first was a short letter informing Cat of the legalities of the contents and the avenue for questions or concerns. Nothing big there, though Dell's constant scrutiny annoyed. Her back stiffened like it did with the foreboding of a thunder clap.

She laid the cover sheet down and scanned the second page. *Sound mind ... property and assets.* Blah, blah, blah. She saw Dell's name.

To Dell Tate, my friend and confidant, I leave all of those guns in my collection that you've been coveting these good many years. Now you need to repent. And I want you to have the ivory chess set that I've beaten you on so many times. You could use the practice. Ha. So like Dad. Her nose tingled as tears stung her eyes.

Dell still watched.

"I don't have any problems with you getting Dad's guns and chess set. Is that what you're worried about?"

"Keep reading." He sighed, but his expression didn't waver.

More blah-blahs. Something *pursuant* and *contractual obligations* ... She found her name.

The rest of my worldly possessions go to my baby girl,

Cathleen. You already have the best I could share with you, your faith in Jesus. Honor Him with the rest. I'm so proud of you.

The tickle in her nose returned. She looked up at Dell and spread her lips in a sad stretch. "I'm okay. I'm glad he was proud of me." Tears neared. She dare not say more.

"In between. Did you understand all of what you read?" He took the sheet from her. "The part about Heath?"

She'd skipped that. Dad's silent partner in Mac's had always been an enigma. They seemed to hate each other. How Heath ever finagled a percentage of the business was beyond her.

He must have taken her silence as a *no* because he proceeded to read, stumbling over some of the legalese. "Pursuant to the contracts negotiated six-September, 1984, the partnership of Mac's Diner between me and Darrell Heath of Heath's Point, Texas shall remain in effect with the following adjustments. Should I follow Heath in death, my heir, Cathleen McPherson retains the fifty-one percent—controlling interest—in the business while Heath's heirs continue receiving forty-nine percent of the profits. However, should I precede Heath in death, I bequeath to him two percent of Mac's Diner, giving him controlling interest in the business. Cathleen McPherson, my only child and heir, receives the remaining forty-nine percent of the profits, with or without her participation in the work there."

Wait ... What? The room blurred. Cat's stomach did a slow dive to her toenails. What happened to Mac's, to the folks who relied on the sunset dinners, if skin-flint Heath took over?

This couldn't be happening. *When I said I had nothing more to lose, God, it wasn't a dare.* She lifted wide eyes to Dell. "Did you know about this?"

"Not before I got the letter." He handed it back. "The rest of that is the contract for the partnership. Says essentially what you

47

already know. Basically, Heath takes over thirty days after the probate of the will. Just over three weeks from now."

She stood. She had to move. Had to process this, this … destruction of her life. She shoved through the doorway with Dell on her heels.

"Leave me alone, Chief. I need to … to sort this out." The breeze bit at her as she turned north on Shepherd.

"What's so bad about collecting profits from the place without having to work your tail off for every penny?"

"Not the point." The place did pretty good business, but that was because everyone in town liked and respected Dad. And he cared about them. Tried to offer what they wanted at prices that most could afford. Even gave it for free to those who couldn't. That was how the sunset dinners came about.

Heath would have the power to change everything. Raise prices. Fire the staff. Even throw away the leftovers so they couldn't offer them to those in need each day. She reached the park and hesitated at the crest of a high point on the edge of the tree-lined walkway. She shivered and the wind knotted her ponytail. Why hadn't she grabbed her letter jacket off the hook?

Dell had continued to follow and stepped close. She rubbed her shoulders. "Maybe Heath will let me buy him out?"

"With what?"

"I have a little. I bet I could get a loan on the house in town."

His lips pulled to one side. "You could try, but don't hold your breath. Mac attempted to buy Heath's half at least three times, each with more of an offering. Well over what his half was worth. For whatever reason, Heath refused. I can't imagine him being willing to sell now that he has control over the place."

"Thanks for the encouragement."

"You'd have me lie? I've got a pair of pink sunglasses back at the office if that's what you want."

Grrr. He was right. But she didn't want to hear truth right now.

"They'd clash with your hair color, though." He slapped at her ponytail and wrapped his arm around her shoulders.

She refused to cry but relished his warmth and support. She turned back toward the diner.

"It's not the end of the world, kid. Look at it this way. You can get a different, better-paying job and double your income by still getting the profit from Mac's. Without the work. Actually seems like a pretty good deal."

Except this was her parents' legacy they were talking about. Did Heath even want to run Mac's? Maybe he wouldn't be bought out, but could she purchase back the two percent that gave him control? The immediate hope that rippled through her warped. She'd have to speak to the man. Make him understand. Surely she could find a price that he'd accept for that small percentage, to allow things to remain the way they were?

The bands around her stomach loosened, if only slightly.

"Everything okay here?"

Cat spun to stare into Ray's face. His tender look leveled another layer of bricks on her chest. As much as she wanted to throw her arms around his neck, his appearance at that particular moment splintered all that remained of her will to hold back her tears. She pushed through the door of the diner and didn't stop until she found her way into the little office.

Ray had parked near the diner intent on making his apology. He hadn't meant to procrastinate in seeing Cathy, but his dealing with Dell changed his priorities. Still, she deserved an explanation. As much as he could give anyway.

The sight of her had stirred up forgotten longing. He only caught a glimpse of her face as she whirled and fled inside. A pout tracked her normal smile in the wrong direction. Her beautiful eyes, drawn and half-lidded. He wanted to soothe her sadness. Comfort her in his arms. Instead he'd blown the attempt and chased her off.

"What's going on?"

Dell's mouth flattened. "Well, I suppose everybody's going to know soon enough. Unless Cat can persuade Darrell Heath to sell his part of the business to her, she'll lose control of Mac's in a few weeks."

A vice pressed against Ray's head. "What? Why?"

"Part of the business contract they set up years ago. Surviving partner gets control."

No wonder she was upset. "I guess seeing me made her day even worse."

"Give her some time, boy. Probably would have had the same reaction to anyone." Dell wheeled and headed back to the PD. "I'll send Danvers back to keep an eye on her."

"No need. I'll watch her for a while." Last thing he needed was the good-looking cop hanging around.

He stared at the caramel-colored glass on the door. The chipped gold lettering still held together well enough to announce the name of the place and reflect the intense sunlight. His chest lurched with a sharp intake of air when Cathy crossed the room. But her rejection was too fresh. What had he hoped for? A welcoming, all-is-forgiven embrace? For all he knew, she was seeing someone. Maybe that cop? He eyed her bobbing red ponytail, her pert chin, and enchanting eyes. Mom hadn't mentioned a guy. Surely she had to beat the men away.

The thought twisted his gut. But he'd ruined his chance with her when he left for Mexico. Still, he hoped that once Cathy grew accustomed to having him around again, the icy air she held would thaw. After a while. He only needed a little time.

The torn photo from his wallet haunted. He had no time. Foreboding stitched a line across his forehead as real as the sutures on his left cheek.

The paper sign still showed the *Open* side, though the last of customers exited. Before he changed his mind, he shoved the door open.

"Ow." Cathy stumbled backward, her hand flying to her face. A set of keys jangled from one finger.

"Oh, I'm so sorry. I was just coming back in to talk to you."

"So you thought you'd smack me first?" She set the keys on a nearby table and pulled a napkin from the dispenser. Tears already shined her cheeks.

Ray reached for her, trying to get her to uncover her face so he could see the damage. "It was an accident. What were you doing with your face up to the door anyway?"

"The lock doesn't work very well, so I have to set the key in just right to make it turn."

"What happened?" Daisy rushed over with a stack of napkins.

"The door hit me." Cathy lowered her head.

"What's going on?" A loud voice boomed from the kitchen followed by Grady.

"Ray hit Cat." The blonde answered while Ray tried to coax Cathy to uncover her injury, pulling gently at her hands.

Grady advanced on him. "What're you thinking? When did you start hitting women?" Grady brushed away Ray's hand, inadvertently swatting Cathy in the nose.

"Ow. Will y'all stop?" She pushed away from the group.

Ray trailed her into the kitchen. "You need to get some ice on that."

"I figured that out all by myself. Just like I've done everything else while you've been gone. I didn't need your help then, and I don't need it now." She opened the top section of the refrigerator.

Ray ducked under the large arc of the silver door. "At least let me see your eye."

She grabbed a bag of frozen corn and slammed the door shut. "Fine. See?" She paused, setting her gaze on the ceiling and holding the position for a moment.

A small vertical dent marked her right cheek, and her eye squinted and flinched, showing slight swelling. The apple of her cheek reddened, speaking of other colors to appear. "It doesn't look so good."

"Gee, thanks." She slapped the bag of corn on her eye. "Ow!"

Grady and Daisy appeared at the doorway. "Son, if you keep hitting my girl, I'm gonna hafta take you outside."

"I didn't hit her." Ray tossed a glance over his shoulder.

"I smacked myself with the bag of corn." Cathy returned to the dining room and sat on a stool.

Grady went back to cleaning his grill. "It coulda been worse. The corn coulda still been on the cob." He punctuated his joke with a loud laugh.

Ray didn't think it funny, but Cathy burst into a trickle of giggles as he joined her at the counter. He'd forgotten how the sound enchanted and relaxed him. "So you're all right?"

"I'll be fine. Just colorful, I guess."

Daisy emerged from the kitchen carrying a pink, leather coat and a matching shoulder bag. "I've always told you that pale skin of yours is unsightly, but it's much better than the black and blue you're gonna have." She passed them as she headed for the back door. "Welcome home, preacher man."

Cathy's laughter faded as Daisy exited.

"Don't listen to her. There's nothing wrong with your coloring."

A rueful chuckle huffed out. "Yeah, and I'm not too short, and my nose isn't too small, and my voice doesn't sound like Smurfette."

"Where did you get all that?" Ray didn't remember her so self-conscious before. As the head cheerleader who always ended up at the top of every pyramid, she'd come across with utter confidence as long as he'd known her.

She rose, still pressing the frozen vegetable bag to her face. "Daisy was teasing. No big deal."

"I hope you don't take anything she said seriously."

"I'd like to lock up." Cathy stood and returned to the door.

And get away from him. The forced sweetness of her tone made that clear. He made a beeline for the exit. "I truly just came back inside to say a proper hello. I didn't mean to cause trouble."

"Now hold on a minute," Grady thundered from the kitchen. "I still need to shake this man's hand." He gripped Ray's right hand and encircled his shoulder. "Glad you're back. Safe." He glanced at Cathy. "We all are."

She stood near the door and concentrated on inserting the key. Grady might have claimed they were all glad he'd returned, but one of them didn't seem to care much.

She opened the door when the key finally rolled into the lock, "Thanks for coming by." Her quick smile didn't reach her eyes. He stepped out, and she shut the door behind him. The bolt turned.

That wasn't quite the way he'd heard the conversation in his head.

But at least he could stand guard over the girl inside her locked building.

Discretion will watch over you,
understanding will guard you. ~ Proverbs 2:11 ESV

Chapter 5

"Think you coulda been a little nicer to that man? He been through an awful lot." Grady clicked his tongue at her as he scraped the grill.

Cat sank her hands in the sudsy water. "Maybe, but he *is* the one who left."

"For good reason. How long you gonna hold on to that hurt?"

Before she could speak, someone banged at the glass on the front door. She flung as much of the bubbles into the sink as she could and wiped her arms and hands with her apron as she rounded the corner. Dell stood outside, stomping and rubbing his gloved hands together.

Beyond him, Cat caught sight of Ray's blue F250 truck parked on the other side of the street. Probably running an errand somewhere. Still, the sight of it sparked a glow.

But thinking about the past was a waste of time and energy. She hoisted a virtual bucket of water over her heart.

She unlocked the door and let Dell inside. The little cluster of noisy silver shaved down the raw edges of her nerves. Maybe she should put the cowbell back and get rid of the ding-a-lings.

"The closed sign is up, Chief, but I haven't emptied the coffee yet. That make you happy?"

Dell held open the door, and Ray stepped inside.

Cat sucked in a breath and turned for the coffeepot. "This some type of intervention?" She poured a cup, begging the remnants of control to weave a barrier around her heart.

"Sort of." Dell pulled a baggie out of his jacket pocket. "Ever seen anything like this before?" He exchanged the bag for the mug.

She felt like she'd been transported into one of those cop shows on TV. "I know what a bullet looks like, Dell. Am I supposed to break down and confess to something now?"

Ray closed the gap. The sight of his injured arm and especially his face knotted her stomach. He eyed the bag. "From the tire?"

The chief nodded.

Cat stiffened. "What tire?"

"Your tire, Kitten."

Ray jerked around and moved toward the window.

Dell sipped the coffee. "You're not going to like this—"

"That's been my whole day."

"—but you've had a threat on your life."

"What are you talking about?" Her brain hovered near overload.

"I'm sorry, Cathy." Ray rejoined them. His low voice spread over her raw nerves, wrapping them in a layer of warmth. "I made a powerful enemy, and he wants to hurt me by hurting people ... around me."

An enemy? "Then why aren't you worrying over your mom?"

Dell held up a torn picture. "Because this accompanied the

threatening letter he received."

She recognized her senior photo even without the face attached. "This is ridiculous."

"I'd agree with you. Except ..." Dell took the baggie from her and held it up.

Like chasing fog. How could Ray and the others hope to protect Cathy against someone they couldn't see? Couldn't anticipate?

"What about this man you ticked off?" Dell's question seemed easy enough, while they waited for Danvers to show. He pulled a chair away from one of the front tables. The vinyl seemed to exhale as he lowered onto the cushioned seat.

Ray sat across from him. "Sevilla is a sociopath. He considered the area where I worked to be his little kingdom."

"And that was?" Cathy faced them, wiping down the counter, but Grady came in from the kitchen.

"Chiapas in Mexico, near the Guatemalan border."

"Dangerous?" Grady sat on the chair between him and Dell.

"Very. People disappear and nobody asks why or where they went." His own experience threatened to encroach his thoughts, but he shoved the nightmare back.

"And this Sevilla guy was in charge. The cartel leader." Dell sipped from a coffee mug.

Danvers tapped on the door, and Cathy hurried around the bar to let him in.

Ray watched them. No words exchanged. No odd looks. Maybe he'd been wrong about what he'd thought?

The man joined them at the table. "I guess you're the

missionary I've heard about."

Dell introduced them. "Ray was telling us about this guy who threatened Cat."

"Yeah, and about that. Why me?" Cathy paused in her table cleaning.

Somehow, the whack-job that hated him found out who he cared about most. But how could he explain that? Here? With them?

Dell answered. "Ray had your picture. Simple as that."

Or Dell's explanation worked. Not the whole truth, but close enough.

"We're going to need round-the-clock attention for Cat." The chief folded his arms across his chest.

"Come on, Dell. That's insane. How could anyone possibly guess where I'm living right now?"

Where was she living? Ray had assumed she'd still be at her Victorian landmark in town.

Dell rubbed his jaw. "Don't you realize that someone's been watching you?"

"You're trying to scare me."

Danvers spoke up. "You should be scared. Assuming Alexander is right, the person who shot out your tire knew your car, your route, and your habits."

Cathy's eyes widened. She backed against the booth table. "Someone's been watching." She glanced out the window. "Here at Mac's? At Sunrise Inn?"

Ray reached her in a moment. His good hand stroking her upper arm. "Don't be afraid. We're going to be here for you, Cathy."

Her wandering eyes found his and hardened. "Like you have over the last several years?"

Slapping him would have felt better and had a shorter effect.

She stomped into the kitchen.

Ray bowed his head. *I don't deserve her forgiveness God, but she needs to forgive me for her own sake.*

"Leave it, boy. She doesn't mean what she says. Too much emotion today."

He believed her godfather, but the truth of her words weighed on him. Along with regret.

Dell stood. "Grady, you and Ray stick with her until she gets to the inn. I'll set Billings out there overnight. Danvers, you can relieve him around midnight and take Cat back here tomorrow."

"Where I can watch her during the day." Grady nodded. "I like your plan, Chief. Gonna work for a couple a days. 'Til we hit the weekend. Cat's gonna throw a fit about all of the attention then, though."

"Let her throw one." Dell took a long stride to the door.

Ray hadn't seen a Cathy-fit since her first year in high school, but he had a feeling he was in for one soon.

Cat could swear she wore some type of psychological straight jacket. Having body guards was bad enough. But why did Ray have to be one of them?

She tried to keep her mind on her tasks. At least the weather cooperated, though a slight chill arrived with the declining day. Smiling, she engaged the folks who gathered at sunset, but her mind refused to cooperate. The faces became blurs.

Someone had been watching her. The thought sent a shiver up her spine. Then she felt the pressure of Ray's hand, his soft words comforting her.

Before she told him off. Such mean words. What was wrong with her?

Ray. Grady introduced him to everyone who came through the line. He greeted each with a water bottle, an offered handshake, and a compassionate look in his warm eyes.

Something she couldn't seem to muster. But maybe that was an effect of the shell shock that today had become. All she really wanted was her pillow. Waking up in the morning might make this nightmare disappear.

Lord, these people deserve more from me than the least I can do.

She slunk into the kitchen. Grady and Ray were great with the folks. Her sour face wouldn't help anything. The men cleaned up outside while she claimed dish duty. Her insides shuddered when Grady said good night. Ray locked the front entrance behind him. Didn't seem to have nearly the problem with the bolt that she had.

"How's your cheek?" He tugged her letter jacket—correction, his letter jacket—from the coat hook.

"A little sore but better than yours." Her battered mind and broken heart were the real problems. Along with being trapped alone with Ray's soft voice and kind words.

"Looks good. Not too much bruising." He chuckled. "I'll have to remember to use frozen corn next time I get injured."

He handed her the jacket. "Sorry I can't hold it for you."

She shrugged on the coat, willing the open wound on her heart to scab over again. "How'd you get hurt?"

His face darkened. He started to say something and stopped.

Wow, sensitive subject. The prospect of Ray's deep pain ignited a new desire to ease his hurt. She struggled for a diversion, but came up empty.

"I better get you to your place. You're staying at the inn?"

Distraction accomplished. "Since Dad died. Hard to believe so much has changed in a couple of weeks." If only she could avoid her painful topics.

"I'm sorry about Mac." He pushed the door open. "He was a good man."

"The best." She braced herself against the emotions and the cold. Numb. An explosion couldn't have rocked her world.

Ray held the door, and she scooted underneath his arm. He touched her back and every nerve in her body responded. And yet his nearness brought back years full of ache and silence.

"I'd forgotten how beautiful this area is. And I've sure missed dry, chilly weather." He paused and leaned against the bed of the truck. "Happy to see you kept the sunset dinners going. The people I spoke with tonight would put you up for sainthood."

She shut her eyes. "There won't be any more sunset dinners when Mr. Heath gets control of Mac's."

"Dell told me about that. Surely you're not giving up already."

Why not? Too much had happened. A huge mountain arose with the partnership agreement, and Cat couldn't even begin to think about that problem under her current state of pseudo house-arrest. She stared at the deep shadows on the outskirts of the lot.

Was God even hearing all of her prayers?

"It's gonna be okay, Cathy. We'll work all of this out."

He had no idea that *he* was part of the *this* she needed to work out. Near the edge of the lot, an orange dot flared. For a moment. Then disappeared. "Did you see that?"

"Yeah. Let's go back inside."

She thought of a similar image that morning. Chills shot across her shoulders.

At that moment, the chief's cruiser crawled into the lot blocking the view of anyone who stood at the edge. Ray ran to Dell. The chief switched on his floodlight and scanned the area. Empty field beyond the gravel lot. The back of some office buildings past the field.

No people at all.

"You sure you saw someone there?" Dell shot Cat a squinty-eyed look.

"I'm sure."

"We both are." Ray's support washed over her. Her skin tingled.

"Get her home. We'll talk tomorrow."

Oh, couldn't Dell take her? She squeezed her eyes shut. She couldn't ask. Couldn't make such an issue.

Ray opened his passenger side door for her. *Groan.* She mustered a soft thank you and hoped he kept his talking minimal.

He said nothing until they passed the place where her car went into the lake. She gazed at the darkness. Nothing in the overcast sky for the lake to reflect.

"I'm glad you weren't hurt last night."

Oh, she'd been hurt all right. But with everything else today, she'd not been able to think about the pain in her knees and chest all that much. "Thanks."

Officer Billing's cruiser sat at the front gate.

Ray parked near the porch. "I'm sorry about all of this trouble."

She sighed. If only he was sorry about leaving her in the first place. But this mess wasn't exactly all his fault. Certainly the trouble with the diner wasn't. "It's okay."

Even though it wasn't. She climbed from the truck cab. Felt like things would never be okay again. Certainly not good. Halfway up the stairs, her trot became a trudge. Maybe he wouldn't notice.

She set her eyes on the front door. Craving the isolation of her suite, she'd avoid talking to Myra and Ellis tonight. Hot chocolate or no hot chocolate.

Tomorrow had to be a better day. What else could go wrong?

The light frost still edging Ray's windshield didn't compare to the chill he'd felt from Cathy last night. He couldn't blame her. But he wasn't going to walk away either.

He watched the diner after Danvers left. The sky pinked and lightened, but only barely against low hanging clouds. With the temperature hovering near freezing, the morning promised a clammy hand against the backs of anyone unfortunate enough to be out in it. Like him.

Finally, Cathy appeared at the front entrance and flipped the sign to the *Open* side. About time. His growling stomach amplified in the closed-in truck cab.

Claiming a table in the back of the room, he had a great view of the front door and most of the tables.

Cathy moved in his direction. The pleasant look on her face fell away almost immediately. "A little early for you, isn't it?"

"Thought I might enjoy one of Grady's omelets." He stroked his stubble, grimacing when his fingers touched the sutures along his cheek. "And coffee?"

Her lips pressed in a firm line. Probably as disgusted with his appearance as she was with him in general. She turned away.

The front door jingled, and he eyed the two men coming in. Bulked up in heavy-duty work clothes. Likely from the highway expansion. They took a center table. Cathy brought them coffee, offered them real smiles, and chatted for a second. Not flirty like Daisy could be, but genuine kindness. Like he always found in his girl.

Strike that. No longer *his* girl. Still as warm and friendly, though.

Daisy trotted in sputtering apologies. She and Cathy

63

disappeared into the kitchen. When they emerged, Cathy handed her a tray and nodded in Ray's direction without meeting his eyes.

So she couldn't even stand to wait on him? Great.

Daisy brought his breakfast. "Had any recent knockouts, champ?"

He chuckled. "Not since I took on a redheaded brute yesterday."

"She doesn't look too worse for the wear." She eyed her boss. "But I'm worried about her. Something's up that she won't tell me. Is she okay?"

Gossip wasn't his style, despite his much-loved mom and her habits. He shrugged. Cathy would have to inform her workers about Mr. Heath's new position of power eventually, but that was her place, not his. "I think she's hurting." True enough. "I'd tell you to pray for her, but …"

"Ha. I like to have too much fun, preacher man. I don't think God will hear too much from me until I'm blue-headed and driving twenty miles an hour down the freeway. I'll be nearer to Him by then, anyway." A trickle of laughter followed her back to the kitchen.

He prayed over his meal, over the waitress who needed Jesus, and over the redhead who needed protection. *Give them both what they lack, even if they don't recognize their desperation.*

As the morning rush amplified, Ray had no problems scanning the room and watching people. Some of the strangers even stared back at him. No one came in alone, except him. And no one looked the least bit suspicious or treated Cathy as anything except a waitress. Several folks spotted him. A few came over and chatted. He didn't invite them to stay. He had a job to do.

By the time the rush subsided, his doubts took over. Was he wasting his time? Maybe the letter itself had been Sevilla's revenge. But the bullet in her tire wouldn't be silenced.

After silently slipping the tab on his table, Daisy left him to himself. Cathy ignored him outright, setting up an orange ladder to the side of the front door. She perched atop it.

He refilled his coffee at the bar and paused to admire the view. Her wavy hair was caught up in a high ponytail, and the pink uniform hugged her petite curves. Even her legs, what he could see of them above her cowboy boots, still looked toned. Hard to believe so much time had passed since he'd left.

Grady came to the kitchen door. "Careful up there."

Cathy needed help at the top of a ladder no more than she had at the top of a pyramid of cheerleaders in high school.

"I'm fine." She fiddled with a screwdriver and disconnected the passel of sleigh bells that hung above the door. She tossed it down to Grady. "Dumpster that baby."

"You'll be sorry. You'll want it next Christmas." Though he argued, he made his way out the back door, nodding to Ray as he passed. "Brother Alexander."

Ray waved at the older man. Grady's encouragement to follow the Lord's leading proved invaluable when faced with leaving for Chiapas or staying behind. But neither of them would share that information with Cathy. No need to include Grady in her anger.

Cathy wrestled with a configuration of the cowbell and the doorframe. She pushed it all the way closed and the spring-loaded latch above the door clamped over the handle of the bell.

"I think that does it."

The door opened quickly and Cathy lurched back. "Whoa."

Ray jumped, but she regained her balance without his help and climbed down.

"Funny place to store a ladder, kid." Dell's voice echoed against the blue and white tile that covered the dining room floor.

She folded and handed the ladder off to Daisy. "Mean thing to

65

do to Danvers, making him sit out in the cold all night."

Danvers again. Ray winced.

"Not that cold, and it wasn't all night. He split the time with Billings."

She rounded the bar, filled a mug with coffee, and slid it into his waiting hand. "Still seems pretty brutal, considering the cushy shift hanging around here all day."

Ray caught the jab. Also that she'd rather have Danvers or Billings here. Anyone but him.

"Yeah, but they work for me." He glanced at Ray. "Ray and Grady are volunteers."

"Hmm." Cathy flounced into the kitchen.

Ray clamped his jaw for a moment. "She doesn't make this *cushy shift* any easier, does she?"

"Oh, no. Not if she can help it." Dell shook his head. "Should be fun to watch her try to make you squirm, though."

"Thanks." He drank from his cup. If Mac were here, Ray'd unburden himself. He'd always been able to tell the man anything. Easier than speaking to his own dad.

But Dell was different. He saw too much. Judged too much. Then again, maybe that's what Ray needed. "You think Cathy'll ever forgive me for leaving her behind?"

The man's eyes crinkled in the corners. "The forgivin's done, boy." He raised his finger. "Trust. Now that's a different issue." A slight nod and he thumped the table before lifting his mug. "Entirely."

Trust?

That would never happen.

With the men chatting about her future, Cat set to cleaning.

The power washer churned away on a load of dishes like her thoughts tumbling through her head.

Why'd Ray have to be her guard? All day long? His low, soothing voice jellied her insides. His gaze followed her all morning, causing her palms to sweat so bad, she thought she might drop something.

If she had to be under guard, couldn't she have someone she didn't care about doing the duty? Let Ray stare at the inn all night long where she couldn't see him and wouldn't think about him while she slept. As though she ever successfully kept him out of her mind. Or her dreams.

Still, she wished he'd stay away from Mac's and let her make the best of her final few weeks.

She ran her hand over her father's checkered apron that still hung in the doorway. How could she let this place go? Gripping the fabric, she shut her eyes. The murderous crazy using her as target practice distracted her at the worst possible time. *Lord, help me keep Dad's place. Don't let Heath take it away.*

The opening door in the other room summoned her. She released her hold and smoothed the garment. Turning, she found Dell alone at the table. Ray was gone.

She relaxed her straightened spine. Though she'd been wanting his absence, it left her with a hollow place inside. "Are you my new guard dog?" She topped Dell's coffee.

"I hope you didn't call Ray a dog."

"No, but I considered the title." She sighed. "I'm sorry. That was uncalled for."

"Your statement? Because you sure treated him like one." Dell's eyebrows furrowed.

Her cheeks warmed. "I didn't intend to be ugly."

"The anger you've indulged in just popped out?"

"Something like that." She had harbored angry thoughts. No wonder she'd been so mean.

"Think you can focus on him as the man trying to protect you instead of the one trying to kill you?"

Sounded simple. Ludicrous that she should get them confused. "Of course."

He rose. "I'll check in on you later. Stay inside."

She glanced at the bare, wind-swept street. No problem there.

The LORD is a stronghold for the oppressed,
a stronghold in times of trouble. And those who
know Your name put their trust in You, for You, O LORD,
have not forsaken those who seek You. ~ Psalm 9:9-10 ESV

Chapter 6

Ray attempted a nap after leaving Mac's. When he did fall asleep, machete-swinging terrorists filled his dreams. Except Cathy had been one of those falling under the attack. He awoke, damp from sweat and freezing after kicking off his blankets.

Just as well. He wanted to meet Cathy back at the diner at sunset.

He turned on the highway toward town when his ringtone started. He clicked the speaker button and laid the phone on the dash. "This is Ray."

"Ah, I hoped this was your number, but I was not sure."

He pulled to a stop light and glanced at the name. Just a number from San Diego. *Wait, San Diego.*

"Miguel?"

"*Sí, amigo.* It is so good to hear your voice."

"How in the world did you get this number? I just got the phone yesterday."

"The board put me in contact with your transfer agent, Pastor

Slaughter."

Philip Slaughter, Ray's mentor and closest friend, had been his first call on the new phone. "Clever. I'm so glad you called. Are you in the states?"

"Visiting my sister in L.A. right now. I bet all of your family and friends were glad to see you."

Maybe not all of them. "My parents especially."

"How is your shoulder, your injuries?"

Ray shared a few of the details of his hospital visits. "But they aren't giving me too much trouble."

"Something is bothering you, my friend. I hear tension in your voice."

Going through the fire with the man had bonded them. Ray's neck heated. He'd not thought about calling Miguel at all. With his friend on the phone, he unloaded recent events. Including the letter and gunshot. "I think Sevilla has sent someone up here."

"Not likely. Sevilla is in prison."

"When did that happen?" He pulled onto Shepherd Street.

"Hard to say. I heard from a contact."

"Good. It's about time."

Silence followed. "True. But I am concerned such a powerful man might find an escape. A connection to freedom."

"You don't really think he could get out." Ray parked in front of the diner.

"I think Sevilla can do whatever he wishes. Look at what he did in Asmirandu."

Images of the nightmare danced across his mind. He winced. "Any word on the mission?" If anyone knew, Miguel would.

"I have had no contact so far. I am sorry, my friend, but I believe the church was destroyed outright. I will continue to reach out to them." The man's voice broke. He was such a natural encourager.

The bad news must hurt to share.

"I'll keep praying that you hear from one of your contacts soon."

"Is there nothing else I can do for you and your lady?"

"Besides pray, no." Though he'd love to have the guy who saved his life watching his back.

"That I will do, my friend. Keep me updated."

Ray rang off. Funny how news of Sevilla's jailing didn't lift his spirits much. Miguel was right. The man could do as he pleased.

"Okay, guard dog. Time to go." Cat switched off the dining room lights.

"Woof." Dell tugged her ponytail.

She locked the front door and paused at her parents' picture. How could she let them down? But this had been her dad's choice. His agreement with his partner. None of the arrangement was her responsibility. And yet …

I'm sorry, Daddy.

"Coming?" Dell waited at the back door.

Cat tugged on the jacket. "I have a stop to make before you take me home. We're doing dinner for the Boy Scouts tonight at the inn. Eagle ceremony, and I need dessert."

"Thought you and Myra made everything fresh."

"We did. We do. But my timing's off a bit." She flattened her collar. "I'm going to blame old man Heath, Ray, and whoever shot at my tire."

"Noted."

Dell groused when he realized her stop was at a Costco in suburban Dallas. "I'm way outta my jurisdiction here."

"What? Your lack of power makes you feel uncomfortable?"

He scowled. "No, the HPPD on my door makes me feel conspicuous. Smarty."

"Mm-hmm. And the gun on your hip certainly gets attention." Cat made her purchases and hauled them out to the car in a large box.

"If I really wanted to get noticed, I'd stick you in handcuffs. Bet people would stare then."

"Think I'll pass." They chatted on the way to the inn. About anything except the most important topics. Mac's, Ray, and some stalker watching her from the shadows. A wall of ice covered those subjects, making them impossible to visit.

She barely had the chance to say hi to Myra. "I'll be back to help with the banquet after I serve at sunset."

"We're fine, dear. Love on the people who need you." Myra was a special lady.

Cat hurried back to Dell's cruiser.

"Your carriage, milady." Dell smirked when she climbed in.

"Dinnertime. Think you might do the devotion and prayer tonight?" Cat fiddled with the snap on her jacket, then gave up. It wasn't cold enough to button it anyway.

"Who usually does them?"

"Daddy did." With him gone there was no such thing as usual, now. "Different folks have taken over since ..."

"Why don't you do it?" He eyed her.

"I never knew you to be afraid of talking to groups. Or of praying out loud." Pressure layered her shoulders. She stared at her hands.

"*I'm* not." He glanced at her.

Cat stared at the roof liner. She'd never even been successful at saying grace at a family meal. "I don't need any new pressure, Dell. I'm just not any good at sharing my faith."

"You could be. If you tried. But I won't add to your troubles."

"Thanks." She knew better.

Dell parked next to the blue pickup. "Looks like Ray's ready to take over."

Not again. Insecurity to insecurity squared. "Does he have to? I mean, I appreciate his generosity, but I don't want to be such a burden."

"I don't think he feels that way."

Of course he did. Yet here he came with a kind face and guilt-ridden eyes. Cat almost wanted to cry.

She stepped into the street. People already gathered, in spite of the chilling mist in the air. Faces, many she'd known since her school days, nodded in her direction. Clara Donavan and her new baby. Dash and Rip who were veterans. Mrs. Dupree who used to own an alterations shop before her arthritis took over.

The Duprees went to the church, but the others stayed away. From everything and everybody. Except Daddy and his sunset dinners. *I guess these dinners are his real legacy, Lord.* Yet, Cat could only step into part of that role. She'd never be the one to evangelize.

But with the *other* partner soon to be in control of Mac's, how would the sunset dinners continue at all?

Ray's heart skipped when he spotted the spunky redhead getting out of Dell's police car. She seemed to be thawing some, and he hoped the trend continued. He followed her to the door.

"You know you don't have to hang around like this. You've just gotten back." She stared straight ahead.

"I don't mind." He trailed her inside and took a case of water off the kitchen counter.

"Well, since you *are* here. And since you have experience that *I* sure don't have, maybe you would do a little devotion and a prayer?" She stepped away.

Now what had she meant by that?

Cathy engaged everyone on the street with a bright smile and a boxed up meal of leftovers. Men, women, even a few children stood around in the cool air and responded to her. The delighted faces and chatter among them all looked more like a potluck at the church instead of a group of homeless and hurting on the streets. He'd noticed something of the same attitude last night with Grady.

"Here you go, Mrs. Dupree. Is that a new coat you got there, Darius?" Cathy handed over a large box to a thin, older lady, gray hair against her dark skin, who stood with a small boy. Her pink, translucent raincoat waved in the breeze as she spoke to Cathy. Baggy jeans hung below several flannel shirts.

The boy, probably about five, grinned at her and chimed in with a proud tone. Their faces glowed with gratitude. Easy to see Cathy's effect on them.

Ray introduced himself and handed out a couple of water bottles to the two.

"Saw you last night. Did you just move into town, young man?"

"Returned a couple of days ago. But I grew up here."

"A friend of Cat's?"

"Most of my life."

She twisted her black eyebrows. "Strange that she never mentioned anything about you." She ambled to greet another woman.

Ray flinched. The memory of Cathy's hardened face came to mind. *I didn't need you before, and I don't need you now.* Wasn't that what she'd said?

Cathy handed a meal to a Hispanic teenager wrapped in a

green blanket. "Welcome. Are you here with Dash?"

Dash. His name must have fit him during younger, slimmer days, but he gave a broad, buck-toothed smile. The tall, black man stepped up and put a hand on the young man's shoulder. "This here's Frankie. He don't speak much English, but I told him you'd give him something to eat iffen he came along. I don't think he's got much in a while."

She spoke to Frankie in broken Spanish. "Pleased to meet you, Frankie."

Ray's mouth dropped open. What a ministry she had here, all on her own.

She handed him a large, wrapped box. "You hungry?"

"*Sí, gracias.*" He gave a slight bow after taking the box, and Ray handed him a water bottle.

He stepped to the side where he could still view the people and engaged Frankie in a little conversation. The man responded with enthusiasm to his own language. Once the faucet turned on, it gushed in a Latin-laced stream. Ray learned about his family, the job he'd just lost, and the walls around an air conditioning grate that kept the wind off him at night.

Cathy continued passing around the meals until her audience stood silently waiting.

Ray rejoined her at the door. "I can't believe they stand out here instead of going somewhere warm and eating."

Cathy nodded. "Even when the weather's really bad, they come. And this was part of Dad's routine. Can you say a few words? Doesn't have to be very long."

He remembered Grady's short devotion the night before. "Sure." He turned to the small crowd. "I understand you all stay to listen and pray before you leave to get out of the cold. I don't take that lightly, and I believe the Lord considers your actions an offering."

He picked up an extra boxed meal. "He's been most kind to bless us with the things we need. Jesus even said that we don't need to worry about what we're going to eat or what we're going to wear. God dresses the flowers and feeds the birds. And He loves you so much more than them."

Cat glanced around at the people. A few children huddled together, stamping their feet.

Ray said something in Spanish. Probably repeating what he'd just shared specifically for his new best friend, Frankie. Cat noticed how the young man's eyes glowed with Ray's attention.

Ray's attention had always made her feel special, too. Her heart ached with memories of times not to be revisited.

A woman carrying a little girl came closer as Ray spoke. Cat met her eyes and held up a box, meeting her in a parking space in front of the diner. "Are you hungry?"

"Very." The dirty cream material of her jacket was pocked with cigarette holes. The little girl clinging to her under her coat wore only a pair of jeans and a flannel shirt.

"Do you stay here in the area?"

She glanced down the street then looked at Cat. "Do I have to fill out a form or something?"

Cat smiled. "No. Not at all. And you don't have to tell me anything either. I'm just hoping you have a warm place to sleep."

"Yes'm." She looked away again and backed up several slow steps.

"Are you all right?" Cat followed her further onto Shepherd Street.

"Uh-huh. Do I need to stay? I wanna get my little girl inside."

She shifted her weight and stepped backward again.

"By all means."

"Thanks." The woman stretched out one hand to receive Cat's box.

A screech of tires erupted on the street. The woman snatched the box, spun, and fled into the darkness. Cat turned to find a set of headlights blinding her.

She leapt back toward the diner. Several hands pulled her to safety. Heavy metal bass pounded from an old, blue Mercury Comet. Two teenage boys bounced inside as it passed. They hadn't even noticed her.

Ray met her instantly. "Are you okay?"

"I'm fine. This was nothing. I didn't see the car is all, and on these dark streets, there's no reason for him to see me."

He grimaced. "If you say so." Turning, he offered a short prayer over the group and their meals.

Cat closed her eyes and forced the threatening tears to hold. She could only think of how she'd treated Ray since his return. Dell was right. She'd been such a jerk, ruled by pride and insecurity.

Lord, help me do better.

After a short cleanup, he met her at the back door. "Maybe I should go out first and bring my truck closer."

"Don't be ridiculous."

"We both saw someone the other night. Someone smoking."

She pulled her jacket collar tight. The whole thing seemed foolish and surreal, and she had more important things to worry about. "I guess you can. But I'm not afraid."

"You're afraid, all right. You'd be stupid not to be." His eyes softened along with his tone. "It's okay to admit your feelings."

Her phone chimed a text alert as she waited inside the door. Myra. Cat read the brief note and bit her lip. A moment later, with the sound of tires on gravel, she darted out and climbed into the cab. "This feels so silly."

"All that matters is that you're safe."

His words tracked a course to the center of her being. Did he mean that? A bolt of electricity skimmed over her, but she suppressed it. She couldn't dwell on unfounded romantic notions.

"Myra texted that Ellis hurt his knee."

"I'm sorry. I guess they've been pretty good to you."

"I've been helping out there for a while. When Dad passed, they invited me to stay. Gave me a sense of family again. And I enjoy the work."

"Don't they have family?"

"Daughters. One's in Seattle. I get the feeling she's not too involved. The other is in Dallas. I've only seen her once a few years ago … that last Christmas." Why did she have to mention that?

Cat took a deep breath, wishing he'd figure out what she needed before she had to ask. "Anyway, I have to host a Scout banquet. With Ellis injured, you think you could come with me?" She rubbed her cheeks with her chilled fingertips.

"Sure."

The simple answer resulted in loud thumping from her chest. How could he not hear that?

She rode in silence the rest of the way. Had some Hollywood hero been driving the truck, she couldn't have been more star struck. Her knee wiggled and she stared out the passenger window. A cold bubble expanded in her chest.

So childish. So inane. Yet she couldn't stop her reactions. By the time they reached the inn, she was sure she'd explode. He had to notice the effect he had on her. He wasn't blind.

"I'll get your door." He popped out and jogged around the car.

She shut her eyes. First date fidgets controlled her body. As soon as he opened her exit, she slipped out and practically ran inside. "I've brought reinforcements."

Myra's presence eased her nerves. Even when Ray stepped into the kitchen. "Raymond Alexander. I'm so glad to see you're still in one piece. Virtually anyway." She wrapped him in a hug and kissed his uninjured cheek. "Your momma called me yesterday. I think your arrival added at least thirty years to her life."

"It's good to be home. But I hear you need some help?"

Cat slipped her arms from her jacket. Ray advanced and took it by the collar. His close proximity called to the goose pimples across Cat's arms. They popped out with a shivering sensation.

"Yes. That old man of mine spent most of the morning on his knees painting one of the upstairs bathrooms."

"No wonder he's sore." Cat began pulling Myra's lasagna pans from the double ovens and setting them on the dumb waiter.

"What can I do?" Ray asked.

Cat eyed him. Something that didn't require the use of both arms. "Can you toss the salad?"

"Salad makings coming up." Myra rummaged in the fridge.

Between the three of them, they set up warming bins in the upstairs dining hall with lasagna and bread, and an ice-filled salad cart with Ray's expert creation. Myra left Cat and Ray filling glasses.

"You suppose we scared her off?" Ray's eyes twinkled.

"She'll be back with the guests. She always greets visitors, even those who don't do an overnight stay."

"I bet she has some stories to tell."

Cat held his gaze. "I'd rather hear yours."

He looked to the floor and cleared his throat. He had something specific in mind. Something that upset him.

She waited.

A couple of families came in. The Scout leaders, adding

decorations to the tables.

Cat let her gaze linger on Ray for an extra moment, but he moved to help the Scoutmaster unpack a box.

Unfortunate timing.

As the evening progressed, she visited the different tables and took drink orders while Ray offered salad and rolls. He chatted with the guests in his easy manner. Light sparkled in his eyes when he made the people laugh. Then he glanced at her between servings and caught her staring. She dropped her head and turned to the table nearest her. "Anyone need more tea?"

For the better part of an hour, she and Ray served like they'd been doing it for ages. As the meal wound down, they cleared the plates, packed up the leftovers, and sent them downstairs in the dumb waiter a load at a time.

Myra worked with the dishes elbow deep in soapy water. "Everybody satisfied up there?"

"Yes. They started the ceremony."

Ellis sat on a bench at one side of the table. A bag of ice rested on his knee. "I feel plum useless. I'm sorry you had to work, Ray. Glad to see you back though."

"No worries, Mr. Stone. Happy to help."

Cat packed up the leftovers, while Ray helped Ellis to his suite. With the express washer filled, Myra chatted with the Scouts and their families as they made their exits.

Ray returned and popped a piece of a leftover bread stick in his mouth. "She's quite the hostess, huh?"

Myra's laughter echoed against the high ceiling of the entry hall. "Yeah. And she'd chew me out if she knew I'd not offered dinner to you. Can I get you a plate?"

"You don't have to wait on me, Cathy." He chuckled. "At Mac's, yes, but not here." He leaned against the counter. "But about the diner. What's your plan?"

Pain gripped her chest and a sob that she'd been stifling all day burst out.

Instantly Ray's arm was around her. "Aw, honey. Don't cry. You know God wasn't surprised by your father's agreement with Heath."

She hated the tears, but the warmth of his arm cuddled her like a baby. "I know. I wish I'd had some clue, though. Three weeks. It's not enough time to do anything." She stepped back and wiped a finger under her bottom lashes, not daring to look at him. "I'm sorry. Overwhelmed I guess."

"I don't mind."

The warmth and strength of his embrace felt familiar and right and comfortable. Why couldn't she just indulge in those feelings and forget the nagging worries that tickled the back of her neck?

The front door closed behind the last of the guests. Ray dropped his arm as Myra puttered back into the kitchen.

He reached for his jacket. "Billings will be here soon to take my place. I guess I should wait in the lot."

Cat slipped on her coat and walked out to the front porch with him. "Thanks for your help tonight."

"I enjoyed it."

"So your being here wasn't just another guard duty?"

He brushed his fingers through her hair and laid his hand on her shoulder. "Cathy, I'm the one who brought all of this on you. I can't tell you how sorry I am."

"I'm not trying to make you feel guilty."

"I know. And I'm glad you have a place to stay. Mr. and Mrs. Stone need you now more than ever."

She nodded. "Myra insists that the attic suite is mine. Though I hate the thought of imposing, I do love that room. And it's not like either of their daughters intend to step in and assist them."

He moved and propped his hand on the porch railing. "The one in Dallas. Hasn't she had anything to do with her folks at all?"

Cat observed him as he leaned against the wooden brace. A stance so familiar her heart turned with memories again. She pushed them deeper to maintain control. "Not much. Myra calls her a workaholic. She's some exec at a marketing company. Her job is all-important to her."

"I guess I can see her point."

She tensed. "Her point in abandoning her parents?"

"She has her own life. Has her own priorities. And you don't even know if Myra asked for her help. You could take a lesson and stop trying to save everyone else."

"Save every … is that what you think I'm doing? Feeding some glorified Wonder Woman complex?"

"I didn't say that, but I think you're far too concerned with the decisions others make. They don't have anything to do with you. Meanwhile, your life is in jeopardy."

"There's no real reason to believe that."

"How can you say that?" He raised his volume. "The letter I got. And the bullet in your tire."

"This is stupid, and I'm not going to argue about it." She whirled around, heading for the door.

"Fine." He stomped down the steps to his truck.

"Fine." She turned back toward him.

He paused at his truck. "Go inside so I can leave."

She wanted to tell him off, to scream. Instead, she shoved through the door. When would she ever learn to make her emotions behave?

Deliver me, O LORD, from evil men; preserve me
from violent men.... ~ Psalm 140:1 KJV

Chapter 7

Leaning against a large live oak, the man raised the telescopic sight to his eye. The light beside the entrance illuminated enough. Their angry voices carried from the porch, but the man blocked all sight of the girl.

She showed in the crosshairs but not long enough for him to fire before she moved. This time behind a square, white column. No problem. He'd be patient.

Voices rose and the man moved toward a blue pickup.

He set his sights again, but the girl spun and re-entered the house. He cursed and lowered the gun. No clean shot of any bedrooms from this angle. Except for all of the windows on the third floor. They viewed three of the four directions. He hadn't studied her movements long enough to know her habitation but felt it unlikely that she'd stay in what must be the best room in the house.

Glancing at the lot, he noticed the truck hadn't moved. Hairs stretched on the back of his neck, but he didn't need to worry. No one could see him without night-vision goggles.

He clicked the safety and began to dismantle his rifle when the light at the top of the house clicked on.

Fortunate indeed. Quickly reassembling the weapon, he kept his eyes on the glass. The shadow of the woman moving around the room gave him hope. He wished for a higher vantage point and considered climbing the tree he leaned against. But the height would doubtless slow his escape.

The top of a head came into view. Enough to hit and probably kill but not enough to be sure. This time, he'd better not make a mistake. How could he explain the need for another opportunity?

The head bobbed in and out of his vision until the woman stepped closer to the glass and glanced down at the truck still sitting in the lot.

Bingo. He pulled the trigger, relishing the explosion in his ear and the sight of the target going down. The echo of the discharge and crack of glass made him smile. He snatched up his gun case and picked his way back through the woods to a driveway on the other side of a hedge. He climbed into his Charger and pulled onto the tar road, heading away from the inn and away from town.

Assignment completed.

Adrenaline coursed through Ray at the blast, igniting every nerve. He burst through the door. "Cathy!"

"What was that?" Myra scurried from the kitchen.

He charged up the stairs. "Which way to the attic?"

"Stairs are next to the dining room."

Ray sprinted for them, meeting Cathy coming down.

She fell into him. "Ray! Someone's ... the glass ..."

"Are you hurt?" He tilted her face to look into her eyes and inspect for any blood. Little red marks and lines sprinkled across like freckles.

"You're bleeding." Mrs. Stone fished a tissue from somewhere and dabbed at the marks. "Bring her to the parlor."

She switched on the light and stepped out of his way. "I called the police."

Ray eyed the front door, which had a large beveled glass design and two long windows on either side. "Stay away from windows."

"Oh, dear. Yes." She hurried into the interior room.

Ray half-carried Cathy to the couch and knelt in front of her. "Are you hurt?" With her mouth hanging open a bit and her gaze traveling around the room, she wavered close to shock. "Cathy, look at me. Are. You. Hurt?"

She settled her eyes on his for a moment. "I don't think so. The window broke."

"Didn't you hear the gunshot?"

"Someone shot at me?" Her face paled.

Mrs. Stone worked on a scratch near Cathy's ear that kept bleeding. The older woman shot him a that-was-stupid look.

Great job, Ray.

"You're all right." He couldn't fathom how but sent up a prayer of gratitude.

"I dropped my earring." She held up the gold dangle previously clutched in a tight fist.

No coincidence there. God's own personal protection agency. *Thank You, Lord.* He choked back more praise lest the depth of his emotions spill over in liquid form. He rubbed heat back into her icy hand.

"Do you suppose the person shooting is still out there?" Mrs. Stone held Cathy's other hand, sitting beside her on the sofa.

"I doubt it."

She glanced at the parlor entrance. "But why would anyone shoot at the inn, Ray? We don't have any enemies."

"It was me." Cathy practically whimpered, igniting Ray's deep desire to pull her into his arms. "Someone's got the crazy idea that killing me will get revenge on Ray." She sniffed. "It's a silly notion."

Not a silly notion. It would destroy him. He couldn't make his mouth admit what his heart knew to be true. Had been true throughout his term in the field.

"I'm so glad you're okay, dear." Myra continued to pat her hand.

A siren split the uncomfortable silence. Ray stood and peered out through the doorway glass. Lights tracked the walls a second before the heavy pounding of Dell's footsteps on the porch.

"Myra?" The chief bellowed as he entered. "Cat? Is everyone all right?"

Ray motioned. "We're all in here, Chief. And all okay. Someone shot through Cathy's window. She's pretty scared and the glass cut her some but nothing serious."

"I think a gunshot is pretty serious, boy."

"I meant no real injury. Of course the shot is serious. Deadly."

He stepped into the room, and Cathy glanced up at him with the countenance of a naughty puppy. "I didn't go off the property."

The man's jaw muscle tightened. "See that you don't. Mrs. Stone, d'you have an interior room where Cat can stay tonight?"

"Oh my, yes. I have a suite that will work. It has a high gable window over the bathtub, but the glass is frosted."

"Good. Billings is here now. Shoulda had him here already, but I thought having a whole mess of Boy Scouts in the place would dissuade anyone from giving you trouble." The lines on Dell's face betrayed the depth of his chagrin over his judgment error, but Ray would've made the same assumption.

"I'll get Cat set up, Chief. Don't worry about that." Myra stood and pulled Cathy to her feet. Ray frowned. He should have been the one supporting her, but instead, he held up the doorframe like an adolescent too scared to dance.

"Danvers can take you to the diner in the morning. He'll stay with you until Grady arrives. No reason to think you won't be safe after that, right?"

Ray finally found his voice. "I'll keep an eye on her, too."

For as long as necessary.

Even tucked inside the interior room, Cat had slept poorly. Every sound in the creaky historic house startled her. And the heat didn't collect nearly as well in the building's second layer as it did in the well-insulated rooftop suite.

She stopped at the foyer mirror to make sure her cover-up lightened the raccoon circles under her eyes.

How Danvers sat in a cold car for hours went beyond her imagination. She expected to find a blue-clad popsicle topped with a tan cowboy hat. Instead, he smirked when she reached his car.

"Heard you're so small, not even a sharpshooter could hit you."

Cat stared at him. Her mouth dropped open. A joke? Really? Poised to give a sharp retort, she noticed his worried look. When she handed him the thermos of coffee she'd made, she caught his eye. "I'm okay."

He bobbed his head with a half-smile. "I'm glad." Taking the lid off, he poured a cup. "Dell would have all of our heads if anything happened to you."

After a silent drive into town, Danvers walked her into Mac's and checked out the empty diner. When he left, even after Grady's arrival, the creepy feeling of trouble lingered. The phantom of fear drifted around her in foggy wisps as she tried to concentrate on setting things up and dealing with her customers.

Through the morning rush, the gruesome truth of last night's terror hovered just under her consciousness. Only to revisit when the crowd thinned. Cat wiped down a table for the fourth time. The breakfast rush, if it could be called that, started late and ended early, doubtless due to the turbulent sky and the diving temperatures.

Someone had actually tried to kill her. No mistake about it. Cat lowered herself into the booth that she'd been cleaning.

And Ray. He'd been so scared. So worried about her. And so determined to make sure of her protection. Could he still have feelings? Didn't seem possible.

His certainty of her danger gave her a semblance of teetering along on some apex. Whether she balanced along the edge of a swimming pool or a cliff had to do with how long she thought about her predicament. After practically shining the paint off of the table, her skin prickled with foreboding.

The fact that Ray's long-kept picture of her stuck her in this mess in the first place still floored her. Why would he have that picture on his mission? The thought perplexed but sparked hope.

"Can I talk to you a minute?" Daisy's voice shook her from her reminiscence.

"Sure."

Daisy sat opposite and stared at Cat. Not a glimmer of the joking, flirty girl that normally wandered the diner. "I think you need a distraction."

"A what?"

"Look, I can tell you're scared spit-less and I don't blame you one bit. But since the accident, and after Ray came back and all, you're not yourself."

"There's nothing wrong with me." *Except for losing my father's legacy, letting people on the street starve, and hiding from a murderous maniac, I'm great.*

She smirked. "I will never agree with that statement, but you were already skinny. Now you're just plain gaunt. When was the last time you ate?"

Hmm. She couldn't consider breakfast. And she hadn't even snacked on a bread stick the night before while she served dinner.

"I'm worried about your health."

"You're not worried that I have a target on my back?"

She chuckled. "I'd have worried if the target was on my back, but I'm not nearly as worried about yours."

"Uh. Thanks a lot."

"That didn't come out right." She looked at the ceiling. "It's simple, Cat. God likes you."

Cat blinked. Daisy? Talking about God? "I didn't think you believed in Him."

"Oh, I believe in Him all right. I'm just not ready to join His club. I figure if I stay outta His way well enough, He won't notice I'm around until I've had my fun." She shrugged. "But you must be one of His favorites. Look how He's protected you so far."

Cat shook her head. "Wait a minute. That has nothing to do with anything. That's saying that God doesn't like people who get hurt or … die. Like my dad."

Her gaze shifted downward. "I didn't consider Mac. And I'm not so much into religious stuff anyway. You know that. But I'm thinking maybe you should take a vacation or something."

Cat squinted. "Are you crazy?"

"No, think about it, Cat. It could be fun. Could get your mind off of things. And it would keep you protected. Don't think I didn't hear about that gunshot thing last night. It's all over town."

So *that's* what this was about. "Daisy, the last thing I need to do right now is leave. I'd feel like I was running away from my problems, and that isn't in me."

"Before you dismiss the idea, think about how it might feel to not have a single thing to worry about. Nobody to serve or clean up after."

"And just how do I get to this paradise?" She had to admit, the picture Daisy drew sounded heavenly, but she knew better than to entertain the thought for long.

"Well, I haven't worked out all the details, but my momma has a place in Florida, you know. And she lives there some of the time, but she travels a lot and goes fishing and such. Could be you could stay there for a weekend. Sun, surf, handsome men."

"Tempting."

"And I got an uncle who could get you a good deal on a flight. He's a travel agent. This is the best time to get away for something like that. Break out of the cold-weather clothes."

The more Daisy talked, the less dreamlike it felt. The pressure started rising as the conversation leaned toward the hard sell. Time to end this. "I don't want to talk about it anymore."

"But ..." The entrance of a new customer hushed Daisy's comment. Mrs. Heath and her daughter strutted in and took the center table like they owned the position.

But they didn't own Mac's ... not yet. Cat's neck stiffened.

"We'd like slices of your Magnolia Pie and two cups of coffee." The older woman announced her demands to the entire room, training her eyes on the far wall.

Cat stood and moved to the bar. "Sorta cold out there today,

Mrs. Heath. What brings you here in weather like this?" Cat filled two mugs and brought them to her table as the cowbell proclaimed another visitor.

"We had some items to collect from the hardware store. Can't imagine why Rupert Burrows won't deliver. We'll think twice before purchasing from him again."

The fact that Mr. Burrows would have to close his store in order to deliver anything since he didn't have a second worker didn't occur to Mrs. Heath. But then she didn't mean her threat either. A lot of bark, but she seldom showed any follow-through.

Her daughter sulked and tapped away at her iPhone.

"How are you today, Lila? Is that a new eyebrow ring?"

The girl paused, giving Cat a silent stare before re-engaging her media.

Daisy brought the pie and the check and pulled Cat into the kitchen. "You don't have to be sweet to people like that all the time. They don't care, and they sure aren't going to be nice back. Unless it's just business?" Daisy's manicured brows angled upward in a look filled with hope, though Cat couldn't fathom why.

She matched her friend's whisper. "I don't treat them any differently than I treat anyone else. Do I?"

"That's just it. They are your enemies. Buzzards waiting to steal this place away, but you don't talk to them any differently than you talk to the homeless folks who come by here every night."

"You're not making any sense, Daisy. And how do you know about the Heaths taking over Mac's?"

"Is that a secret?" She straightened, her pink fluffed ends bounced against her collar.

"Not anymore, I guess."

"I just want to know why you're nice to mean people." Daisy raised her voice a tad.

Cat took her arm and tugged her into to the office.

Daisy pushed the door almost closed. "I can only guess it has something to do with that church thing, 'cause I see the same thing in Grady and Pastor Slaughter. Ray, too."

Cat didn't know how to respond. How could she explain things like that here, now?

"At first I thought the stuff you learned at church was like a political opinion or something, but you're different than most people. You actually go out of your way to be nice to others. You're even nice to folks who are rotten to you."

Daisy would know. They'd both had some pretty rude customers. The remarks flattered Cat, but she struggled for the words to answer her. She couldn't even pray out loud. How could she share what she so deeply believed?

"I wondered if you acted like you do because of your rules from God." Daisy stared at the door. She'd obviously been giving this some thought. "I mean, you and Grady talk like He's a real person or something."

Cat bit her lip, verses whirling through her mind, but where did she start? This was exactly the sort of situation when her dad used to lead people to faith in Jesus. He'd ignore the other customers and start in with his own experience. Sometimes, he just gave the people something to think about. Other times, he'd sit down with them, pray, cry, and have a full worship service.

Her words jumbled on her tongue and her mind blanked. She sighed. How could she possibly expect to follow her dad's path? Instead, she responded to Daisy's direct remarks. "I don't know where you got the rules part, or the politics. God *is* real, and I try to be nice because ... well ..." Memories flooded back. "Because God loves me even when I'm not very nice."

She snorted. "When have you *ever* not been nice?"

"Plenty of times." Shame slumped her shoulders. "Remember when Cassidy Gonzalez couldn't find her shoes before cheerleader tryouts?"

"I heard about that. She slipped twice on the tile floor." Her eyes grew big. "You took her shoes?"

Cat stared at the floor. "I'm not proud of it. I told Cassidy about it a few days later. I even planned to quit the squad, but she'd decided to go out for the drill team instead." She looked up at the blonde. "I've done other mean and ugly things, too. Even said some horrible things to Ray just this week." She touched her arm. "But the point is, God still loves me. I'm His baby. He forgives me."

Gulping air, Daisy's gaze intensified. "You think He'd … I mean …" Her chin lowered, and she crossed her arms. "I've never really done anything good before."

"That's not why He loves me. The Bible says that He showed me His love when He died in my place, even though I wasn't a good person." Cat wished she knew the verse.

Grady's spatula hit the bell. "You got some new customers out here."

Shootfire. Cat prepared to let them wait, but Daisy backed awkwardly away.

Still, she'd shared. A little anyway.

The lunch rush, though smaller than normal, ended all opportunity for further discussion. Just as well. Cat couldn't fathom broaching the subject again.

Through her scurrying about, she sent up a silent prayer for her friend. *And please let me know what to say if another opportunity comes along.*

As more people drifted into the diner, Cat wondered who might be the shooter from the night before. Several of the men with the construction crew casually turned their eyes in her direction. She recognized one or two of them, but they came in and out so regularly that she couldn't be sure.

Toward the end of the rush, a man came inside. She'd seen him before, an angry customer the morning Ray had returned. He scowled at her and scanned the room. Then he turned on a bright smile that didn't reach his eyes and took a seat at the counter. "I'm looking for a beautiful, redheaded lady named Cathy McPherson. Do you know her?"

Cathy? No one called her Cathy except Ray. She wished he were there.

She gave a tight-lipped smile. "You're teasing me. Who told you to call me that?"

"Not at all." His perfect intonation hinted at radio or television training. "We have a mutual acquaintance. Merely a connection, really. A missionary who worked with your friend. I was surprised to learn that he'd returned already."

The hairs on the back of her neck rose. Everything about this guy seemed false. Maybe if she delayed him, she could get Grady's attention. "Have you talked to Ray? I bet he'd enjoy meeting you."

"Precisely my intention. But while I'm waiting for him, I thought I'd enjoy a piece of your Magnolia Pie. I'm told it's the best in the county."

The man had the appearance of a billboard model. His smooth voice reflected international travel. Between his syrupy tones and the way he called her Cathy, she felt an intense need for a shower. And thoughts of the gunshot weren't far from her mind.

"And a cup of coffee for such a chilly day."

Still, he couldn't do too much in a room full of people. She glanced through the kitchen window. Grady had his back to her.

Bad timing. She decided to play stupid until she could catch Grady's eye. "Are you meeting Ray here?" She collected a mug from the stacked column.

"Why don't you join me?"

Not on your life ... Or mine. She smiled. "Need a slice of Magnolia here." She called through the window. Maybe that would make Grady take notice. She set the mug on the counter and filled it from the pot, then pushed it toward him. Lightning fast he thrust out his hand, grabbing her wrist in a steady grip.

She almost dropped the pot. "Let go."

The man's grip tightened.

Cat doused his lap with the steaming liquid from the glass carafe.

He released her and jumped up with a howl.

That got attention. Grady moved to the doorway, a large knife in his hand. "Problem, Cat?"

"I am so sorry." Cat's pretended apology gained a couple of chuckles, but the diners began to ignore her again.

A hard edge came to his features like an anvil forming on a bunch of fluffy, white clouds. Hate filled his eyes, and the muscle in his cheek twitched. "Next time ..." The sing-song of his voice vanished. Rasping whispers replaced the debonair tone. "I won't miss ... kitten." Glaring at her, the man tossed a few bills on the counter. "For the coffee."

Cat left the bills where they lay for fear that he would grab her again.

He took off. She bolted toward Grady. "What were you going to do? Mince the man?"

"Iffen I had ta. But I didn't want to make a scene until ..." Grady shook his head. "Until I seen him grab you. But you got a quick reaction. Bet that hurt." He smiled but worry filled his eyes. "I called Dell when I seen him come in."

A cruiser zoomed down Shepherd Street about the time that

Danvers crashed through the door. "Everything all right in here?"

His jolting entrance collected the stares of the entire room. "We're all just fine." Cat smiled and looked around. "Aren't we, folks?"

"Anyone want some pie?" Daisy turned on the charm, probably to return things to normal.

But normal was long gone.

He sits in ambush in the villages;
in hiding places he murders the innocent.
His eyes stealthily watch for the helpless; ~ Psalm 10:8 ESV

Chapter 8

Ray hitched his stride across the street. His errands took way too long. So much for the late lunch he had wanted.

"What do you mean you can't return to the inn?" Dell's bellow resounded to the sidewalk as Ray neared the door. He stepped into the warmth of the room.

Cathy straightened and stared almost straight up at the chief. "I can't. I have some business I have to take care of at the house."

"Why today?"

She folded her arms. "Daddy's will and that partner agreement. That shouldn't have been such a surprise. I thought I knew everything about Mac's. Now, I realize there are all sorts of files I've never looked at. A whole cabinet full, as well as boxes. Then, there's his desk—"

"And all of that can wait." Dell mirrored her stance a foot or more taller than her.

"Before I got the will, yes. Now, not so much. I've got to go through all of that to get Heath papers, receipts, warranties. No time to waste on that."

Ray loved the way she stood up to the old man, head high and chin up as though she measured six-feet instead of five-one.

She gave a slight shrug. "And I don't mind telling you that I hope to find some legal document to rescind what Dad's will says."

"You can give up that pipe dream."

Her shoulders lowered slightly. "I know. But especially with things the way they are, I need to find a way to keep serving dinner to the homeless. You know Heath isn't going to help me."

"I'll go with her, Dell, if that's what you're worried about." Ray stuck his hand in his blue jean pocket.

The chief's frosty brows met in the middle of his forehead. "What I'm worried about is some guy coming in here and grabbing her, telling her he won't miss next time."

"What?" Ray went cold.

Dell explained the visit from the stranger, with Cathy interjecting comments. She downplayed the whole thing, but Ray saw fear in her eyes.

Dell shoved his cowboy hat on his head. "What? You think you're gonna find some long-forgotten receipt from where Mac paid Heath off?"

"Maybe."

His cheeks sagged. "Why don't you give me the night to work on finding the guy with this new lead?"

She shook her head. "No good. It's only for a bit. I need to get through all of this today."

The chief turned his piercing blue gaze on Ray. His right eye squinted like it hurt to think so hard. He sighed. "All right, here's the deal. You two work there until sunset."

"But I don't do the dinner tonight. Grady and Daisy do."

"'Til sunset. I want you back at the inn before dark, and one of the officers will meet you at the gate. Got that?"

"Uh …" Cathy's fist landed on her jutted hip.

Ray couldn't help his chuckle. "*I* got it." He relished spending more time with her, especially alone.

"And I can give you some good news for a change." Ray handed her the plastic-covered garment. "Your coat."

"How'd *you* get it?" Dell straightened.

"Mom sent me to the cleaners. Mrs. Flores found out I was coming down here." He shrugged. "She did a pretty good job, too. Doesn't even smell bad."

Cathy sparkled and shrugged on the scarlet, full-length wrap. She pulled a green scarf from the coat rack and slipped it around her neck. "It's perfect."

"Sunset." Dell pointed and tapped her nose.

"Yes, sir." She followed Ray to his truck.

Opening her door, he had an odd déjà vu moment, like the old date nights they'd had. He climbed in and pointed to the scarf. "Didn't my mom give you that?"

"Yes. She knitted it for me that last Christmas we … the one that I …" She reddened.

He remembered. Their last Christmas together. His senior year in college. She and Mac had come out to the ranch. He'd promised to return home for her. And she promised to wait.

Instead he had jumped on an amazing opportunity without giving her so much as a telephone call.

She stared out the passenger window and avoided his eyes.

Just as well. What could he say to her anyway?

Cat stared out the side window until her childhood home came into view. She didn't give Ray the chance to open her door for her, not this time. Why had she brought up their last Christmas? The whole month had been magical, full of gifts and promises. Well, almost-promises.

Ray probably imagined her as a bride. Mr. Perfect watching her come down the aisle, an overgrown kewpie doll enmeshed in white tulle growing around her like some sort of kudzu. No wonder he turned tail and ran.

As she opened the door, dust particles swirled and danced in the late afternoon sunbeams fighting through the slats of the Venetian blinds. Cat slid a finger along her dining room table. "Hard to believe this place got so dusty so fast."

"Are you okay? Being here, I mean."

"First time after Daddy ... I'm okay." She opened the top drawer of her desk. "I'll be excellent if I can find something useful."

Ray sat at her dad's desk, sorting through drawers full of papers. "Remind me why we're here again?"

She started to slip off her coat, then thought better of it with the draftiness of the house settling in. "I need to go through Dad's files. I haven't done that. And now ... Well, I guess I need to get things in order to hand them over to Heath."

"Unless you can find something to change that part of the will. Is that what you're hoping for?"

She clamped her jaw, but she couldn't tell him he was wrong. Long shot or not, she wouldn't give up the wish. "I have no idea what might be in there. Likely comic books, knowing Dad."

"Ha! Maybe they'll be valuable."

Cat shrugged off her negative expectations and dug into the desk drawer. Receipts and warranties for the new appliances Dad had purchased last year filled a file folder. A listing of specialty food sources went in as well.

Ray attacked a wooden filing cabinet. A few minutes later, he laughed and pulled out a Captain America comic.

Cat loved the musical sound of his chuckle, the delightful curve of his mouth and show of his straight teeth. She joined him. The ice that had gripped their relationship began to loosen its hold.

They commented from time to time and chuckled over Dad's various collections. A clay bowl painted green and red that Cat had given him for Christmas candy when she was eight. A binder full of baseball cards he hoped she'd be interested in someday. Tourist pamphlets from every road trip they ever took, even the one to downtown Dallas.

Daylight dimmed, and they'd found nothing with Darrell Heath's name on it at all. Cat glanced out the window at the clouding sky. "I need a few things upstairs. Then we should go." She unloaded a lapful of trash into a box.

"I'll load up the files we didn't get to." Ray sauntered out the front door with the box. Cat jogged up to her room to get a quilt from her cedar chest. The new room Myra had given her was considerably colder than her suite at the rooftop level.

Then there was that bottle of perfume that Ray had gotten her for their last Christmas. She'd left it here, barely able to keep herself from smashing the thing against the concrete outside. Now, she had a reason to apply it. She carried her quilt into the bathroom and opened the cabinet under the sink, feeling around for the bottle.

While the darkness obscured her view, she knew the bottle sat just inside and reached for it. Not finding it, she tried again, but still came up empty.

She turned and flicked on the light switch. Whirling back around, she halted, facing the mirror.

Sorry I missed you.

Her scream echoed against the walls. Steps pounded up the

stairs. She should hide, escape, but the words, written on her mirror in crayon-red clamped her feet to the tile floor.

The shooter. *He wants to kill me.* The startling memory released her captured feet. She stepped backward through the doorframe. Into Ray's arms.

"The mirror. A message."

He glanced in the bathroom then did an about-face, pulling her to the steps. "We're getting out of here."

"Shouldn't we call Dell?" She clutched the quilt as he pushed her ahead of him and followed her down the stairs.

"When we get on the road."

Halfway down, the house went dark. Cat let out a squeal and halted, dropping the quilt. Ray pushed closer to her. "You know this house, Cathy. Don't stop. Lead me to the front door."

She fled straight across the room and opened the front door. A clamor sounded in the room behind her. Ray jerked the door shut.

They bolted to his truck, but a black Charger had parked behind it. Ray grabbed her hand and tugged. They ran past the corner of the house next door and headed toward downtown.

He turned his head.

She followed his gaze and saw no one. "You heard him. He was right behind us."

"I heard him."

Cat looked again. The nose of the black car pulled into view. "We've got company."

"Need to get to the PD."

The glass doorway of the always-open station lay ahead, several doors down and across the street.

Cat struggled to keep up with Ray's longer stride. "Will he come after us if we cross?"

"We need to chance it."

She turned again. Still the car sat. Too long. The driver had to be watching. She eyed the large cement planter across the street. The only barrier besides the curb on the whole block. "Better sooner than later."

"Good idea. Let's go now, before he can accelerate."

Without hesitation, she dashed into the empty street. The car squealed its tires in the right turn and roared down on Cat. Ray's hand touched her back. She stretched out her stride, leaning into the sprint. Hopping the curb, she hurdled the decoration in front of Betty's Beauty Barn. Ray pushed her against the glass of the shop front.

A crash sounded behind them and rocks pelted the glass around her. Ray's body protected hers completely, but she predicted he'd been hit by the debris.

"Go." He pushed away from her and grabbed her hand for a second.

The black car had destroyed the planter, but with smoke rising from its crumpled hood, the chase was done.

"Come on!" Ray shoved her ahead of him.

She put her head down, ignoring the burn in her lungs and thighs. She didn't turn until she reached the door to the police station.

They both paused, looking down the road. A couple of cars stopped and two or three people came from offices and shops along the street to see the source of the ruckus. The sedan backed off of the stones and turned in the opposite direction.

Ray pushed her through, then came huffing a step behind her.

Cat gasped for breath and bent double with her hands on her knees. "Why ... do you suppose ... Why didn't ... he shoot us?"

"Who tried to shoot you?" Dell stormed through the doorway at the end of the room.

Ray puffed. "No one."

"Chief, hit and run at Betty's." Mrs. Hawkins called through the gap in the glass window.

"Do we need an ambulance?"

"I'll check."

Cat still struggled for air and put her hands on top of her head, pacing the little waiting room and willing her heart to slow to a subatomic speed.

Ray shamed her, already breathing more normally, even in his injured state. "No one was hurt, Chief. Black sedan. Didn't get the license."

"What do you know about this?"

"Tried to run us down." He glanced at Cat. "We're okay, though."

"This time. What about next time?" Dell turned bright pink and walked to Mrs. Hawkins's window. "Send Vasquez and Evans down to check out the accident site."

"Yes, sir."

"Not gonna be a next time, Chief."

"That's right." Dell's neck splotched and a vein stood out on his forehead. "She's staying right here."

"Here? You have to be kidding?" At least Ray was on her side.

Cat straightened. "You can't put me in jail."

"Don't tell me what I can and can't do. And you'll do what I say, little girl."

Little girl? She fisted her hips. "Keep that up, Dell, and I'll walk out of here right now."

"You listen to me, missy ...." He stuck his finger in her face.

"I won't until you stop talking foolishness." She stamped her foot, feeling ridiculous, but unable to control herself.

"Both of you stop." Ray pushed between them. "Cathy, settle down. The chief is just worried and trying to protect you."

"Yeah, so you'll do as I say." Dell spoke from behind Ray's

head.

"Wait a minute, Chief. Putting Cathy in jail doesn't find the guy trying to kill her."

"You think hanging her out like some glorified minnow will catch this fish?"

"That's not what I mean. But if we can hide her, thoroughly, then you can follow up on some of the trails he's left and continues to leave while he looks for her."

"So we hide her in jail."

"Oh, no, you don't." She crossed her arms. And he'd better not try.

"You know the town better than that. Every detail that happens around here might as well go up on a neon sign."

"So what do you propose?" Dell spoke a little quieter, and his color adjusted to nearly normal.

"Let her stay at my parents' place."

Dell snorted. "Oh yeah, with the gossip queen herself? That'll work."

"Mom keeps her mouth shut when she has to."

"Name one time."

He turned to Cat. "How much did you know about my mission?"

"Nothing." What did that have to do with Vi? His direct gaze penetrated her fog and his full meaning burst forth. "She knew you were going and didn't tell me?"

His mouth flattened, and he nodded. "She also knew where I was the whole time. Any hints?"

No. How could she have kept that secret all these years? "Why didn't she tell me?" A sharp pain stabbed through her chest.

Ray faced Dell. "The place is off the main loop, quiet, and highly secure. And since I used the last name of Johnson while in the field, they have no clue of my real name or to my parents."

A few moments of uncomfortable silence made the tension rise, but Cat still ached from the revelation of Vi's betrayal.

"All right. She can stay with your folks."

Cat chimed in. "Maybe I don't want to. Why can't I stay with Daisy, or maybe Donna?"

Dell snorted again. "Donna doesn't have the room, and Daisy is an obvious connection. Until something changes, you stay on the ranch with Ray and his parents. If you don't, I'll put you behind bars so fast your eyebrows will have to catch up."

Cat's gaze hit the ceiling. That didn't even make sense.

For I know the plans I have for you, declares the LORD,
plans for welfare and not for evil,
to give you a future and a hope. ~ Jeremiah 29:11 ESV

Chapter 9

Ray flipped in his bed. Finding a comfortable position was useless. His body ached from the unexpected exercise of the evening. But sleep evaded him, even when he did find a cozy configuration.

Kicking off the covers, he crawled from the bed and shrugged his plaid robe on over pajama pants and a t–shirt from a long-ago Christian concert. He paced along the front windows overlooking the driveway. Silence. An unmarked brown cruiser sat just outside the gate. Nothing traveled on the little used road.

Everything seemed normal. So why couldn't he settle down? A tempting aroma drifted on the air, coaxing him further awake. Barefoot, he crept down the stairs and entered the kitchen, startled to find Cathy.

"What are you doing?" Ray rubbed his hand through his hair. Bedhead ruled. Expecting to score a cup of Mom's coffee before taking a shower, he hadn't reckoned on Cathy being up so early. Or in his kitchen wearing a cute, frilly apron.

"I got bored so I thought I'd do a little baking. Casserole in a couple of minutes and muffins following."

"You got bored? At five in the morning?" He chuckled and filled a mug with a fresh brew. Cathy's sparkling eyes enchanted him along with her brassy hair curling around her cheeks. He liked to see her wear her hair down.

"Did you forget where I work? I'm always awake by now, usually earlier. And I'm used to cooking for people. It's the least I could do for your mom and dad for letting me stay here." She glanced at him shyly. "For you, too."

"I …" *I love having you here. Say it, stupid.* "I just want you to be safe." He mentally slapped his forehead. How lame.

He pivoted. "I'll be, um …"

"Upstairs?" Her confused expression didn't rival the twisted feelings that affected his mind.

"Yeah."

As Ray showered, he flinched at how dumb he'd sounded.

New rule. Never speak to Cathy before being fully alert. He hustled into clean clothes and ran his fingers through his wet hair.

The smell of fresh-baked something and bacon drew him downstairs. He met Mom and Dad as they chatted over plates with bacon and squares of breakfast casserole as well as blueberry muffins with crumb topping. "Mm. Cathy, this smells amazing."

"Is amazing." Dad agreed through a mouthful of muffin.

Cathy handed him a laden plate then reseated herself across from him.

"If you ever want to hire out, Cat, Vi could use the help." Dad chuckled.

"Thanks a lot." Mom threw her napkin at him. "Truly, though, I hate cooking. I don't know why it never appealed to me."

Cathy kept her eyes on her plate. Obviously uncomfortable. Ray shouldn't have told her about the secrets. Had he forever spoiled their friendship?

She took a swig from her Diet Pepsi. "I'd be happy to do the cooking while I'm here."

"I can't let you do that, Cat." Dad wiped his mouth. "You're our guest."

"At least let me take care of some meals? If I don't have something to do, I'll go crazy."

"Okay." Dad nodded and pointed at her. "You're hired. Take care of dinner tomorrow. Nothing else, though. Agreed?"

"Agreed until after dinner tomorrow. Then we'll talk again. Yes?" Cathy held up her soda and Dad *thunked* it with his coffee mug.

"Done."

Ray took a final bite of the egg casserole. Delicious. He wanted seconds, but an idea took shape. "I think I have a solution to your boredom. Why don't we exercise the horses a little this morning?" In high school, Cathy came over to the ranch to ride every day just before sunset.

Her eyes sparkled. "Really?"

"Dell said to stay on the ranch. He didn't say you had to stay in the house." She'd be safe. No one had a clue where she was.

"I'd love to." She bolted toward her room.

"Good on you, son." Mom took hers and Dad's plates to the sink. "But I noticed that Cat is a little … I don't know, colder?"

"I had to tell her about the secrets."

She slowly turned to him. "She must think me a monster."

"No." He took his dish to her. "She's hurting a little, but she'll get over it. She'll feel a lot better once we ride. You'll see."

"I hope so."

Ray took his time changing to jeans and boots. He still beat Cathy to the stable. He greeted his dad's horses and pulled the tack off the wall where it hung in order. The scent of leather and hay settled peace on him. He hoped for the same effect on Cathy.

"Thought you might take Misty," he suggested when she came into the barn. She'd changed. Long-sleeved plaid shirt over a green turtleneck. Brought back all of the times they'd spent mornings doing this very thing.

"That'll work. I suppose Prince is going to be your mount?"

Memories of her teasing came back to him. Her accusations of riding the horse so the royalty would rub off. And that Ray had purposely turned the palomino against her, so he didn't have to give up riding rights. "Maybe."

He glanced at her. Did mischief shine out of her eyes?

She turned her back and led Misty to the watering trough. Climbing on the edge of the metal tub, she mounted the horse.

He quoted their typical banter from yesteryear. "I thought after cheerleading for so long, you'd just swing yourself onto Misty's back." He let Prince chew on the bit.

"I would, but I still can't reach the horn for leverage." She smirked. "But thanks for reminding me about my height. Wouldn't want to forget that I'm challenged in that area, you know."

"You? Short? I never noticed. I just thought I was above average."

Usually that elicited her sweet smile, and she'd reply, *You are above average, Ray Alexander*, but this time she just spurred Misty into a trot toward the open fields at the back of the property.

He followed her at a walk through bare trees with a few live oak and some pine sprinkled among them. Some of the trees needed trimming to keep them passable. He made a mental note to discuss things with Dad. Side by side, they loped across the hay lot, barren at this time of year. Her ponytail sparkled in the rays of the sun, bringing back memories that made his chest ache.

She slowed near a pond, and he caught up. "At least you don't have to worry about Misty rolling in the cold water. Even she's not that stupid."

Cathy laughed. She could always laugh at herself, even after Misty took her into the pond that summer day so long ago. She'd been covered with mud and sludge.

"Good thing, too. I didn't learn my lesson the first time and brought her right back here. Would serve me right to be waist deep in a near frozen tank." She tugged on the reins. "But then, I've already had my polar bear plunge this year."

Ray sobered. What if the first attempt on Cathy's life had succeeded? Or the second? He scanned the area. *Sevilla can do whatever he wishes.* Miguel's statement haunted. But Ray would do whatever it took to keep Cathy safe. "I'm sorry about your car. About … everything."

Everything. The word hung between them. Her shoulders stiffened. She dropped her gaze and nudged Misty into a trot.

He shifted the reins to his left hand, took off his black felt cowboy hat, and wiped the sweat on the back of his flannel sleeve. His apology had upset her.

How was he going to apologize for the apology?

By the time they returned to the barn, the sun angled toward the west and Ray's stomach growled. He tied Prince to the post and took Cathy's reins, walking Misty to the barn to let Cathy get off at the big crate that they used to secure the oats.

"Thanks." She dismounted and reached for the leather straps, laying her hand over Ray's. Her touch caused his breath to catch. He turned slowly toward her, seeking her ivy-colored eyes.

She stared at their hands. Had she felt the spark? When she looked up at him, her expressive gaze held … fear?

"Cathy."

She didn't turn away at his low whisper. He stepped closer,

111

not missing her slightly parted lips. Her brows puckered as she lifted her hand to his injured cheek, stroking it like a warm feather. Wishing he had both of his arms to hold her, he released Misty's reins and stroked the curve of Cathy's smooth jaw. Hairs that had escaped the ponytail rolled across the back of his hand. He moved in to claim her lips.

A car horn jolted them. Ray stepped back. What was he doing? A lousy protection job, that was for sure. He'd been so distracted, he hadn't noticed Donna's monstrous old Chevrolet bouncing up the road. Dad must have let her in, but how had she known where to find Cathy?

He might be a failure as a boyfriend, but even if he destroyed their friendship, he couldn't risk failing as a bodyguard. "How did she know where you were?"

She widened her eyes. "I wasn't thinking. Donna called late last night and asked if I was up for some girl time. I told her and Daisy to come."

Great, Daisy, as well. The opening of car doors and girlish laughter poured ice water on him. That and the fact that anyone could have followed them. "No more phone calls."

Cathy nodded and rubbed her hands over her upper arms. She strolled over to meet Donna and Daisy at the barn opening.

"Sooo, what's going on in here?" The latter eyed him suspiciously, but he gave her his back and loosened Prince's saddle.

"Stop dreaming. I'm under house arrest. Ray just gave me a little freedom is all. Anything beyond that is just ridiculous."

Her words stung. Whatever happened between them, she waved off like an annoying mosquito.

"You go on in. I'll take care of the horses." He needed to be away from her for a while.

"Hmph. Like I'd let an injured man carry all of that stuff by himself?" She loosened the cinch and hoisted Misty's saddle.

Donna and Daisy insisted on helping, as well. One took Prince's saddle from him and the other grabbed a brush and shooed him into the house.

Ray's injury forced him to lose his manhood. Lousy boyfriend. Lousy bodyguard. Now he was a weakling. He stormed into the kitchen.

"Boots!" Mom's call halted him. He retraced his steps to the mudroom. Just inside the back porch, he slipped the dirty things off with a wooden boot-jack attached to the floor.

"You two have fun?" Mom passed him as he headed upstairs.

He stopped, his raw feelings piercing what little pride he had left. Words poised on his tongue. His eyes shifted. He opened his mouth then closed it again, nodding. He continued up the stairs.

None of them had purposely insulted him. Of that he felt sure. Cathy had made her feelings obvious. She had little respect for him at all. But her thoughts didn't matter. He had a call to make. He hoped Dell would just send a cruiser this direction to check things out and not haul Cathy back into town for putting herself in danger. Again.

Donna hopped into the floral-covered wingback in the Alexanders' formal living room like she'd regressed to high school age. "We've got a great idea, but we need to jump on it or the rest of the town won't have a chance to join us."

Cat brought in mugs of hot chocolate and let herself be drawn into the exuberance. "Okay, tell me."

Daisy shifted on the loveseat, leaning forward, over her long legs. "Remember when you begged your dad to throw a fiesta for your eighteenth birthday?"

"You want to throw a fiesta?"

"It will be great." Donna matched Daisy's body language. "We can set up at Mac's or even outside in the gravel lot. Have a band and do some line dancing."

"In January?" Though the weather would be the least of Cat's issues with what sounded like a wake for her losing control over Mac's.

"Forecast says we're going into a warming trend. If it's only a little nicer than today, it would be okay." Donna's eyes sparkled. "And we can hang a piñata. Molly will be so excited."

Donna's precious four-year-old had more personality than most teenagers Cat had encountered. Molly's snaggle-toothed smile flashed across Cat's memory. She loved the candy-filled punching bags.

"If memory serves, your sweet girl's begging to hit the piñata was the only thing that lured you to church, to that block party last year."

"Would have taken a lot more than that for me." Daisy turned away and took a drink from her mug.

"Good thing, or I would never have realized all I missed in my life." Donna and Cat turned toward Daisy, but the blonde didn't bite.

Cat relished the diversion. She didn't want to talk about a party. "So how does Molly like preschool?"

"She loves it. And I love that she's only there half-days and can play in the back room of the salon the rest of the time. I'll really miss having her nearby when she gets to first grade. She'll be gone all day then."

"I can't believe you're already fretting about something that is two years off." Daisy chimed in, not turning.

"A year and a half, but who's counting?" Donna took another drink from her mug and toyed with an M&M in a crystal bowl.

"For pity's sake, stop playing with the thing and just eat it."

"Heavens, no. Do you have any idea what's *in* one of these little innocent babies?"

Donna's dedication showed in her skill with her business, her relationship with her daughter, and in her svelte physique. "Just one of these can lead to all sorts of issues. I'd have to learn to cut hair while working out on the elliptical."

Daisy giggled. "As long as you're not cutting mine."

"Yeah, I'm thinking I should do that with Mrs. Heath, or maybe with Lila?"

"By all means, do that with Lila. She'll never notice." Daisy burst into a fit of giggles. Donna joined her along with Cat, though more subdued.

Mention of the salon brought back the nightmare from last night. Cat concentrated on relaxing her shoulders. "Speaking of the Beauty Barn, does Dell have any leads on the guy that rammed into your planter?"

Her friend's pert mouth flat-lined, and she gave a shake of her head, ruffling the dark stylish bob of her hair. "No. Not so much. Just some guy. Too dark to see." She pushed her bangs out of her eyes. "I hoped someone had seen something. The planter is ruined."

But it saved her life and Ray's. Cat kept the little tidbit to herself, thankful that Dell removed that part of the story from the verbal headlines.

Daisy squinted at Cat. "How do you know about her planter if you're supposed to be under guard out here?"

"Under guard?" Donna turned to Cat for confirmation.

"Did I say I was under guard?" She knew better than to discount the accusation.

"House arrest, remember?" Daisy squinted at her.

"Oh, that." She forced a laugh. "Not really that big a deal."

"So you're staying at Ray's place for the scenery?" The pink ends of her hair danced on her blue scarf as she let out a trickle of laughter.

Cat threw a pillow at her. "There's nothing between us."

"Right." Donna tilted her head and arched an eyebrow.

"What about the threats?" When would Daisy learn to shut her yapper?

"Threats?" Donna straightened. "What are you talking about?"

"Danvers and Dell have been hovering a lot more than normal, and it's not because of Grady's cooking." Daisy set her mug down on a stone coaster with a thump. "You're gonna get leg cramps jumping to such long conclusions." Cat sipped from her mug, but the smooth chocolate suddenly tasted bland.

"Maybe the guy who's threatening Cat is the one who hit the planter." Daisy pulled Cat's mug away from her mouth. "I'm right, aren't I."

Where had she come up with that crazy scenario? And how could Cat keep her from realizing its truth?

"Who is he?" Donna directed her question at Daisy.

Cat took the opportunity to go into the kitchen. "I'm getting some more hot chocolate. Anyone want chips or popcorn?" Surely she'd seen something like that in Vi's pantry.

They continued their chat, voices animated by the excitement of intrigue. Didn't matter the questions or who the story included. Didn't even matter if all the facts landed in the right places. Events like last night would fuel the Heath's Point imaginations for days, maybe longer.

Funny how Cat knew these girls from childhood but never really socialized with them until they all got out of school. Donna, a couple of years younger, had been a wild child, scoffing at the goody-

goody cheerleaders. And Daisy, tall and beautiful, had been homecoming queen and basketball champion a couple of years before Cat. She never paid any attention to those she considered beneath her. Literally and figuratively.

Now, and especially with Dad gone, every friendship felt so essential.

Cat found some celery sticks and a half a bag of baby carrots that she dumped into a bowl. She rummaged through the fridge and found a half-used jar of spinach dip which she spooned into a dish. Grabbing a bag of pretzels and refilling her mug, she carried it all back to her spot on Vi's leather sofa. "Got the munchies?"

Donna claimed the bowl with a squeal.

Daisy snatched a fistful of pretzels and dunked them in the dip one at a time. "So if we close the back parking lot, we can take the whole day to decorate and set up the stage at one end."

"Close off the lot?" Dell would never go for that. "Don't you have to have all sorts of permits?"

"Already spoke to the chief about it. He says he'll make sure the civic forms are done up right."

"He's okayed it?" Were they talking about the same Dell?

"Yep. He loves the idea. And all of the downtown shops are good with the plan as well."

"Wait a minute, y'all. Whoa-back. You know we can't do a party. Heath would never go for it."

Donna popped a baby carrot and spoke through her crunching. "'Snot a wake. T'sfunser."

"She means fundraiser." Daisy dunked another pretzel. "And it's not Heath's decision. Not yet. Besides, we've already planned it all out."

Ugh. How did she break this easily? "Girls, even if we do raise a lot of money, the chance of Heath selling me his controlling interest is minimal." She put her fingertips to her forehead. "I can't let you waste your time tossing pennies in a bushel barrel."

Daisy rose and stood in front of Cat. "Must be tough to lose something you've had your whole life."

Funny how she could sum up such a wrecking ball with one little sentence. With a hollowed out chest, Cat kept her gaze on the floor. "There's more to losing Mac's than my livelihood."

The woman lowered into the seat. "I get it. Your father's legacy. All that you have left of your parents."

Another strike. Was Daisy trying to destroy her? A tear dripped. "Mac's is all that, but the diner means survival to Dash and the Dupree family and a host of others." She shouldn't expect Daisy to understand. Wiping her cheek, she looked up at the pastel-blonde. "I appreciate your idea, but I want to save everything I can to keep the meals going at least a little while longer. Even if dinner becomes hotdogs or cold cuts."

Donna leaned forward, a glow of joy shining from her face that had been absent during high school. "That's what the party is for. If we can persuade Heath to give you back control of Mac's, great. But we're doing it to raise as much as possible for continuing the sunset dinners. Folks all over town are planning to help."

"The Tex-Mex place by the freeway is donating food, and Fresh Greens is sending over salad fixings." Daisy bubbled. "And the Chicken's-a-Must owner is offering tea, lemonade, and extra wait-staff."

"That's right. They're doing all the waiting. You, Daisy, and Grady get to sit and relax."

"I'll go for that." Daisy laughed. "And there are several businesses that are donating services for a silent auction. Even the Superstore manager is kicking in a bunch of gift cards."

"How did you do all of this?" Cat looked at the same Daisy

she always saw, but there was something different about her.

"Come on, Cat. I just act like I'm stupid and talk like a hick. At the risk of blowing my cover, shall I remind you I was valedictorian?"

"Ha! Out of a class of forty-seven." Donna slapped her thigh.

"Funny, I didn't see *you* getting anywhere close." She flung a pretzel at the other girl.

Donna giggled and flounced out the room. "Anyone need a refill?"

"I'm good."

Daisy stayed silent, staring at Cat. "You think this is ... I mean, I know this little thing isn't enough." Her eyes glistened. "But you think, maybe God would like me a little with this party?"

Cat bit her lip. "Oh, Daisy, is that why you're throwing this party?"

"No. Not at first. But since I was already thinking about it, I thought maybe God would give me a credit or something?"

Her eyes, opened wide and hopeful, made Cat's heart break. She shook her head. "God's not a great big calculator that keeps track of your good and bad." She laid her hand on her friend's. "He loves you. Adores you. And wants so much for you to know Him."

A mirthless chuckle emanated. "Me?" She sniffed and wiped a finger across her nose. "No, you're confused. I've never done anything worth loving." Tiny lines appeared between her brows. "Not since basketball in high school. I don't suppose He's a fan."

"He's a fan of you." How did she explain God's love, grace, mercy, all of it?

Daisy hopped up and turned her back to the kitchen as Donna came bounding toward her chair.

Cat swallowed. Again, she'd missed her chance.

"So we're all set to jump in on this, then?" She gulped her

drink. "I've already talked to Mr. Canzoneri at the high school to borrow some staging platforms and stuff."

Wow. They had done so much. "Do we have time to pull this off? I have to be out in just over two weeks."

Daisy spun. "Oh, honey, we're already on the job." Gone was the vulnerability of a few moments before. "We've planned everything for this Thursday night. Hopefully the weather will be as nice as they are predicting."

"Spring-like, if you believe the forecasters." Donna chomped on a celery stalk.

"But if things turn cold or wet, we can use the elementary cafetorium. Not as roomy as the lot, but the place will work in a pinch."

They had all the details covered. "Sounds like you two have put a lot of thought into this. I won't stand in the way. Just tell me what you need me to do."

Donna squealed. "Oh, that's the beauty of the whole thing. Everything's done. You can just enjoy the fun and reminisce about all of the special times we've had at Mac's."

Reminiscing was exactly what she didn't want to do. She mustered a smile and begged the girls for the opportunity to shower. They left just as giddy as when they arrived.

Cat hated to rain on their parade, but storm clouds were gathering.

Trust in the Lord with all your heart,
and do not lean on your own understanding.
In all your ways acknowledge Him, and
He will make straight your paths. ~ Proverbs 3:5-6 ESV

Chapter 10

Ray heard Cathy and the others in the living room and steered clear. Using the back stairs, he crossed the large family room at the rear of the house. Dad sat in his study, so Ray chose the morning room, a glassed-in back porch with a hot tub in the corner and space heater near some lounge chairs. He turned on the heater and opened his laptop.

Thankfully, he'd spoken to Lt. Estrella when he called about Cat's visitors. Juanita was serious about police work, but she didn't go over the edge like Dell did. But then, Mac hadn't been her best friend. And Cat wasn't her goddaughter. Either way, she downplayed the issue and sent a cruiser to make wide security circles.

The stress levels he'd been entertaining required a little time to veg. While Cathy sat perfectly safe in the other room, he worked to shut his frustrating notions down. He surfed on the Internet to wherever the waves took him.

His stomach growled again as he flipped to a sports site. No lunch. "Won't do." He listened for the girls. Still there. Still talking.

After more than an hour, he thought they'd be gone by now.

Sneaking into the kitchen proved no problem. In fact, he thought he heard Donna and Daisy leave while he made himself a turkey sandwich.

He hoped so. Desire begged him to rekindle the flame he and Cathy shared in the barn. He wanted to do something to put them back in that place, ready to make that connection. But the other side of his brain hoped the very thing he wanted most wouldn't happen. Not while Cathy still stood in the face of danger. He couldn't protect her while his heart turned somersaults every time she smiled at him.

When she smiled, which wasn't nearly often enough.

He took his sandwich and peeked into the living room. No one. Not the noisy friends. Not the precious redhead.

Collecting a bottle of water, he returned to the morning room. He started to sit on a wicker chair but caught movement out of the corner of his eye.

Cathy sat on the ledge of the hot tub. Her head rested in her hands and soft sobbing rose from her.

Instinctively, he stepped closer but stopped. What could he do? Obviously she sought privacy. His arrival would just embarrass her. And besides, no matter how badly he wanted to stir the feelings between them, he couldn't let himself get so caught up. He needed his head clear of emotions while her safety remained his responsibility.

Donna's honking car reminded him of just how quickly he could fail if he let her get too close. And failure could prove disastrous.

He retreated, softly, and turned when he backed through the doorway. Best to leave her alone this time.

What a lousy friend she was.

Here they were, planning a party on her behalf. And she only craved them gone so she could puddle into self-pity.

Surely planning her funeral would feel less painful. *I can't do this.* As much as her heart wrenched at the thought, she had to try. Had to do whatever she could to continue the dinners. Until some of the churches could step in. If they would.

But what if they didn't?

She sat on the steps of the hot tub as a wave of regret washed over her. Her life plummeted into a downward spiral. Her dad, her car, the diner. All gone. And now a perfect opportunity to tell Daisy about Jesus. The chance to step into her father's place—his talent for sharing his faith to any who needed hope. Instead, she let Daisy leave.

Then there was the lunatic who hunted her.

And Ray. Their close encounter ignited a spark she believed long dead. Did she dare hope? Could she risk her heart again?

In that small corner, with all of the plants and curtains to dampen the sound, she gave in to her pent-up emotions.

Wiping her nose on a tissue, she sniffed, breaking the silence of the room. She dragged a fingertip under her bottom eyelashes. The last thing she needed was for Ray or his parents to witness her inability to control her emotions. And Ray had always been so protective over her. He'd likely fuss. She smiled to remember his arms about her, coaxing her to abandon her tears.

A shuffle caught her attention and she turned in time to see Ray exiting the room. So much for the memories of his attentiveness.

Her neediness probably turned him away from her in the first place. Likely, he left without her because he didn't think she could cope in the mission field, and he didn't want to deal with the tears.

She lifted a prayer that Dell would solve this case sooner rather than later. The Alexanders needed release from their promise to protect her. And a quick resolution allowed Ray to return to the life he chose without the trouble of having her around.

Sunday morning started with an argument. Ray sided with Dell. Of course, Cathy couldn't go to church. It would be the first place anyone would look for her.

But he kept his mouth shut and let the chief do the ramrodding. Not like he needed Ray's help.

By the time Ray left them to sort through the details, Dell's lady-friend, Juanita Estrella, had soothed Cathy's worries about missing services.

Squeezing through the doors of the filled foyer of Shepherd Street Baptist Church, he immediately slipped his coat from around his bad shoulder and off his one arm. Whether from the overworked heater or from the crowd that shuffled around the little room, the stuffiness made it hard to breathe. Even with the scent of coffee in the air. He looked across the expanse for Dad's gray head.

"I heard you were home." An exuberant blonde whose name escaped him threw her arms around his neck. He stiffened. A rosy floral replaced the coffee smell. He sneezed.

She released her hold and smiled at him.

"Um, hi." Who was this girl?

"I want to hear everything about your adventure, sugah." She stepped back and tossed a length of straight hair over her shoulder. "That is, unless Cat McPherson still has you branded." She spilled over with a ripple of laughter.

Branded? "I'm not sure …"

A dark-haired girl stepped next to her. "I'd like to hear about your ministry in Mexico."

The two looked like a set of equal opposites. The blonde, tanned and slim. The brunette, same form and figure, even the same hair length and style, but pale. Both overdid in the makeup department.

"I don't think Cat's even here today." The blonde looped her arm around his. "So we've got you to ourselves."

Ray peeled her hand away, trying a polite laugh.

"It's not like she's gonna care that you were talking with us." She reached for him again. He dodged.

"I think I see someone." He pointed and escaped backward, swallowed by the worshipers.

He moved to the counter where a half-dozen volunteers filled steamy mugs for anyone interested. "I'll take a hazelnut, please."

Mrs. Dupree entered with the boy from the other night. They seemed to be wearing the same clothes they'd worn at the sunset dinner. Two teenagers stood nearby. He lifted his hand.

"Well, then. Here you are again, young man." She introduced her kids, the boy about fourteen, thin and shy. The girl a few years older. She gave him a bored look before following her brother into the sanctuary.

"Sorry about that. Micah has trouble with people he doesn't know. Melody just has trouble."

He set his cup on the counter to help her remove her lightweight overcoat. The woman needed more protection from the cold than that flimsy thing. At least it wasn't supposed to be too cold for the next few days. "I understand. I think raising kids has to be the hardest job."

"And when they get Melody's age, they's wanting freedom, independence. But they go about it all wrong. Get all moody and striving after the wind." She folded the coat over her arm. "But I keep praying. Spirit's gonna have His way with her someday. I just know."

125

"Like some coffee? The hazelnut is outstanding."

"Don't mind if I do. And thank you."

He ordered and retrieved the paper cup for her.

"So now, you said you was friends with Cat. How long you gonna wait?"

Ray started to nod then halted. "I beg your pardon?"

"Young man, I've seen enough to know the difference between looks of friendship and full-out attachment. How long you gonna wait to tell her you are in love with her?"

Oh wow. Maybe speaking with that blonde girl would have be easier after all. "I'm ... well ... that is ..."

"You don't need to answer. Just make sure you have my name on one of the invitations is all." She nodded her head and followed her teens.

Where had she gotten such a crazy .... For a moment, he indulged in the thought of invitations and flowers and Cathy in white lace. He blew the thoughts out across the surface of his coffee and snapped a lid around the rim.

The blonde made another beeline for him. He turned toward the sanctuary, but worshippers blocked his path.

The girl caught up and squeezed in front of him. "Since Cat's not here, you think you could join us for lunch?"

Her teammate stepped alongside, making a short wall. "You could share your stories."

Myra Stone neared and gave Ray a worried look. "What do you mean Cat's not here?"

The blonde gave her a half-second glance. "She didn't come today." She kept her eyes on Ray, answering the gentle woman through the back of her head. "Maybe she's willing to release the stranglehold she always had on Ray, here."

Wow. Could she be any more direct? And repulsive?

Mrs. Stone's brows rose with a wrinkle in between them. She laid her hand on Ray's arm. "You don't think anything has happened to her do you?"

How could he answer that? He wasn't supposed to know anything about her, but he didn't want to make the woman worry more.

Her husband stepped closer and fielded the question. "I'm sure she's fine. Maybe she's taking a day off?"

"Cat doesn't take off days from the diner, much less from church."

Ray dropped his chin.

"Do you know where Cat is?" Mrs. Stone stopped a man whom Ray didn't know.

"I got a call from her a bit ago, asking to be replaced in the third-grade class this morning."

So Cathy worked with the children. A slight smile played across Ray's face. How he'd love to watch her with her class.

"Did she say why? Was anything wrong?"

Donna Fuller stepped up behind Myra. Ray gave her a helpless look.

"I think Cat's visiting. Doesn't she have some cousins in Canton?"

Ray nodded. He'd met them once. Her mom's family, though he couldn't remember their last name.

Donna shrugged, grabbed a coffee, and scooted.

The blonde giggled. "Problem solved." She leveled her gaze at Ray and advanced with a pout. "And you, sugah, are free for lunch."

He took Mr. Stone's arm as the man passed, following his wife. "Should be careful with your knees and all."

"They're much better today."

"Glad to hear that, and if you let me help you to your seat and keep that blonde off my tail, I'll promise to paint your next project."

"You sure? You don't know what the next project is." He chuckled.

"As long as the job doesn't involve a blonde bloodhound, I'll take it." He walked the man toward the front then settled in next to his mom.

"Everything okay?" His mom spoke low, even though energetic music flowed from the speakers.

He sipped from his lidded cup. "Some girl setting her sights, I think."

"Oh, you must have come across Angela." His mom rolled her eyes toward the arched ceiling. "Sugah."

He squelched a laugh.

"She's been asking about you since you left."

"I don't even know her."

"She's Bubba's younger sister."

"Oh, man." Romantic attention from his friend's baby sister? His whole face cringed.

Pastor Slaughter stepped to the podium and offered a prayer before the worship set began. A band took their place and the chords started the moment he spoke the *amen*.

How different from the Chiapas meetings. Songs broke out all the time. No one really led, though one of the first converts had a good strong voice and opened a song if no one else offered one. Without video screens or instruments, how had they managed? Ray shook his head.

Leaning against the cushioned pew on the left side of the brown and burgundy worship center, utter luxury surrounded him. The environmental control kept him comfortable enough. A sound system amplified the message and music. Thick carpet cushioned his feet, and the roof covered his head. The patter of rain echoed around the room as the gray clouds that greeted the dawn finally squeezed themselves out.

He'd heard the sound in Chiapas many times. The regularity of the rain, usually during their services, was one of the reasons many of the villagers attended. A particularly loud storm had also masked the approach of the machete-toting men who attacked.

He wiped his hand over his face to erase the memories and concentrate on Pastor Slaughter's message. Another luxury—sitting here listening instead of standing there talking. He'd been the Lord's mouthpiece to the Lacandon people as well as His feet and hands.

Ray's heart warmed. *Thank you, Lord, for allowing me to serve. And for Miguel. Giving him the ability to get us to safety.* The Lord had protected him well, despite his minor injuries.

Near the end of the service, Pastor Slaughter changed directions. "We've been praying for some time about our erstwhile missionary somewhere in the tropics. You might remember how he and his ministry partners brought down the dictatorial regime of a drug cartel leader in the area."

Ray's cheeks heated.

"When we lost contact awhile back, we feared the worst but prayed for the best. I'm here to tell you that the worst tried to happen, but God thwarted the intentions of the evil one. Raymond was wounded in a brief attack, but he is here with us today."

Applause erupted.

Please don't make me stand.

He gritted his teeth and stared at the floor. How ridiculous that they ignored his utter failure, his cowardice and defeat.

"Stand up, Ray. Say a few words if you like."

Ray stood for a half a second. He gave a pressed smile and a wave, shaking his head at the pastor. No words came. Opening his mouth would surely have emptied his stomach.

Philip gave vague concluding remarks. Ray breathed out his relief. His friend had let him off easier than he expected. If things worked as he hoped, he'd make a quick escape. With Cathy safely in Dell's care, Ray had some things to consider, and he needed solitude to do it.

"Be blessed as you go out." Philip was wrapping up. "And after we pray, make sure you come down front to chat with Ray a bit and truly welcome him back."

So much for sneaking out.

Cat rearranged the condiments in a little tray in the center of the table. Force of habit. Somewhere in the back kitchen of the chain restaurant, a dish clattered on the floor. Not like that didn't happen at Mac's from time to time, but the customers usually whistled and clapped. Here, nobody paid attention.

Just like Dell hadn't paid attention to her arguments to go to church. Of course her salvation wasn't wrapped up in church attendance. And yes, they could likely find someone to take her place. But he missed the point. She wanted to be there. Needed to be there with her church family. To indulge in worship that forced everything else to fade away.

She stared at the man on the bench cushion across from her, whispering something to his on-again/off-again girlfriend. Talk about third-wheel syndrome.

Purposefully removing the scowl from her face, she tried to rework her thoughts. This whole thing was a new form of worship. Obedience. Since she couldn't alter Dell's plan, she needed to find joy in the situation. She relaxed in her chair and let a waitress place crepes and over-easy eggs on the table in front of her.

"Not so bad letting someone serve you for a change, right?" Juanita smiled across the table while Dell, sitting beside her, asked for some ketchup for his omelet.

The round-faced woman rib-poked the big man. "On eggs? That's disgusting even for you." Her glasses hid her dark eyes, but Cat bet there was laughter there.

"No different than salsa, without the kick."

Juanita stretched her deeply tanned hand between her plate of waffles and the condiment tray. Cat grasped it as Dell spoke a short prayer of blessing over those at the table, the food, and their friends.

Cat echoed his *amen* and picked up her fork. The mixed smells of sweet and savory began to erase her annoyance at missing her worship service. "Thank you both for bringing me out here."

Dell smirked. His cheeks pink under bright blue eyes. "I didn't think you'd relish spending Sunday morning in front of a TV."

"You know where I'd rather be." Okay, she'd obey. But she didn't have to thoroughly embrace being absent.

"I'm glad you realized the folly of that action."

She let Dell's comment go. No more argument necessary. Though given half a chance, she'd be teaching her third graders right now.

Juanita buttered a biscuit. "Don't mind him. He's grumpy because the leads from the accident didn't pan out."

Cat had already heard and didn't want to think what that fact meant to her.

She continued, "But don't you start worrying. I'm following up on every detail."

"I thought you worked at Emmittsville, now."

Dell cleared his throat. "Lieutenant Estrella has returned to HPPD. Guess she couldn't get enough of us." He lifted his chin without a smile.

Juanita's mouth tightened, and she let her eyes drift upward to the man before giving her head a swift shake that bounced her shoulder-length black hair.

Hmm. Juanita had moved to the Emmittsville department when she and Dell started seriously dating. Did they break up?

Cat contemplated their relationship and popped a piece of crepe into her mouth, letting the cream cheese and strawberry flavors mingle. Maybe that's why they wanted her with them. To ease tension?

Wow. If Cat was the one to ease tension, they were in serious trouble.

"So I heard about the fundraiser." Juanita broke the uncomfortable silence as she cut into her waffle.

"Daisy's doing." Dell took a bite of his omelet, covered in red goo like an icing job on a cake.

"And Donna's. I'm not sure what they hope to accomplish, though." Cat's shoulder muscles flexed.

"At first, Daisy set to saving Mac's."

"Not possible." Cat hated admitting defeat without a fight, but her diner couldn't be the first priority. The people who depended on her meals deserved all of her effort.

He continued, "So she thought to raise as much as possible for the homeless folks who come eat." He sat back and wiped his mouth. "They've canvassed most of the downtown merchants. Even Mr. Havesheim is donating something to the silent auction."

Juanita sparkled when he mentioned the other businesses. "He's right. I heard that most of downtown will stay open late on Thursday to help the celebration. Many of them are doing giveaways and having special sales."

"Yeah, and the hardware store is giving away blankets to the needy. Anyone who comes in until they run out."

"Wow." Tears bit at the corners of her eyes. So many people had been touched by both the diner and the man. Mac's legacy was even bigger than Cat realized. She set her fork on her plate.

Dell didn't move but kept his eyes trained on her. "I know you're hurting."

Tears pooled. The pastry took on a Van Gogh appearance. "He touched everyone he met. Why would God take him? Why now?" She rubbed under her eyes with her napkin. "I shouldn't question. I know that. I ... just ... miss him."

Juanita leaned forward. "Cat, honey, God understands that. And His shoulders are way big enough to carry your questions."

"I don't have answers for you, Kitten." Dell's eyes looked moist. "Wish I did. That's where your faith and trust come in. Tell me this. Have you felt alone at all since your dad died?"

She internally winced at the word but shook her head. On the contrary, she'd felt pampered and fussed over. Almost babied.

"Christ said He'd never leave you without comfort. He's kept that promise, because He's a promise-keeper. And He'll keep all of His other promises, too. Like the fact that you can't do anything or go anywhere to get away from His love."

Cat sniffed. "I know all those things."

"But it still hurts." Dell put his hand over hers. "I know. Me, too."

A deep breath assuaged the heaviness. "But about this security detail."

He shook his head. "That's a done deal. You're staying under wraps until we find this man who's been trying to hurt you."

Her back muscles tightened. Surely, Dell didn't mean to keep her away from the diner. Not when she only had a few days left there. "I'm working at the diner tomorrow." On this topic, she'd not relent.

He visibly tensed, fisting his knife and fork. "You're willing to throw yourself into harm's way so you can sling—"

"Dell." Juanita laid a hand on his arm. "Your blood pressure."

Cat steadied her gaze on his face. "I'm not putting myself in harm's way. I'm waitressing. For the last few days in which I'm allowed to run Mac's." She laid her hands in her lap.

"Stubborn. That red hair of yours is showing a bad side."

Had nothing to do with her hair. She'd not miss a moment in her father's place, serving the people he cared about. People she'd grown up with.

At her lack of response, he crossed his arms. "I suppose I'll have to transport you."

"You can't let Ray do the toting?" Juanita sipped her coffee.

"Already thought of that. I don't want her to be seen coming or going with Alexander."

That was a relief.

"Seems like the trick will be returning her to the ranch." Juanita fingered the brim of her mug.

"Yep."

The couple seemed to have forgotten Cat was even with them.

The lieutenant leaned her elbow on the table. "Trackers, multiple vehicles?"

"You and I think alike." His mouth curved in a tender smile. Definitely something special simmered there.

"You could probably use some backup?"

"You don't have to. I can take care of things."

"Never said you couldn't." She glanced toward the window next to them. "Thought I could tag along. Maybe get a bite afterward."

Dell's gaze rested on Juanita's head. "I s'pose."

A genuine smile broke out across Cat's face. There might be hope for Dell yet.

But they who wait for the Lord shall renew their strength;
they shall mount up with wings like eagles;
They shall run and not be weary;
they shall walk and not faint. ~ Isaiah 40:31 ESV

Chapter 11

No more, Lord.

If Ray had to endure another pat on the back or admiring glance, he'd sprint right out of the worship center.

He eyed Philip. His *friend* set him up to be cheek-pinched by every dear little old lady in town. And his mom stood there beaming at him.

The donut he'd eaten soured. Mom would adore him no matter what he did, but these people. They congratulated a fraud.

He smiled and tried to give cordial replies to the well-wishers. At the first sign of a gap, he excused himself out the side door. Even the chill of the courtyard didn't chase away the nagging truth.

To have these sweet people believe better of him than he deserved was one thing. To have Cathy think of him as a hero was another.

Something she said about him speaking at the sunset dinner the other night struck him wrong. He couldn't remember the exact wording, but he felt like she was commenting on his grand experience. His high missionary status. He had to set her straight.

"There you are. You altogether vanished."

Great. Bubba Crane's sister again. She followed him through the exit he'd taken. At least she'd shed her shadow. "Needed some air." Needed solitude. He couldn't be rude. However, standing in the ornate and way-too-empty walkway with this girl, he'd rather be in a crowd.

"Lunch?"

"No, thanks. I've got—"

"You have to eat, sugah." She looped her arm through his and tugged him toward the parking lot.

He could do rude if she continued to persist.

Mom trotted down the steps from the foyer. "Oh, good. I was hoping you wouldn't be too long. Your dad and I wanted to go over a few things with you."

"We're going to lunch." Angela stuck her chin toward Mom.

Self-absorbed. And her insult to his mom begged a reply. He struggled with how to give one without upsetting his mercy-filled mother.

"Oh, dear Angela …" Mom pried the girl away, inserting her own hand into the curve of Ray's elbow. "Never try to come between a man and his mama. If he really wants you, he'll make the separation himself."

Wow. For all of her leaning toward mercy, she knew when to stand and fight.

"But what about our lunch?" Angela fisted her hips.

Ray looked over his shoulder. "There is no *our*." Tempted to say more, he turned and put his arm around Mom. "When was the last time I said, I love you?"

"I don't know, but certainly not recently enough."

"Thanks for the rescue." He gave her a squeeze.

She led him toward Dad's car. "Rescue from the star-struck teenager? That's nothing. Actually, son. I need your help."

He frowned. Mom chatted away, but his mind honed in on her phrase. Star Struck? Did the girl think of him as some celebrity? He had to squelch that idea fast.

"... so we're going to visit with Aunt Eleanor. Thought you could keep an eye on Cat for us."

"Wait ... what?" No. Not yet. He needed to think through the conversation. To rehearse.

"You weren't listening were you?"

"I was ..."

"Well, Angela is a beautiful girl."

He snorted. "Creepy-stalker-chick."

Mom halted, her eyebrows rising. "Raymond Wesley Alexander."

"I'm sorry. I wasn't distracted by her looks. I didn't like the way she spoke to you. Or how she invited herself to lunch with me, like I owed her the date."

Her posture relaxed. "I probably should have dissuaded her before." She shrugged. "She's got it in her head to claim you."

"Already figured that one out." He opened the passenger door.

"So you can keep an eye on Cat?"

He opened his mouth. Then shut it with an exhale and nodded. In truth, having an afternoon alone with her would be his sincere pleasure. Until he had to speak. Which he'd have to do at some point. And he had no idea what he was going to say.

How could Cat be a third wheel with only her and Ray in the truck? As strange as it seemed, the atmosphere in the pickup felt the exact same as in the sedan with Dell and Juanita. At least there, she'd had a reason for feeling extraneous.

With Ray, she felt more like a babysitting chore. And the feeling started as soon as Dell dropped her off at the ranch. Ray had been lacing hiking shoes. She could swear he'd scowled at her. But even if she'd imagined it, he'd said precious little.

She sat in the heat-filled cab for an extended moment as the abbreviated conversation spun through her head. No explanation. No purpose. Going for a walk.

She exited his truck, resisting the urge to slam the door. Even without the extra muscle, the sound echoed from the bank of trees on the edge of the empty parking lot at the Heath's Point Nature Preserve. "You'll remember, I didn't ask to come." She spoke to the back of his head. He couldn't even look at her. The air wrapped its clammy hands around her shoulders.

Instead, he eyed the side mirror and picked at something there. His jaw muscle tensed. "I know. I know. But since Mom and Dad are both gone, you have to come with me."

"Why are we way out here?"

"I have some things I need to ..." He paced away then turned toward her like he was going to finish his thought. He reached for her then tilted his head back and turned away. "Just follow me, okay?"

"I thought I was supposed to stay on your parents' property." Not that she didn't like the lake area, but being with Ray again, so soon after the way he'd turned away from her the night before ... her back stiffened. She couldn't let his presence or their solitude get to her.

"Technically you still are. Grandpa deeded this part over for public use." He pulled a wool cap over his sun-kissed waves.

She slipped on her white winter-weather jacket and pulled the fur-trimmed hood over her head. The preparation felt like the senior ski trip she and Ray had enjoyed at Red River, New Mexico.

Only this time ghosts hung between them.

And *this time* he turned and walked off without taking her hand or even glancing in her direction.

She shoved her hands in her pockets and followed down what seemed more like a wash than a trail. Moist sand streaked the limestone with patches of brown grass and weeds on either side of it. Ray set a pretty brisk pace, and Cat struggled to keep up.

Exercise always helped her attitude. Maybe Ray had the right idea. Though the Pollyanna in her faded as he distanced himself.

Why was she doing this? She preferred a tour through town and greeting people instead of climbing through nature. Especially at the jog she had to use to keep up. She slowed to her own speed.

Ray walked over a slight rise and turned a corner, disappearing from view. The isolation crawled up the base of her neck, but she shrugged it away. No one knew their plans. She hadn't even known until they got there. And with no cars in the parking lot, there was nothing to fear. Maybe it would be good for her to be by herself for a while.

Hadn't she been longing for a little seclusion? Time to think?

But then again, thinking too deep could prove disastrous. She glanced over her shoulder again. Would she see another cigarette flare?

Why did she have to look so fetching in that little white coat? Ray focused on the trail and listened for her to follow. Sure enough, her light footsteps padded behind him.

Good. He raised his eyes to the sky and stretched his stride. God had to calm his heart if He expected Ray to protect Cathy. He could barely even glance at her without feeling his chest flip.

He should have waited for his parents' return, so he could've taken this trip by himself. All he could think about was being with her. Having her alone.

But instead of taking advantage of the opportunity—of speaking his feelings and failings—he rushed across the rocky trail hoping to escape what he refused to face.

Mom and Dad likely planned the visit with Aunt Eleanor before he even arrived home. Then again, his mom had a penchant for matchmaking. Did she throw him and Cathy together on purpose, hoping to find them rekindling the flame by the time she came home? Mom's perfect dream had always been to marry them off.

Ray shook his head. Cathy had been a vision in pink lace on their prom night. How much more beautiful in white. He hurtled the thoughts away.

"I can't do this." He kept his voice to a throaty whisper, unwilling to let Cathy hear him. *Lord, I can't keep her safe if I can't keep my mind on her safety.* The attack washed over his memory. Sweet, gentle people at the end of machetes. He couldn't let that happen again. Not to anyone. Especially not Cathy.

The walkway narrowed through trees covered by a bed of pine needles. Ray glanced back to see how she fared.

Where … he whirled and retraced his steps at a run, catching sight of her as he rounded the turn out of the trees. She gasped, her cheeks flushed and her eyes widened.

"Are you okay?"

Her brows furrowed. "Scared of silly ghosts." A wisp of red curled around the edge of her hood, taunting him to tuck it inside.

"I guess I went a little fast."

She kept her eyes forward and didn't alter her pace.

"I didn't mean to leave you behind."

She stopped, and her eyes met his for a moment. Questions filled them. What had he said?

"Why are we here, Ray?"

He lifted his head, seeking the treetops, anywhere to keep from looking at her. "A stupid idea. I needed to calm my brain."

She exhaled long and deep. "I should have guessed that. You always used to run whenever we had an argument." She crossed her arms. "Only I didn't realize we were arguing."

She *would* have to remember that. He let his gaze drift back to her. "We're not. I'm doing a fine job of arguing with myself."

"About what?"

The feathery red strands of her hair called to him again. He reached out and fingered them. That last Christmas. When they talked of their lives together. He'd all but proposed to her. And intended to as soon as he returned. But God called him to Mexico.

And he cowardly left without explanation or even a goodbye.

He shut his eyes and let his hand drop as he turned toward the woods. "I'll slow down."

"If you head toward the right when you get to the fork, you'll get to the other parking lot. Maybe by then you'll be tired of walking? We can cut across on the road and get back to your truck."

"You really hate this, huh?"

"Hate is such a strong word." She padded behind him. "But I admit that walking around in the cold wilderness wasn't anywhere near my bucket list for today."

Ray took the right fork. The atmosphere seemed so different than the jungle environment he'd returned from. There, the sound never stopped. The breeze rustled slapping leaves constantly. The birds and animals always had something to holler about. And the damp woodsy scent permeated every trail. In the towns and villages, dust, mold, and septic smells took over, but the trails cutting through the jungle had a clean, natural aroma.

Here, he smelled nothing at all. And the quiet creeped him out. Nothing but the padding of Cathy on the trail behind him, and that silenced for a while as they walked through a pine-needle carpet. Everything felt so dead.

"Is this the way you wanted to go?" He turned toward her, more to check on her. His question gave him an excuse.

"Yes, the lot is ahead over there."

The edge of it appeared behind a rise in a barren field.

She trotted a few steps and came up on his left "So have you chased away your demons?"

Fat chance of that happening. Might as well head to the house. If he didn't, he'd risk getting drawn even deeper into his feelings. "I'm fine."

"Good." She took the lead rounding the curve into the empty parking lot.

"Ray?" Cathy stopped so suddenly he almost plowed into her.

Not empty.

"I see it." The black Charger that tried to run them down sat parked close to the hill they'd skirted.

"What do we do?"

He pushed her behind him, and they backtracked a few paces. "Keep a look out." He turned toward the hill.

"What are you planning?" Her whisper trembled.

But explaining might waste precious time. "Watch the path." He pointed along the way they had come, and climbed up the steep slope that made one end of the parking lot. He lay on his belly and peered over the ridge. The sedan sat there, the busted grill and broken headlamp had pieces sticking out in odd angles. Even the hood had a huge crumple, but not so bad as to block a driver's vision.

Where was that driver?

Unless the man reclined across the rear seat, he wasn't in the car. Ray decided to find out. He picked up a few stones and flung them as hard as he could into the windshield. They popped against the glass with a muffled clatter. Not large enough to crack it. He wished he'd had a brick.

No one appeared in the car or otherwise. Nothing moved.

He broadened his scope, rising to his knees in the dead grass. "I don't see anyone." His whisper cut the silence.

Cathy tilted her head, looking up at him with her hood hanging down. "Not a soul." She spoke louder.

He put his finger to his lips. Where was the driver? Ray needed to sight him in order to avoid him. "I think we better go, while whoever drove that car is missing." He jogged down the incline and collected her hand as he passed.

Circling the hill, the lot appeared silent. He stepped off the sidewalk, making a point to walk behind the vehicle where he hadn't had a good view. Still nothing and no one. The light penetrated the interior but showed no signs of life. He paused.

"I don't want to see inside, Ray. Let's go, please?" Cathy tugged at his hand.

She pulled him to a wide sidewalk. He followed her to the place it ended, where the hill eased into the edge of the woods. The last squares of cement rose over a gully of sorts. A pipe, traveling under the lot, pushed through the rock to create a drainage ditch.

Ray made use of the high vantage point to scan the trails below for movement.

Instead he saw a man lying in the gully.

He halted. Cathy's hand slipped from his. "What?"

Instantly alert, he rushed forward, pushing her ahead of him. "Checking out the trail is all."

He'd moved her to nearly a jog by the time they reached his

143

truck and climbed in. She didn't even peel off her jacket.

She breathed hard. "What did you see?"

He pulled off his cap. "You saw the car."

"You saw something else, Ray. Don't try to lie to me. You could never get away with it."

How well he remembered his attempts to avoid her in the past. He hadn't even been able to keep her surprise eighteenth birthday party a secret.

But he wasn't an adolescent anymore. He pulled out his phone and dialed Dell's cell number.

"What's happened?" Anxiety colored the chief's voice.

"Cathy and I are fine." That would calm the man a little. "But I think I found a body. And I think it might be the guy that tried to run us down Friday night."

Beloved, never avenge yourselves,
but leave it to the wrath of God, for it is written,
"Vengeance is mine, I will repay,
says the Lord." ~ Romans 12:19 ESV

Chapter 12

A body?

"Where?" Cat's question blurted out as soon as Ray hung up. She opened her door.

"What are you doing?"

He had paused at the water pipe. His face had clearly paled. No wonder he stopped. "Did you recognize the person?" She retraced her steps.

Ray blocked her way. "You can't go back there."

"I want to see."

"No, you don't." He rested his hand on her shoulder. "I promise."

Sparks tingled at his touch. "Maybe he's not dead. Maybe he needs help."

He shook his head.

"You saw a man, right? Not a woman."

"Yes. A very dead man."

"How could you know? You never got near him." She edged

145

around him.

"Cathy, that area is a crime scene."

She rushed to the edge of the lot. "Really? Now, you've decided a crime was committed? You can't even be sure he's dead."

He jogged behind her and caught her arm. "I know the symptoms of dead."

Pulling away, she kept going. "And I'm saying you can't tell from way up here." She reached the pipe and looked over. A body did lie at the bottom of the ravine. But not so far away to hide the fact that most of the head was gone.

Bile hit her mouth, and she turned away with a whimper.

Ray cradled her in his arm. "Honey, I'm sorry."

Tears spilled over her cheeks. She paused a moment to counter the sob that rose. "No. I'm sorry. I should have listened."

With his arm around her shoulder, he led her to the car.

"Why do you assume that's a crime scene?"

"The guy didn't get that way from a fall."

She couldn't argue his point. Why hadn't she listened to him and accepted his protection?

Cat had to hand it to Dell. He wasted no time in getting his people to the preserve. And they sure seemed to know what they were doing once they got there.

Danvers reached the lot first. He left Ray in his truck and put Cat in the rear seat of his cruiser with an order to stay.

Hmph. Like a family pet. Her red-haired attitude threatened, urging her to hike through the woods to Ray's house.

She calmed herself. After all, the house was almost three miles off.

Ray exited his truck as soon as Dell pulled into the lot and stood by the door until the chief parked his car.

Juanita rode with him. Interesting that they stayed together all afternoon. Cat wondered about their relationship. At least the musing kept her mind off the body in the woods.

The female officer got out of Dell's cruiser and climbed into Danvers's seat beside Cat. Pulling the door shut, she leveled her gaze. "What are you two doing out here?"

"Ray needed to walk. You know how men get when they're upset." She'd seen Dell do it enough. Juanita must understand.

"So you want me to believe you found this guy by coincidence?" Suddenly Cat found herself speaking to Lt. Estrella instead of her friend.

Technically Ray found him. Had he known the guy was there? As soon as the thought crossed her mind, Cat dismissed it. No way. "Ray needed to walk, and Vi and Denny were both gone, so I had to come with him."

Juanita's perfectly shaped eyebrows rose. "How did Ray happen to see a body, especially in a preserve this size?"

She shrugged. "It was me who suggested we take the shorter route through to the other lot. That's where we saw the other car. And when we cut through the trees, he spotted the body."

"How do you know he hadn't planned on taking that path on his own?"

"Well, I don't. But Ray hasn't been out here since they created all the walking paths. He wouldn't know one from another." Cat preferred talking to Juanita, her friend, rather than Lt. Estrella.

"Is that what he told you?"

"He didn't have to tell me anything. They finished this paving two summers ago while he was away. And anyway, we were both surprised to see that car sitting in the lot. Ray even went up on the hill to make sure no one was hiding in the car."

Lt. Estrella lifted her chin. "So since he couldn't see the body from the top of the hill, he walked you closer to it?"

"He climbed the hill to check out the car. He didn't even look in the direction of the walkway." He didn't. Did he? She struggled to remember exactly. "I'm the one that wanted to cross the lot and take the short cut to the truck. He didn't even know where to find the path."

"But he could find a dead body?"

"He saw the guy because he kept glancing over his shoulder to make sure no one followed us."

"All of your answers are only opinion, Cat. You have no idea what Ray thought, or what he knew. He could have been looking for the place where he left the body of the man he thought tried to kill him. And you."

"You can't believe ... Ray would never do something like that, and you know it, Juanita."

"I know a lot of things. Right now, I hope that Raymond Alexander has better answers to those questions than you did." With a stern frown, the lieutenant exited.

Cat shivered. Dirty cotton batting layered the sky, giving the appearance of a cozy blanket, but the clouds didn't fool her. The humidity wrapped everything in a sticky chill, including her, and wouldn't let her loose. Her toes numbed as the cold took possession of Danvers's cruiser. She stepped out of the vehicle and jogged in place, willing the rushing blood to warm her up.

"What are you doing outside, Missy?" Dell's voice startled her, booming up from the tree cover at the side of the lot. "I thought Danvers told you to wait in the car."

"For pity's sake. Are you spying on me, waiting for me to step out of line?"

He approached her with thunder on his face, saying nothing.

"I got cold. I stayed right here, in case you didn't notice."

"Get back in." He pulled the door open and slammed it behind her. Circling to the other side, he folded himself in, peeling off his white cowboy hat and setting it between them.

When he turned on the engine, Cat gave him a side-long glare. "Are we going somewhere?" She hoped he didn't intend to make good on his threat to stick her in jail.

"Turning on the heater's all." He settled in the seat and turned to her. His face, recently shaved, had little divots at his jaw and deep paths along the sides of his mouth. Funny how she never noticed how old he'd gotten.

"Why did Ray bring you up here?"

Ugh. "You already know, Dell. Surely you've talked to Juanita."

"Yeah I did, but it doesn't add up. S'pose you tell me yourself."

Cat glanced around and noticed that no one sat in Ray's truck. "Where's Ray?"

"I'm asking the questions. Why did he bring you up here?"

Her thoughts whirled. What was Dell after? "He wanted a walk, but I had to come, too, because his folks went out to visit someone."

"That what he told you?"

"That's what happened. Would you rather he left me at the ranch alone?"

He stared at the steering wheel for a couple of ticks. "And how do you know Victor Marienas?"

Cat let the name float through her mind, but it didn't connect anywhere. She shook her head. "Never heard of him."

"Had a receipt from your diner."

"So? I know regulars, but unless folks stand out, I don't usually remember one-time visitors."

Dell turned his head slightly and squinted at her. "Then how'd you know he'd only been there one time."

149

"Because you said *a receipt* as in one." She blew her curling bangs out of her eyes. "You gonna tell me what this is all about?"

He stared at her for several moments, his face an unreadable mask of controlled emotion. Or was it disappointment?

"You don't think Ray or I had anything to do with some guy's death, do you?"

"Murder." He looked at the steering wheel and sighed. "The guy in the gully is Victor Marienas from Mexico City, and he has a picture of you in his wallet."

"Me?" The icy hand had started to fade away, but instead it grabbed a stranglehold around her neck. "Where'd he get a picture of me? I've never been to Mexico."

"School picture. The top-half of the one Ray got in the mail."

Some stranger had Ray's picture and now was dead? Cat's thoughts spun again, physically dizzying her. "Where's Ray?"

"Now see, what I think is that Ray and this guy had a fight. And Ray kills the guy. Then when no one finds the dead guy, he brings you up here to innocently stumble on the body."

Her mouth dropped open as she eyed the big man. Had he lost his mind? She straightened her shoulders, checking the rant that threatened to explode. "Chief, you're talking about a huge coincidence. Ray happened to come up to this out of the way place, recognize a man he'd never seen, fight with him, and with his injury, win the fight?" Cat felt the pressure explode around her ears.

"Rifle blast. Not much of a fight. And I didn't say he happened to wander up here. Maybe he arranged to meet the man."

"Well, when did he do this? He's been with me almost exclusively since Friday night. Or do you think he came here instead of church this morning?"

Sift out the sarcasm. It won't help.

"So instead I believe the coincidence that he brought you here

150

on a lark?"

"That's what happened." She all but shouted. "Sorry. I didn't mean to yell, but you're not being reasonable."

"There's another option, but it's uglier. Maybe Ray brought you up here to let the guy finish the job."

The close quarters restrained her. Dell's idea was ridiculous. She struggled for breath and kept her voice low. "If Ray wanted me dead, the car trying to chase me down would have done a fine job, leaving him to appear as a tragic hero." She punctuated the final word, hoping he'd take the hint and leave the subject alone.

"That may be …"

"You're not even making good sense, Chief." Her eyes squinted as she glared at the man. "Why would Ray plan to kill me, but make sure you knew about it beforehand?"

"Stranger things than that occur all the time."

"You forget who you're talking about. He would never hurt anyone, especially not me."

Dell sniffed. "Been gone a long time."

"Moving away doesn't automatically change your character. And nothing he's said or done since he's returned has shown any hidden agendas whatsoever." The rant warmed her. She needed to escape the stuffy car and the infuriating man who sat next to her. How dare he attack Ray simply because he'd come home?

"I still think we need to keep a close eye on the man."

She clamped her teeth. "Fine. You do that. Since you don't have other important work."

Dell opened the door, grumbling. "Talking to you wastes my time."

Hers, too. Cat watched him traipse into the woods. She worked to steady her breathing. Tried to remember that Dell worried about her. Worried too much, but he had a good heart, even if it led him to incorrect conclusions.

Could Dell really suspect Ray of something so horrible?

She hugged herself and glanced out at the darkening sky. Dell's insinuations nauseated her. Ray would never try to hurt her.

And he hadn't killed that man.

Had he?

The sun hung low by the time he returned to the parking lot. He glanced in her direction, locking his pain-filled eyes with hers, before climbing into the truck.

The motor gunned about the time that Danvers reached the lot. Two black-jacketed men followed him to a county van, pushing a long, black bag on a gurney. Juanita met him at the back doors and handed him her keys.

Cat stared at the floorboard and jumped when the door beside her opened. "Get in the back." The chief's gruff voice and their previous argument urged her to obey this time. Juanita waited as Cat extricated herself and took her spot in the passenger seat.

Peachy. Third wheel again, only they weren't going to brunch.

And this time, she got to sit in the criminal compartment of a cruiser, instead of Juanita's sedan. Cat stared out the side window and tried not to touch anything.

The old man checked his mirrors and pulled onto Bushward Road. "You saw something horrible, Kitten." His softened tone made her want to cry. "We're trying to get to the bottom of what happened. I know you don't like the questions. Neither do I, but they're necessary to uncover the truth."

"Ray had nothing to do with that man's death." She couldn't hold Dell's job, his investigative duties, against him.

"Murder." Dell glanced over his shoulder. "The man was shot in the head."

The nightmarish image seeped into her mind. Served her right for insisting to see for herself.

"Dell, maybe tonight isn't …" Juanita put her hand on his arm.

"Tonight is a perfectly good time to talk about this." He eyed her over his shoulder. "You should be scared out of your stockings."

She was. Terrified. "What makes you think I'm not?"

"You have to take the threat seriously. Especially after the gunshot and that car that tried to run you down."

But wasn't the guy who tried to run her down … "Wait a minute. If that guy is dead, the danger is gone, right?"

"Someone killed that man, Cat."

She shut her eyes and shook her head. "There are murders in Texas every day."

"Too much coincidence. I don't buy it."

Whoever killed the man did Cat a favor. Why couldn't Dell see that? "I don't like what happened, Chief. But I'm not ignoring the gift. This frees me to return to the inn."

"You will do what I say, exactly as I say it, or I'll plop your fanny in my jail cell and forget you're even there."

Juanita twisted in her seat. "You don't mean that." With hushed tones, the older woman chided him.

"I mean every word and what's more, that man probably wouldn't have died if Cat had listened to me before."

Cat flinched.

"Enough!" Juanita laid her hand on Dell's shoulder. "You're going to be sorry for the things you're saying, Dell Tate. You stop now and let this be. You hear me?"

He opened his mouth, but shut it and growled instead.

Cat stared out the window as the car turned down the farm-to-market road toward the Alexander ranch. Dell only wanted to protect her, but she'd been smothered for days. Was he right about that man? Was his death her fault?

Juanita blew out a loud exhale. "Let's just relax the rest of the way. Okay?" She mustered a half smile and glanced at Cat. Her eyes focused past her out the back window, and she frowned. "Dell, check your six."

Six? Cat followed the woman's gaze. A set of headlights followed about a hundred yards behind. "It's probably nothing but a farmer going home."

"Maybe." Dell kept eyes on his mirrors as much as he looked out the windshield and drove right past the turn into Ray's ranch.

"I thought ..."

"We're going around again." Juanita patted Dell's dashboard, and he accelerated.

Cat turned and noticed the lights becoming minimal in size until they disappeared altogether.

"Clear," Dell announced, like he'd actually chased someone away.

Of course. Since there's no one left to stalk me. She tried to take Juanita's advice and sink into the corner.

Silence filled the car as Dell made a three-point turn in the middle of the county road.

She waited until they parked in front of Ray's house. She needed, more now than before, to confirm her stand. "I still plan to go to the diner in the morning."

Juanita glanced at Dell. Surely Cat could count on her support.

Woe to those who devise wickedness and work evil on their beds!
When the morning dawns, they perform it, because it is in the power
of their hand. ~ Micah 2:1 ESV

Chapter 13

Gut-punched. Seeing the body shocked Ray. Nauseated him. Then Cathy's reaction shredded the edge of his heart.

But Dell ... His questions. Ray barely answered. He just stood there with his mouth hanging open. Did the chief really believe Ray killed that guy? He'd known Dell all his life.

And insinuating that Ray might have brought Cathy there on purpose? He wanted to hit something.

He could hardly look at her on his way to the truck. And went straight to his room at the house. When he did come out, he couldn't meet her eyes.

How could he face her doubt? Hearing suspicion in her voice would tear him apart.

So much for trying to separate himself from his feelings for Cathy. But as much as Ray wanted to make her happy, Dell was all wrong about letting her go into work at Mac's. Especially since she'd gotten into her head that she was safe.

Ray wanted to follow her in, but Dell wouldn't allow it. "Too much risk. I don't want anyone guessing she's out here." So he stayed behind and used the opportunity to spruce up before vising Mac's for breakfast.

When he made his way downstairs, both of his parents ambushed him as he filled a mug with coffee.

"Have a seat, son. Your mother and I are concerned about you."

That never sounded good.

Mom sat on a leather lounge chair while Dad stood at the sofa, using the table behind it like a podium. "Raymond, now that you've completed your ministry in Mexico, we feel it's time you stepped into the business with me, at Alexa Corp. I could use a man with keen logic. And frankly, son, you need to get a job."

Mom examined her nails. "And you need to stop hovering around our houseguest all the time."

Ray wished for a set of reins to whoa them down. "I intend to get a job, Dad. But who's going to hire me in this condition?" He pointed to his arm held by the sling.

"That's not an issue if you work with me." Dad had always pushed Ray to join the business. He practically glowed when he spoke about fluctuations in the market and acquisitions.

Why didn't he recognize the same spark in Ray when he contemplated mission work? Not that his desire for the field mattered anymore. That door had closed forever.

"I appreciate the offer, and I'll think about it, but I want to be free to make my own choices."

His father nodded. Ray expected him to understand, considering the way he'd bailed on Grandpa's lumber company to start his own brokerage firm. At least Ray's offer to think about the change gave more hope than Grandpa got.

And he did think about it, until he climbed into his truck and turned toward Heath's Point. A certain redhead surely had a delicious breakfast ready for him. Or soon would. And maybe he could sort out his feelings enough to discuss things with her.

The chimes of his phone made him pause at the intersection to the county road into town.

He answered and heard the smooth sound of Miguel's lilt in response. Not that it didn't shove horrible images of the attack into his head. Still, he could be nothing but grateful to the man.

"I hope that I am not bothering you, my friend, but I have been worried over your threats from Señor Sevilla."

"There's good reason to worry. Be better to pray, though. I think I found his hit man yesterday. Dead."

"Then your friend's trouble is over? What a relief. I hope you can relax now and enjoy your homecoming."

Ray relished the thought of a smattering of peace. Maybe things could settle to a normal pace. "Relaxing sounds like a fantasy." He told his friend about the closing of Cathy's diner. "And it's a shame. Best food in the area. I'm on my way there now."

"Oh, no, man. Is she all right?"

Ray pulled onto the road heading south. "I think so. We're having a big party in a couple of days. Sort of a fundraiser. Should make some nice memories for Cathy. She's feeling rather low right now."

"I'm sorry to hear that. Is there anything I can do to help?"

"Thanks for the offer." Ray hesitated. Questions about Sevilla and the attack ached to be asked. "I wonder. Do you know anything about the mission in Asmirandu?"

"I tried to make some connections with people there, but they have shut out all communications. Obviously, Sevilla and his men succeeded in their terror plot."

Had that been what it was? "I can't believe the people of that little church would lose their faith."

Silence grew for a moment. "I am not sure that there are any people left from that church, amigo."

Ray flinched. Stunned, he pulled onto the shoulder and stared out through the windshield. Only he wasn't seeing barren trees shaking in a frigid wind. He saw smiling faces of Spirit-filled people who believed in Christ because of Ray's words to them. His charges who trusted him to know what to do for their growth in the Lord and the safety of their church in a volatile environment.

People now silenced because Ray let them down. What of their children? Surely not all of them were dead?

"Amigo, are you still there?"

"Yes." Ray fumbled with the phone and almost dropped it. "I can't believe they're all gone. I won't until I know for sure."

"That is a good attitude to take my friend. I wish you good news at the end of your search."

Ray prayed that would be the case.

The call from Miguel added to his already weighted chest. The man couldn't help reporting awful news when that's all there was. At least he told the whole truth without minimizing tragedies.

Ray pulled into a spot just outside Mac's windows. The lack of information bugged him, though. Surely someone could learn about Asmirandu. He dialed Philip.

"Heard you had an eventful evening." His friend's voice soothed frazzled nerves.

"Good to know the rumor mill is already up and running this morning."

"Nope. Working overtime last night. Mrs. Hawkins spoke to your mom, and she talked to my wife."

Of course. "Can you reach some of the partners in Chiapas?" Ray climbed from his car. "My contact can't learn anything about the mission in Asmirandu. I wonder if one of the partners will travel there and check things out."

"I've got a few people I can ask. Some favors owed to me. Let me see what I can find out."

Pushing off the hood of his truck, Ray hung up and caught a glimpse of the flashy redhead. She smiled and chatted on the other side of the glass. Being so close to her this weekend had completely undone him. He'd kept a distance as much as possible, but he noticed everything about her. The fragrance of her just-washed hair, the laughter that spilled over when she and Mom finally worked out their differences. He even loved the way she stuck her pinky fingernail in her mouth as she read through a novel last evening.

No, not loved. He couldn't go there again. The atmosphere that followed their horseback ride filled his mind. With a shake of his head, he entered the diner and moved toward a table at the back of the room.

Daisy brought him a menu. "You heard about the fundraiser, right?"

He nodded. "I'll be here."

He kept his eyes on the little stick of dynamite that ran the cash register. She giggled while she chatted with Donna, who came in for a to-go sack.

Daisy took his order and stepped away, speaking to Cathy as she passed. The redhead spotted him. He nodded and lifted his hand. With a slight smile, she lifted her chin then turned again to Donna.

He should have spoken to her last night. Aired out all of Dell's accusations. Maybe even broached his other shame. But now wasn't the time for that.

He scanned the other diners, most strangers to him, except for Mr. Havesheim. The print shop owner sat in the opposite corner. The old man's bushy mustache almost looked like froth on his coffee cup.

Highway workers filled a table between them and a booth near the front. One lady in business clothes sat alone at a center table. No one triggered his alarms, but he kept an eye on the door.

With a clatter from the cowbell, Angela and her dark-haired friend entered. Catching his eye, she strutted toward him like a model taking a catwalk. She stuck her fist on one hip and posed in front of him. Her shadow matched her attitude in mirror-like form.

"Well, seems we can share a meal together after all. Mind if we join you?" She plopped in the chair directly across from him with her friend in the next seat. Though everything about her repulsed Ray, he'd not embarrass her by denying her a chair.

The other girl tucked a strand of hair behind her ear. "Tell us about that mission. What types of people did you meet, and what did you do?"

He glanced around, but found no possible means of escape. "There really isn't much to tell. I preached on Sundays and during the week, we helped people wherever we found needs."

"Don't be so modest." Angela reached across the table to stroke his hand. She had to stretch to touch him.

He slipped his hand into his lap.

She flicked her medium-length hair over her shoulder and propped her chin on the backs of her fingers, elbows on the table. "Tell us how you destroyed the drug cartel. From what I've heard, you're an actual hero."

No. A hero was someone who'd take a machete blow and shove you out of the way. The image of Matteo's face drifted before him as he recalled the man's words. *Go my friend. May God Himself protect you.*

Tears stung Ray's eyes, and he blinked them away. "I'm not much at telling stories."

"Nonsense." She raised her hand. "Hey, Daisy. Two specials

here."

She stood, an expectant curve on her mouth. "I think all you need is a little relaxation. Maybe a shoulder massage while we wait for our food?"

He shook his head and looked up in time to see her seductive expression ice into a grimace.

Soft hands rested on his shoulders, smelling of dish soap. "Is everything all right here, Ray, honey?" Cathy's voice warmed him, rescuing him from Angela's unwanted attention and his deep-set guilt.

He glanced up at her and covered her right hand with his. "Think you can join us?"

"That's silly." Angela stacked her hip again. "You're too busy serving us."

Cathy scanned the room. "Not so busy."

Ray scooted to the next chair so she could stay on his good side. He put his arm around her shoulder, silently declaring the possession he hoped for.

"Well. This has been fun." The blonde collected her purse and half-hugged Cathy. "Good to see you, Cat, dear." She turned. "Places to go."

Her shadow hung back. "I didn't mean to make you uncomfortable, Ray."

He let out a relieved sigh. "You didn't. She did. So what can I do for you?" He released Cathy. "I'm sorry. I don't know your name."

She pulled at a strand of hair. "I'm Chloe Heath. I guess I've changed a lot since you left."

"Chloe?" The little sprite had tagged along after her mother and older sister everywhere they went. "Wow. You make me feel ancient."

"Life goes on, you know." She pushed the hair behind her ear.

"I'm thinking about maybe going into the mission field myself. My parents worry, though. Is it always dangerous?"

"No. My experience wasn't typical. Most places are quite open to evangelism."

"I want to go into nursing, but Mother says it's uncivilized."

"So you thought about mission work?" Really? "Wouldn't going into third-world countries and sleeping on dirt floors offend her more?

"When I say mission work, she thinks social work, charity fundraising and such. So far she's not halting my intentions to go on field work in Zambia."

"Zambia. You'll be helping in a hospital there?"

"In an orphanage. My hope is that I'll get there and be able to stay. But is that a terribly dangerous place?"

Ray shrugged. "I really don't know."

Cathy stood. "Sounds like you've got this under control." She took a step away and addressed Chloe. "Do you want your meal here?"

"If you don't mind." The brunette glanced at Ray. "I don't want to make a problem."

"No worries. I'll bring you a Pepsi?"

"Yes, thanks."

For the next hour, Ray gave Chloe the inside story of working with the local folks in Chiapas. By the time the girl stood to leave, they had prayed over her upcoming trip and for leading of the Spirit. Distinctive tears sparkled in her eyes as she turned to the door.

He caught Cathy staring at him, a sweet expression of admiration.

"What?"

She advanced on him with a tray and scooped up the used dishes. "You amaze me, Ray Alexander. How could you see the difference between those girls? I thought they both had man-eater written on their foreheads."

"Me, too, at first." Did his smile look as sheepish as he felt? "The thing is, Chloe kept asking about the mission. Focused on it. She had a different type of energy."

"I'm sold. I wish I had her opportunity." She turned and strolled to the kitchen.

Ray watched her move away, appreciating the view as much as the encouragement she'd given and the glow it inspired.

Ray hung around all day, but this time, his presence warmed Cat. He guarded her, even though she didn't need it. And he watched her with a tender smile in his eyes.

She melted a little every time she caught his gaze.

After lunch, Daisy and Grady worked in the kitchen. Cat took advantage of the quiet. "Thanks for sticking around. You didn't have to, you know."

"I wanted to." He tilted his head. "Listen Cathy. About yesterday. I'm so sorry I dragged you out there."

"Why did you?" She sat across from him. Peering into his eyes. Would they show her any deception? "Dell had some good questions. How is it you just happened to head out there of all places?"

His mouth dropped open. "Are you suggesting—?"

"I'm not suggesting anything." Oh, she shouldn't have started this at all. But having begun, the conversation begged conclusion. She took a deep breath. "So why did we have to go right then? You were in such a hurry to get there. And you happened to glance back at just the right moment."

"Wait a minute. You were there. Heck, you were the one who

wanted to take that trail to the other parking lot. I've never even seen those footpaths."

He was right. She tried to relax against the cushion. "You haven't answered my question."

He closed his eyes. "I needed to clear my head."

She let him have a moment, wishing she'd brought up any other topic. Almost any other topic.

"I would have gone alone if Mom and Dad hadn't decided to do their visiting." He clasped his hands on the table. "Please believe me. I'd never seen that man before, and I didn't know he was at the bottom of the ravine until I spotted him there."

"When you looked back." She didn't question him now. The whole thing sounded too coincidental, but she'd lived through the event.

"We saw the car. I knew the driver was out to get you. He had to be there somewhere. That gap at the pipe gave a high vantage point." He shrugged. "Truth is, I expected to see him."

He had?

"Only I expected to catch his movements as he made his way along one of the lower trails. Thought he might be following us."

She leaned forward on the table, her face lowered into the palm of her hand in a sweet pout. "I'm sorry. This is all so confusing. When Dell suggested that you had something to do with that man, I defended you. But I couldn't get the notion out of my mind."

He stopped in front of her and put his finger under her chin. "Well, get it out now."

She met his gaze, but found hurt there. Hurt that she had caused.

Grady came in from the kitchen, snapping a cup towel against one of the stools. "Boss-lady better not get too cozy. Your ride's waitin' on you." He thumbed the front windows.

Sure enough, Danvers sat in a parking space. Engine running. Lights on.

"You're sure you don't want me to come back for the dinner?" A dinner party at the inn for the rotary club claimed Cat's attention, but she didn't like missing a sunset dinner she'd been scheduled to serve.

"You go on, now. Mrs. Stone put this on your calendar way back. I got dinner. Figure I'd ambush preacher-man here to help me out."

"At your service." Ray stood and bowed. He stroked her chin once again and licked his bottom lip. "I'll see you at the house later?"

Her knees quivered. She nodded and turned, unable to force her voice to work. What had happened to her?

Ray helped wipe down the tables while Daisy and Grady cleaned up and prepared the boxed meals. "Sure I can't do anything else?" He was more than ready to be out of the sling and fully functioning again.

"Nah. We're covered."

Rain started pelting the front glass.

"Oh, no. Not today." Daisy trotted to the windows. "Shootfire."

"What's a matter with you?" Grady hung his apron on the hook.

"My car wouldn't start this morning, so I walked. Guess I'll be late to my date." She cut her eyes at Ray. "Unless you can take me home?"

Uh ... "Sure." He caught Grady's attention. "We've got time, right?" His gaze bore into the older man's. Grady was going with them whether he realized it or not.

The man shrugged. "We gots nothing but time. Least not 'til sunset."

Her apartment wasn't a far distance. On their return trip, the clouds broke enough to let beams of light paint them. Would be a great sunset for the dinner.

Grady leaned up on the dash of Ray's truck and pointed out the windshield as they neared the diner. "What's that?"

Something large and yellow blocked the door. Had Heath somehow forced a closure of Mac's? Ray pulled into the parking space nearest to the street lamp and glanced out the windshield at a large bouquet of yellow roses that sat on the stoop.

Little alarms went off in the back of his head. He hated that the flowers bugged him, but with all the crazy things happening, no wonder his senses went on alert. Shoving into park, he peered out the window at some early-arrivers huddled in a nearby doorway. A group of them broke away and leaned on the warm hood of his truck.

"Hey, guys." Grady stepped out and chatted with the men. Ray made a beeline for the flowers, hoping their innocent appearance matched their origin.

He dug through the fragrant heads, their scent mixing with the damp, stale smell of a frosty downtown. His hand touched the edge of a card as another vehicle pulled up. He held the note out, angling it to catch the full spread of the available light.

With deepest sympathy for your loss. Too late for these flowers to be for Mac's death. Was this a new kind of threat?

"I thought that was you." The deep familiar voice sounded out of place.

Ray whirled and found himself staring in the face of Miguel. Before he could react, the other man grasped his hand and pumped it. "I have missed you, *amigo.*"

"Where … What?" Ray stepped back and studied his smiling friend. "What are you doing here?"

He pointed to the vase full of roses. "Delivering flowers. I did not think this tiny town you call home would have a florist."

Ray laughed. "Why did you bring them here?"

"You said your friend was losing her diner. This is the only diner in town that is not a franchise. And I would have had them here earlier, but I fell asleep at my hotel." His grin turned sheepish. "What are you doing out here in the cold?"

Grady unlocked the door and let them in while Ray explained their process.

"I see. So you feed homeless people and preach to them here. Why did you go to Chiapas?"

"It's not my ministry." Ray shrugged, but the question resonated. These dinners touched many people.

"So your friend is not here tonight. Shame. I hoped to give her my encouragement in person."

"I'd love to introduce you to her." Ray hesitated. He'd normally invite any friend to stay with him, but not with Cat there undercover. "How about breakfast tomorrow morning right here? About nine o'clock?"

They agreed, and Miguel waved goodbye. "Have a peaceful evening, and I look forward to meeting your friend in the morning."

Ray swallowed his guilt over his lack of hospitality, but already too many people knew that Cat was hiding at his house. After loading the cart with the leftover meals, he stepped outside and began talking about the Savior's love while Grady passed around the food.

"Out here in the cold night, you all aren't alone or without hope. The God who created the ground and sky and the stars and the icy air knows everything about you. He knows your name. He knows why you're here. He knows all that's happened to you and all that you've done."

Ray didn't know if the people who listened felt the depth of his meaning, but the words he spoke pierced his soul. "There's a story in the Bible about a prostitute who met Jesus. Even though He knew what type of woman she was, He offered her the same rescue that He offered His closest friends.

"That's the same rescue He offers to you. He loves you. Adores you like a daddy coddles a newborn." Ray's voice broke.

Miguel's arrival brought back memories of the dear friends he'd left behind. God knew his failure. His short-sightedness that caused the deaths of loving people in his mission. And yet He not only forgave Ray, He gently led him to continue speaking and serving.

"And I'm in your shoes. Not in the same circumstances, but I so desperately need to unload the guilt and failure I carry." He paused and swallowed hard. A gust ruffled the curls along his forehead and gave him opportunity to seek better control. "But as much as I crave forgiveness, He wants to lavish it on me even more."

Ray offered a prayer of gratitude when all the meals had been shared. He breathed in a frigid breath that stung his chest and turned the cart backward to drag it to the kitchen.

"Sounds like you been beating yourself up." Grady caught up to him with an empty water-bottle box.

"There's a lot I've not really shared about Chiapas."

"Figgered as much. Also figgered if the mission got itself attacked, and you got hurt like you did, then some of the folks mighta gotten hurt worse."

Much worse. Ray wheeled the cart into the office and shut off the light in the little room.

"But unless you did the attackin' your own self, you gots no business giving yourself any blame."

Ray shook his head. He breathed in slow to measure words

he'd shared with no one before. "I didn't think anything would touch us."

The older man crushed the box and slid it into a large waste can. "Don't add up. I get that you didn't understand the danger. But, Ray, you didn't *make* the danger."

His words connected with a longing in Ray's spirit to have a good reason for exoneration. If only he could forgive himself. He'd think on Grady's words a little more.

Marji Laine

For You bless the righteous, O LORD;
You cover him with favor as with a shield. ~ Psalm 5:12 ESV

Chapter 14

Cat dragged herself into the Alexander ranch way later than she planned. Oh boy, had Myra needed her help. That little rotary club had exploded.

Thank goodness Billings drove her to the house. She'd have fallen asleep at the wheel. And she almost dozed in the hallway. She greeted Vi with a wave on the way to her room.

Unfortunately, the shortened night did nothing to help her get moving the next morning. Not even a second dose of caffeine on ice had pierced the fog, but the breakfast rush escalated quickly.

"You okay?" Daisy paused with a tray full of plates.

"Tired."

"I knew something was wrong. I've never seen you make so many mistakes."

She was right. Missing food, mixed up orders, forgotten requests. *Bear down, Kitten.* She could almost hear her Daddy's voice.

Yet her mind wandered. Would Ray be in? She hadn't seen him the night before. They'd shared such a sweet moment. Faked for Angela Crane's benefit, but held elements of reality. At least, *she'd* had real feelings. Did Ray? Had the sweet sparkle in his eyes been sincere?

"Cat!"

She jumped at Dell's voice and the clank of the cowbell. She balanced a plate of Goldenrod and another of Orange Jacks. "Have a seat, Dell. I'll put your regular order in."

"That's not why I'm here."

She delivered the platters to a table near the entrance. "Well, either arrest me or wait your turn then." She could hear the *hmph* across the room as she trotted to deliver a bill to a table full of businessmen.

The cowbell rang as she picked up another loaded tray. Ray came in. Her steps stuttered, but she paused and regained her composure.

"Who is that gorgeous man with Ray?" Daisy gave them a side glance.

Cat had only noticed Ray, but the man with him was handsome. Deep dimples in a smiling face with curling black hair and a weightlifter's build on a six-foot frame. Maybe a little shorter.

"Yum." Daisy grabbed a couple of menus. "I'll take care of them."

"Sorry. My table." Cat smiled and tucked the menus under her arm.

After delivering the meals elsewhere, she greeted the men with a bright smile. "Morning."

Ray returned her smile, teeth and all. "Good morning."

Cat's toes practically curled in her boots.

"You are correct, Raymond. Your Cathy is like sunshine." The stranger stood.

Was that a blush on Ray's cheeks? He chuckled and dropped his chin for a second. "I want you to meet one of my ministry partners from Chiapas. Miguel's the one who helped me get out of Mexico."

He offered her a hand. "I am so delighted to meet you. And so very sorry to hear about the loss of your diner."

"He's the one who brought the flowers on the counter." Ray pointed to the spot by the register where Grady set them the night before.

"Thank you so much. They're lovely."

"You are quite welcome." He sat as she handed over menus.

"Where are you from?" Cat hoped to switch the topic away from Mac's.

"Order up." Grady interrupted the moment with a *slap-ding* from the bell in the window and his dancing spatula.

"I'll be back. Don't go anywhere." She scooted through the tables.

"Cat, I need to talk to you." Dell caught her arm as she tried to move past him.

"You can see we're busy, Chief. I'll come listen when your meal is ready. Promise." He released her, and she dashed back into the kitchen, eager to reach a lull so she could spend some time with Ray.

Ray looked up.

Dell strolled to his table, taking in the room. "Funny how this place starts dancing days before its death."

"I wouldn't say *death*, especially not around Cat. But the timing is lousy." Ray introduced him to his friend. "Miguel, on the other hand, has perfect timing. He'd only been assigned to my mission a couple of days before the attack, but I wouldn't have survived without his help."

Dell offered his hand though he didn't smile. "We're in your debt then."

"Dell's the police chief for Heath's Point."

"Oh, you run the entire department in Heath's Point?" Miguel raised his eyebrows.

Was that a jab? Ray hadn't known him long enough to get the feel of his personality. "I guess with your being from San Diego, Heath's Point looks pretty small."

Dell's eyebrow rose. "I can imagine. Anything smaller than Dallas would seem like a hick town."

"No offense intended. This is not as small as the villages of Chiapas, but close." Miguel laughed, and Dell chuckled as well.

"Join us." Ray indicated an open seat.

"Actually, I came to tell Cat she's off the hook."

Ray's insides spun. "You're sure?"

He nodded. "Lab boys over in the Lackard office matched the dead guy's prints to one we found at Cat's house. Same prints are all over his rental car. And, I found an XM2010 Sniper Rifle in the trunk of said car. Fires a bullet that matches the one in Cat's tire *and* the one I dug outta her ceiling at the inn."

"Looks like you got him."

"Snipers?" Miguel's smile faded a bit. "What sort of town is this?"

"I'm sorry. I didn't want to worry you. But I told you I received a threat against Cathy last week." Ray explained about the car chase, the shooting, and the shot-out tire.

"And the dead man?"

Dell shifted his weight to his other foot. "Was a hit man sent to make good on the threat against Cat. At least, that's what the bullets and fingerprints indicate." He smiled. "Hick towns know all about them suckers. Course we can only pick 'em up with Silly Putty and coal dust, but we find a way."

Miguel laughed. "You still power the computer RAM with hamsters on a wheel, huh?"

"No, we've graduated to a goat out back that trots around the ring." Dell folded his arms across his chest.

"A goat?"

"Yeah. Kills two birds. See, we can milk the goat."

Ray rolled his eyes. "Good grief." He glanced at the redhead marching toward the back of the room with a pair of filled plates. "Does Cathy know yet?"

"No. She's too busy to stop long enough for me to tell her."

Ray scooted off the seat. "Let me." Without waiting for an answer, he sidled up to the end of the counter. She'd returned to the bar and filled two coffee mugs from the oversized pot.

"I have some news."

"Yeah?" She glanced up through long dark eyelashes.

"Dell got a report back from the lab. Looks like your hit man is dead."

She set the cups down. "He's sure?"

"You're safe."

Cathy flung her arms around Ray's neck. Warmth soared through his middle as he encircled her with his good arm and buried his face into her neck.

But as much as he delighted in her nearness, he let her separate. She gave a shy smile and picked up the two mugs.

His thoughts troubled him as he returned to Dell and Miguel at the table. Someone killed that man. Cold-blooded murder. Why?

What possessed her to throw herself into Ray's arms like that? Cat's cheeks heated once again. She hazarded a glance in his direction. Ray's friend had left. The chief sat with his back to Cat and said something that made Ray laugh. He looked up and caught her watching. His mouth curved upward.

A roar sounded in her ears. Like her blood rushed to her head all at once. She turned away from the room and took a deep breath to keep her emotions in control.

When the chief left, she cleaned off his side of the table and returned to wipe it down.

"Think you can sit with me a minute?" Ray's smooth voice caressed her ear. Nothing she'd like better. Especially with the tenderness in his expression.

She glanced around. Only a few of the breakfast folks were left. She checked the funny-faced cat with the clock in his tummy. Still plenty of time before lunch customers started arriving. "Sure." She lowered into the seat. "Where'd your friend run off to?"

"Dallas. I think this is his first trip this way. He said he wanted to do some of the touristy things."

The cowbell clunked. In strutted the Heath family, most of them anyway. Lila shadowed her mother. Chloe folded into the corner of the room behind the entrance.

"Well this color is hideous." Williora Heath fingered the wall beside the picture of Cat's parents. "I think a nice shell pink."

Ick. She wanted to paint Mac's pink? Folks would think of raw meat.

"Something light and feminine. Perfect for a tearoom." She shoved the frame over. "Ugh. And the artwork."

Cat felt the floor tilt. Heath didn't want Mac's. He just wanted to cannibalize what he could from the place to give his wife another charm for her bracelet.

"There's an empty booth over here, or would you prefer a table?" She struggled to keep her voice even as her temperature rose.

"We're not here to eat, young lady." Darrell Heath strolled toward the kitchen.

Cat trotted ahead and blocked his way. "Then you're not here at all."

"As the controlling owner, I have every right to inspect the premises. And fire any employee who ..." His eyes roved from her toes to her face. "... stands in my way."

She didn't move. He wanted a fight. *Fine.* "You're not in control. Not yet. And you have no rights. In fact, I don't even have to let you come in here."

"Now, see here, young lady ..."

Ray stepped between them. "Mr. Heath, Miss McPherson is correct. And do you really want to make a stink right now? I mean, unless you're *hoping* your wife's new tearoom fails completely. Big tax break for you, but it would make Mrs. Heath look pretty ridiculous."

The woman's mouth dropped open. "Is that why you suggested I change this place to a tearoom. So you could write it off?"

The older man reddened and glared at Ray. "We'll come back another time."

"When you have your own key." Cat followed him to the door. "Unless you want to eat here, don't come back until the control changes hands."

"Hmph."

She lowered her voice, stopping him from opening the door. "I mean it Mr. Heath, and that goes for your wife, too. I will call Dell if either of you return for anything other than ordering food." She

177

stepped back and opened the door for the man.

He lifted his chin, allowing his wife to go first. Three-in-a-row, chins high, haughty expressions.

Then Chloe followed. "I'm so sorry about all of this."

Cat ducked her head. "I'm the one who should apologize. My temper snapped. I'm trying not to think about losing control of my dad's diner. So strange that two men who had such animosity for one another would become partners."

"That wasn't the way it always was. My brother, Elliot, told me that Mac used to come over all the time. He and my father talked about opening the place together, but your mother didn't like Father very much.

"I've never heard any of this."

"Mother's mentioned the situation as well. I don't know what your mom had against our family, but she insisted that Father stay away from Mac's. Started all sorts of trouble between him and your dad."

Why hadn't Dad told her about the conflict? "I thought they *always* hated each other. When I learned that Dad sent monthly payments to your father, I decided it was an agreement for a business loan. I had no idea they had been friends at one time."

"I think he wants to take over Mac's because he was squeezed out before. Wants to prove that he can do a better job of running things than your dad did." She put her hand on Cat's shoulder. "But your dad was amazing. I told Father coming out here was a bad idea. But he wanted to see the inside and plan." She huffed. "He's a little on the stubborn side."

Noted. But knowing the whole story, maybe he had reason. "He'll have plenty of time for fantasizing about this place in a couple of weeks."

Chloe's mouth flattened. "I wish I could help." She followed her family outside.

She already had helped. Cat sighed. Heath wasn't the heartless creep she imagined. Sounded like he'd been hurt somehow. Maybe if she tried to talk it out with him, they could work something out.

It was worth some thought.

Cat drifted toward Ray. "Thanks for standing up for me."

"You're under a lot of pressure right now."

"Less, since the stalker's gone." She'd never been glad for anyone's death. Never. But couldn't ignore the relief she felt from the loss of that man.

He nodded.

The cowbell clanged. Several men from the highway work site entered. Others followed. Lunch rush erased opportunity to talk further. By the time things cleared out, Ray had left.

He hadn't even said goodbye.

Despite the gentle sound of his voice and the look in his eye, he must've needed distance between them.

She needed to keep her head straight. And to get her stuff out of his house and back to the inn where it belonged.

Dell carted her out to the ranch as soon as she set the closed sign in place. "I still think you should be staying out here." He always fussed when he was worried about something. "There's safety that you don't have with the Stones."

"I've been a burden long enough. At least at the inn, I can earn my keep by helping with cleaning and such."

"I know the Alexanders don't think of your visit as a burden."

She exited his cruiser and headed for the door. "Maybe not on the surface. But this whole situation has put a lot of pressure on them." She stopped at the porch. "Sort of like the way you've had to cart me all over the place. Here, to the inn, then back to the diner. You know you're getting tired of being a cab driver."

"True enough, but without wheels, you don't have a lot of choices."

After knocking, she turned. "I appreciate the help. And how you've kept me safe, but I'm not in danger anymore. Right?"

The man watched from the shadows of an alley across the street from the diner. Victor had been stupid, trying to set up some grandiose plan when simplicity served the same purpose. Watch, wait, then act quickly. Easy.

Only two women passed out the little boxes tonight. The heavyset, black man who cooked sat inside talking with a pale thin teenager. Their presence and unknown intentions delayed matters.

At least the bodyguards who surrounded the woman since the ridiculous shooting incident were absent. After all, no one wished to harm her any longer. The threat disappeared when the dead hit man had been found.

A smile crept over his teeth. The big man walked the scrawny kid out the front door and down the street. They got into an old Volvo station wagon and drove away.

The two women remained along with a handful of vagrants.

He touched the cold metal of the Luger in his pocket. Not long now.

His redheaded target carried a lightweight box inside. The chatty blonde woman stayed at her heels. With a short reply from Cathy, she burst into a cascade of further excited words. They pulled a dozen water bottles from the white chest, stacking them into a box. Together, they dumped out ice and water onto the concrete.

This took too long. Why did the other woman stay? She hardly worked. Only talked.

Incessantly.

At least the street people ambled away.

The two women moved to the interior of the diner. His chance became clear. The blonde? Collateral damage.

Stealing from the shadows of the alley, he crossed the street. Avoided the dim spread of a street lamp near the entrance. He paused in a walkway to check his weapon. The diner at his back. A building that housed an empty Laundromat in front of him.

Best opportunity. Complete the plan. Then walk away leaving the missionary to grieve in the knowledge of his careless guilt. He stepped into the light of the windows as a truck turned onto the street. Ducking back into the shadows, he chanced to peek around the brick facade.

The missionary slowed his pickup to a crawl. Had Raymond Johnson seen him? In moments, the car would align with the walkway and give a full view of him crouching there. He fled down the open space to the parking lot at the back, dodging out of view when he reached the white rocks of the other side.

Breathing heavily, he turned away from the diner, taking a roundabout way to his car.

His task abandoned. For now.

Marji Laine

For the LORD knows the way of the righteous,
but the way of the wicked will perish. ~ Psalm 1:6 ESV

Chapter 15

Ray let his truck drift a few more feet and gazed down the open alley. Empty. His imagination raced. He'd seen someone duck into the walkway. Couldn't tell in the dim light if the figure was a man or woman. Might even have been a child.

He backed up and parked then jogged down the dark path.

Coming out of the alley into the white gravel of Mac's overflow lot, he noticed no movement. Not even an animal. Had his recent fears played upon his nerves so much that he made up new threats?

He rubbed the back of his head and returned to the street side. He pushed through the propped-open door. What was Cathy thinking? Anyone could have come in. He swallowed the chiding.

Daisy came out of the kitchen. "I don't mind."

"Don't mind what?" He glanced at the heavy coat she wrestled to fold over her arm. He didn't blame her. With the temperature reaching an unseasonable high in the seventies today, nobody needed the coats they relied on the day before.

"Hi. I was just telling Cat that I didn't mind taking her out to the inn."

"Thought I might do that myself."

Cathy flicked off the light in the kitchen and came through the door.

"Since you moved out while I was gone." Ray locked eyes with her.

She gave him a slight smile and shrugged. "I guess."

He held the door open for both women and followed Cathy to his truck, calling "good night" over his shoulder.

Cathy climbed in before he reached her door. He matched her silence, wondering why the normally talkative lady sat so stoic. They reached the turnoff to the highway and still she hadn't opened up. He sat at the stop sign and turned to her, waiting until she glanced in his direction.

She didn't. Instead, she bowed her head and kept her gaze down.

"I give up. Something's gnawing at you. I can't fathom what. Seems like you'd be happy to have your freedom back."

When she lifted her face, his heart twisted at the sight of the tears on her lashes.

"Cathy, what's wrong?"

Shaking her head made a tear drop onto her cheek. "I failed, Ray. I'm losing Dad's diner. His dream."

"You're his dream. You and the people of this town that he's loved into the faith."

"I'm the nightmare. I can't do anything right. Here you come back a hero. Saving souls and uprooting an evil local dictator. I felt ashamed enough to have you come back and me still working at the diner like before, but now I've even lost control of that." She dug in her leather bag and came out with a tissue to dab her eyes.

"Cathy, none of that's true. You aren't responsible for your dad's business decisions. And as far as me being a hero …" He scowled. Heroes didn't turn tail and run while other people stood in the gap. The guilt cut so deep he couldn't finish.

She sniffed. "I'm just feeling sorry for myself. I'll get over it. I kinda-sorta have to, with the party tomorrow. Then we'll have a few more days before I have to turn over the keys. Who knows, maybe I'll use some of my inheritance to take a vacation."

Never in a million years. However, chatting about a vacation was a safer topic, far from his mistakes in Chiapas. "Where would you go?"

"I don't know. I'm not really a beach lover."

"The mountains?"

"Hmm … not so much. Too cold. And I'm not the rugged type." She fingered the buckle on her green purse. "To be honest, I've never really wanted to be anywhere else."

"What if you invested your dad's insurance in a new place?" He moved forward again, checking his mirrors out of habit.

"Wouldn't be the same."

"Could be better. I can't imagine Mac's doing much business with Heath at the helm. Especially if he transforms it into a tearoom." A coffee house, maybe, but a tearoom? Wasted space.

"Thanks for saying that. Part of me hopes you're wrong. I'd like to always find Mac's in Heath's Point. Even if I don't own the place."

He pulled into the lot at the inn and shoved the car in park near the front porch. "I'll come for you in the morning."

"Not necessary. Ellis said he'd take me."

Ray glanced at her. "I don't mind." Surely she understood his meaning.

185

Her gaze dropped to the seat, and she scooted out. "Thanks anyway, but I'll be fine." She dashed up the steps without looking back.

She might as well have shouted, *I don't need you, Ray. I don't want you around.* If only his heart accepted what his mind instructed. But no. He had to keep trying. Had to keep butting his head against a door he had closed himself.

A door that didn't want to open again.

Cat focused on the customers the next day. Kept a smile on her face and a filled coffee carafe in her hand. She worked at exuding confidence, victory, especially in the face of the evening's fundraiser. The evidence of her personal defeat.

The whole town knew about Mac's by now. People whispered behind their hands. Like she couldn't tell their subject matter with their sidelong glances.

Marlena Lithgow was the worst. The older lady had trouble hearing, so Cat picked up her loud whisper, even though she was facing away and on the other side of the bar. "What's she going to do now? Without a husband to support her?"

Heat crept along Cat's collar. People were concerned. She should feel flattered that they worried about her.

The other woman at the table didn't trouble with a whisper. "Seems to me any girl who looks like that must have deep issues if she hasn't snagged a man yet."

The burn deepened.

"Oh, she had one, once. But he left her."

She shut her eyes. *Great.* Now all of her failures were the subject of idle discussions. She collected the women's meals at the window and delivered them, resisting the urge to reply to their rude conversation. Instead she gave a bright smile and laid their checks on the table. "Let me know if you need anything." Like a new topic.

They were right, though. What *would* she do? No job. No car, though she could use her insurance to replace that.

She paused and sucked in a deep breath. *None of this is a surprise to You, Lord.*

I've never seen the righteous forsaken or his seed begging for bread. The verse from Psalm 37 floated to her on an old song that her father used to sing.

Dad was surely righteous, Lord. I'm claiming Your promise.

She pictured herself opening a fancy restaurant in the metroplex or someplace similar. There, the customers outnumbered the chairs four to one, and wait time averaged an hour and a half. The reservation list spanned months in advance and included this century's social elite.

Not that she wanted those things. Her roots were in Heath's Point. And she'd be happy to keep up with the sunset dinners. If she could support herself. Nevertheless, the fantasy kept her mind away from losing the precious thing she thought she could keep forever.

Forever ended next week.

Thankfully, Daisy and Donna kept their planning and preparation away from her. When the last of the customers left, she had no choice but to turn her thoughts to the night and the party. Her party. Or anti-party.

Fundraiser. Not a party. A way to keep feeding those who needed help. She wandered through the back door and into the gravel parking lot where she stopped short and stared around in wonder. The day stayed warm-ish—as the forecasters had promised—with barely a hint of a breeze. Scents of smoking ham and turkey filled the lot and made her mouth water.

187

Wow.

"Pretty sensational, huh?" Donna gave her a hug. "I know you don't want to lose Mac's. I don't want you to, and Molly's gonna throw a fit if she doesn't get to enjoy Grady's Orange Jacks next summer. But tonight is about good memories, great friends, and exceptional food."

"And raising funds to keep that food for the homeless going as long as possible." Daisy scooted close. "But this is also gonna be a lot of fun."

"I know. And thank you both for doing all this work. I've been a slacker." Cat admired the large colorful lights spanning the lot from the trees on the other side with poles across the middle of the space giving added support. "Where did you get all the decorations?"

Donna giggled. "The lights are from Albert Dorf's Chevy dealership. The poles are borrowed from the high school volleyball team. The principal also donated the stage for the night. Pastor Slaughter sent over the chairs and tables. And all the flowers and lattices are on loan from Mr. Jackson's Nursery."

Cat strolled slowly to the center and turned a complete circle. Full of twinkle lights and supporting hanging baskets, the lattices formed a fake wall along the sides of the makeshift stage. The strings of lights draped from their volleyball poles and gathered in the middle of a triangle truss that held specialized squibs for the stage. "This place looks downright magical."

"And the best part is over there." Daisy pointed to a half-dozen rectangular tables filled with baskets, goods, and note cards. "We've had so many things donated for the silent auction we had to borrow extra tables from the middle school. And look at this stuff."

Quilts, home decor, handmade art, sports equipment, and a number of flower arrangements interspersed with baskets of dry goods, hardware, books, and Essential Oils. Mixed in with all of that

188

were cards. Taped to the tables, they spouted free golf tee times, tennis and swim lessons, hairstyles, and even babysitting. Cat noticed free airfare for two, weekends at Sunrise Inn, and some truly high-dollar items like Dallas Cowboy tickets, and season passes to Texas Motor Speedway and Six Flags over Texas.

"Oh, my gosh. Where did all of these things come from?"

Donna tucked an arm around her waist. "From folks who loved your dad and the work he did for the homeless."

"The work *you* do for the homeless." Daisy stepped to her other side.

Cat's heart swelled. She gave her friends a quick squeeze. "Wow. Thank you for reminding me to make the most of every opportunity. Like Ephesians 5:16 says." Her favorite book. She should apply its truth more often.

"I don't think partying is what the Apostle Paul had in mind with that verse." Donna laughed, though Daisy seemed rather lost.

She shrugged, bobbing the pink edges of her hair. "I don't know Pastor Paul, but I think *make the most of every opportunity* means to think and act as positively as possible, no matter what the circumstances are."

"I like that interpretation." Ray called down from a ladder stationed under the truss. He worked with a wrench on the large lights hanging there. "I always assumed that verse discussed sharing the Gospel, but knowing our Lord wants us to keep a good attitude, I concede to your thoughts."

"Ha. I don't really think that much about the Lord." Daisy shielded her eyes against the afternoon sun behind Ray as she gazed up at him.

"Really? Most people have a strong opinion one way or the other. Either they're a believer or they aren't."

Cat smiled. *You go, Ray.*

Daisy bit. "A believer in what?"

"A believer in Christ as the Son of God." He shifted on the ladder to work on another light.

Donna stole a glance at Cat and shut her eyes. The signal resonated, and Cat lifted a prayer for Daisy's soul.

Maybe Ray could make a dent in her armor.

"I suppose. I never considered Jesus in that light. Is that important?"

Ray descended the ladder and strolled over to the trio. "Paramount."

"Hey, Daisy, where'd you want these balloons?" Kurt, the delivery man from Jackson's Nursery rounded the corner with two, giant bags floating above each hand and lifting his arms higher than normal.

"Over there." Daisy pointed and met the man halfway across the lot.

"And moment lost." Cat frowned. "Had such a promising reaction from her."

"Not lost. Never lost." Ray stepped closer. "You never know when the Spirit's words'll find soil."

Donna grabbed his and Cat's hands, pulling them closer. "Lord, we offer this night to You. We're especially grateful for whatever You're doing with Daisy. Please become real to her. At Your perfect time and in Your name."

All three joined the *amen*.

Hope sparked in Ray's chest. Cathy hadn't pulled away when he put his arm around her.

Of course, she wouldn't. They were praying with Donna. But

even after the amen, he let his embrace linger as he said goodbye.

And she smiled at him. Sincere, warm, even a little wistful. After a quick shower and change at the ranch, Ray returned to the lot as Cathy and her friends came out from changing inside the diner. He couldn't help but admire the view. From her cascading brassy curls, to the frayed blue jean vest over the flirty, short, patchwork skirt, and all the way down to her shiny brown cowboy boots.

She struggled to keep a smile on her face when someone approached with a condolence for her dad. The bright expression and appreciation for the thoughts had to be hard to muster. Ray couldn't imagine having to repeat the words and attitude the hundreds of times Cathy must've since Mac died. She'd always been confident, but now she held a determined courage he couldn't help but admire. If only he could find a way to become part of her life again.

A teenage guy worked a makeshift soda counter. Ray asked him for a glass of tea.

He hadn't had a moment alone with Cathy since the night before. And that one had been far too brief. He sipped his tea. The chill of the iced liquid stiffened his spine. He'd had chances to tell her of his feelings. But the truth about his mission had to come with that conversation. His ultimate failure there.

Tonight, he'd find a way. Somehow. He had to tell her the truth. All of the truth. Maybe then … he dared not give definition to the hope sparking.

Scanning the group, he spotted Miguel entering from the alleyway. What a blessing to have him here.

"Amigo, you're just in time." Ray set down his glass and greeted the man with a handshake.

"This is quite a party. I should have come earlier. Perhaps I could have helped?"

Ray reflected on his struggle to get up the ladder to tighten the light screws several hours earlier. Yes, Miguel's help would have been welcome, but he wouldn't say so. "I'm glad you could join us."

"As am I, my friend. May this be a joyous night, laughing in the face of tragedy."

A kind thought, but Ray hoped Miguel wouldn't voice it in just that way in front of Cathy.

The LORD your God is in your midst, a Mighty One who will save;
He will rejoice over you with gladness;
He will quiet you by his love;
He will exult over you with loud singing. ~ Zephaniah 3:17 ESV

Chapter 16

"Say cheese." Cat clicked the picture of Donna and Daisy posing for the camera. "You guys are my heroes." She had to shout over the loud strains of a recent country release.

"Hungry heroes." Daisy, dressed in as far from her plain waitress outfit as possible, wore a short, jean skirt and a lighter sweater tank with a straight-cut, beige jacket over the top. Thankfully she hadn't worn the high heels she'd planned. Imagining them on the gravel lot pained Cat. Instead, Daisy had settled on beaded flip flops.

Cat elbowed the blonde. "Aren't your toes cold?" Even with the unseasonable warmth of the day.

"Yeah, but these set off the pedicure I got yesterday." Daisy pointed one foot. Her nails perfectly matched the color of fuchsia on the tips of her hair. All Cat could do was shake her head as her free-spirited friend led her to the center table. "You're over there." Daisy pointed to one of the chairs. A little card sat in the place where the plate would go.

"No, this one says Daisy." Cat circled the table. "Here's

mine." Two places down, situated between Ray and his friend.

Cat adjusted a decorative chain and cameo pin hanging from her vest. She felt strange wearing regular clothes at Mac's, but sitting around while her friends waited on her was worse. Donna and Myra wore the traditional pink dresses of Mac's with full aprons. They moved to get plates of food for Cat's table. A handful of teenagers helped them with drinks and plates.

Their busyness made her useless and unnecessary. With the festive atmosphere and Ray at her side, she worked to shed her uneasiness.

Raucous laughter erupted from the table next to them. Several of the diner's regulars sat there, delighting in the beautiful weather, the great music, and huge helpings from Grady's smoker.

"They sound like they're having a good time." Ray leaned toward her.

"I think so."

"Along with some of your sunset customers." He pointed to another table near the stage.

Warmth seeped into her chest. "I'm so glad they came. And for the beautiful weather. If we'd had to move inside, many would've stayed away."

"I've noticed how Dash avoids the entrance."

"Yeah. I have no idea about his life before Heath's Point, but he's never come in. Not even for dad." She glanced over at the big man where he sat chatting with some of the typical sunset folks.

"You know this ministry you have … What a huge blessing."

She stared at him. Was he talking about her third graders? "I don't have a ministry." Cat took a sip of sweet tea.

"Sunset dinners, here at Mac's."

"Dad had the ministry. I only serve the dinners."

He took a bite of his smoked turkey sandwich and a gulp from his glass. "Don't minimize your work, Cathy. You've done good work with these people. They not only trust you, they care about you. And I can tell you care about them."

"Well, I hope we can raise enough to keep the dinners going. At least through the rest of the winter."

"The Lord has taken care of them so far. Don't you think He is able to continue that work with or without you?"

She lowered her chin. Of course God would take care of them. And He didn't need Cat's help to do that. *But please keep using me, Lord.* The sinkhole that began when she received the will from Mr. Norton's office had grown to epic proportions. The pressure thudded with the rhythm of the bass guitar. "I like feeling useful."

"Being waited on is driving you crazy, huh?" Ray chuckled.

"I guess." That wasn't exactly what she meant. If only she really did have a ministry. A place to belong with the confirmation of God's leading. The man at her side had experienced such. And she had no doubts he would again. God had gifted him with speaking talent and a desire to share His gospel.

Cat only had serving skills. And a desire to be helpful. *Please let this fundraiser work, for Your glory and to help these people who so desperately need Your provision.* She blinked away threatening tears.

Wait and see. She'd laid her concern at God's throne. Release lightened the weight she'd been feeling. He loved these people much more than she did. He'd take care of them.

She tapped Daisy's arm. "Are you feeling odd at being served?"

"What do you mean?" Daisy leaned closer to Cat and Ray. Miguel leaned in behind her.

"I should be refilling drinks or getting seconds for people. Or clearing off their tables so they can talk."

"Huh-uh. Not me. I'm having a blast being on this side of the counter for a change." She lifted her hand. "Hey, Donna, can I get a little more of the potato salad?" She snickered when Donna curtsied. "No, siree. I'm happy to be here."

Miguel sat next to her, said something, and the blonde giggled, turning her back on the two of them.

Cat stared for a moment. "You don't suppose Daisy and Miguel …?"

"I can't imagine them together." Ray shook his head. "I don't know Miguel all that well, but I would think a relationship would interfere with his ministry."

"Wait a minute. Are you intimating that forming an attachment ruins a ministry?" Surely she'd misunderstood.

"That's not what I said."

So what had he intended? She folded her hands onto her elbows.

"Not what I meant, anyway."

She lifted her left eyebrow, waiting for the explanation.

"I get the feeling Miguel is serious about what he does. So much so that he wouldn't let a woman interfere." Ray wiped his mouth with his napkin. He left a streak of barbecue sauce across his cheek. "That's him, though, not me. Besides, Miguel has a calling. I can't imagine him connecting with a woman who doesn't have the same strong faith."

Cat felt a smile coming on. She pursed her lips.

"Truth is, I can't imagine Miguel marrying anyone."

"Oh, I see." The smile escaped. "You have a little something..." She pointed to her own cheek.

"Huh?" He wiped at the wrong side.

"No, on the other side."

He stroked his napkin near his chin and left another gash-like mark.

Cat bubbled over in laughter. "Can't take you anywhere."

Daisy let out a ripple of giggles as Miguel went to refill his tea glass. "Ray, you look like you've been brawling." She reached across the table handing him a fresh napkin.

Her fingers upset a glass of tea, hurling the liquid toward Cat's lap.

She jumped, and her chair tipped, folding partway as she stepped backward. Her boot heel caught in the bars and she stumbled and turned, taking another step away from the table and dragging the chair with her.

Laughter exploded around her.

At that instant, an overhead light hanging from the trestle crashed into the empty space where she'd sat moments before.

Glass showered her legs and she tripped, landing on her behind. Someone, Daisy maybe, screamed. Ray appeared at Cat's side in an instant.

"Are you all right? You aren't hurt?" He scanned her face with his warm brown eyes.

"I think I'm okay."

"You're bleeding." Ray stared at her face.

I've been cut? She didn't feel any pain.

Skeet, a young newcomer to the sunset dinners, slid in beside her, dabbing her face with his napkin. "Iffen that tea hadn't spilt …" His face reddened. "Good thing you got the reflexes you do."

A guy in a blue shirt with a Heath's Point Firefighter logo helped Daisy up. She limped against him.

"Glad you wore those boots." Ray helped Cat to her feet.

She spotted several trails of red on Daisy's ankles. "Oh dear, I think she's really hurt."

The firefighter wedged open the diner's exit, and they

disappeared.

"You're really hurt." Ray's tender eyes scanned her face. "Let's get you cleaned up and make sure those cuts aren't deep."

Cat tried not to grimace as Ray walked her into the diner. He helped her into the seat next to Daisy's booth. The party music from the stage barely hesitated.

"You okay, Daisy?"

"Sure." The high cushion blocked Cat from seeing her friend, but the wavering single word told a different story.

"What happened out there?" Grady bustled in, a pallor to his normally warm, brown skin.

Donna followed close behind. "You both could have been … hurt. I mean really hurt."

Cat knew what she meant. "I'm glad Daisy is clumsy." She looked up at Donna. "Or maybe *I* am." She tried to chuckle, but the sound twisted.

Ray's face darkened. "I'm the clumsy one. I hung the lights myself. I wanted to make sure they were secure."

Cat laid a hand on his shoulder. "You can't blame yourself."

"Yeah. Accidents happen." Daisy's voice trembled.

"Accidents?" Miguel came toward them from the restroom hallway.

Cat peaked around Ray's shoulder. "A little one."

He halted. "What happened?"

"A light fell. Crazy things happen sometimes." Cat locked eyes with Ray. She had to make him believe that.

Daisy sighed. "I guess we better figure out how to replace that light for the high school. Those things can cost a fortune." She almost sounded like her normal self.

Dash stood outside the door. "Sorry to bother you folks. Um … can I talk to you, Grady?" He eyed the group.

Cat watched to see if he would take a step inside but didn't expect it.

The new volunteer firefighter, Mark something, continued to work in the booth beside her with the diner's first aid kit.

Grady eyed his work. "I guess y'all have things covered in here."

Outside, Dash glanced at the doorway and lifted a shaky hand. He leaned forward, keeping his head behind the facing. Brows furrowed, he tilted his head as he scanned the interior of the building. Cat wished she knew his story.

"Ray, why don't you come with us?" Grady pointed at her. "You okay for a minute?"

"I'm okay, period. You don't need to worry about me." She took a deep breath as they stepped outside with the big man. If only the room would stop tilting. She'd not been hurt. Not really. But another accident? Now? Why did this keep happening?

Donna scooted toward the door. "If y'all are okay, I better get back to work. I don't know how y'all did this every day for so long."

Not for much longer.

Miguel and the fireman tried to help Daisy up. She didn't hit vertical before her color faded, and she plopped onto the cushion. "Maybe after a few minutes."

Cat didn't blame her. Her own legs felt like Jell-O sticks. Good thing the guys hadn't tried to help her up.

Ray twisted in his sheets, his hair plastered to his head with sweat. Thrusting them off, he sat up and peeled off his t-shirt, threading it around his sore arm.

His shoulder hurt. But not as bad as his conscience. He alone put Cathy in danger. No matter what Dash claimed he saw.

The clock read 4:58 AM. Cathy would be at the diner soon. Probably alone. On the heels of Dash's claim, Ray couldn't let that happen. Especially since the big man didn't want anything to do with the chief.

Had Grady told Dell?

He climbed from his bed. Didn't matter. He had to make sure Cathy wasn't alone.

Showered and armed with a tall mug of coffee, he pulled into a spot in front of Mac's door. He exited his truck when Ellis stopped behind him in his tan Suburban.

Cathy climbed out and thanked the older man for the ride. Then she turned to Ray. "What are you doing here?"

He'd been trying to come up with an answer to that question since last night when he'd determined to meet her. "Couldn't sleep." That wasn't anything near the replies he'd rehearsed. His sweater tightened around his neck, and he pulled at the material.

She paused, her chin cocked toward his face. "Are you worrying again?"

"I don't like coincidences." He followed her into the kitchen.

She switched on the grill as she passed. "But coincidences are real. Look at the car full of teenagers that almost mowed me down."

He nodded. "I know. Lousy timing and reckless driving on their part."

"They were jamming to loud music. Probably never saw me."

"Have you seen the girl again?"

She shook her head. "But I've only done one sunset dinner since then." Opening the freezer, she lugged out large plastic bins.

Ray started to offer assistance, but he couldn't lift. Useless. "Can I start the coffee?"

"Grady will be here in a minute." She began to unpack trays

of wrapped hamburger patties and all sorts of frozen meat. "You don't have to stay."

Yes he did. "I want to stay. I'd like to help." He glanced out the front windows. Even if Dash's information was ridiculous, he couldn't clear the niggling worry. Someone had murdered Sevilla's hit man. But Cathy thought herself safe.

Sevilla wouldn't let that go. Even if he was in prison like Miguel reported. Another would be coming. For her.

And then they'd have another killer wandering around. He pushed against the rear door. Locked. Good.

She hovered at the kitchen entrance. "Is something bothering you?"

Bothering? Was she kidding? "Besides you almost getting crushed last night?" He hadn't meant to raise his voice.

Cathy straightened, regarding him with her expressive green eyes.

He slumped, his breath heaving out. "I'm sorry I shouted."

She tucked her hands into her apron pockets.

Walking toward her, he massaged the back of his neck with his hand. "You could have been killed last night. With all of us sitting around you."

"I'm okay, Ray." She touched his arm.

He shut his eyes for a moment. What would he do if something happened to her?

She returned to her box.

Ray scanned the front windows. Still dark. Shouldn't the sky have lightened a little by now?

Grady hurried across the walk outside, and Ray rushed to open the door for him.

The older man nodded a good morning. "A little early for you isn't it?" He shook off his windbreaker and hung it behind the door.

"A little." Ray reached to shoot the bolt when an orange flame glowed across the street. A cigarette. Like he and Cathy had seen in the parking lot.

Without thinking, he flung open the door and darted across Shepherd Street to a gap between the hardware store and an empty storefront.

A man leaned against the bricks, a blanket covering his features so that only his cigarette showed.

Ray's fist balled as he neared the figure. "Why are you out here? What are you watching?" His volume rose, and he shoved his forearm against the man.

The blanket slipped over his face. Spanish in quick staccato emanated.

He replied in the language. "You've been watching. What are you waiting for? Who are you working for?" With every question, his volume grew.

Cathy approached at a run. "What are you doing?"

"He's been watching you."

"Let him go." She pulled at his arm.

The man trapped against the wall wiggled. "No. No." The blanket fell from his shoulders revealing Frankie. Eyes wide and attempting to become part of the wall he leaned against.

"Ray, stop. You're frightening him."

He knew what he saw. Had Frankie been the man stalking Cathy all along? He let her pry him away. "I'm watching you." He pointed to the small man to make sure he got the message.

Frankie shrank toward the wall and picked up his blanket. He probably would have fled if Cathy hadn't grabbed his elbow. In her broken Spanish, she invited him in for breakfast.

"Cathy, this man—"

"Needs something warm and nourishing to eat." She asked

him again, pressing until he nodded.

Ray growled. This guy had been watching her, maybe for days. And she rewarded him with another meal? But he took Frankie's other arm. If for no other reason than to make sure he carried no weapon.

Grady met them at the door and greeted Frankie. "One o' my especi-als coming right up."

Ray followed him into the kitchen and remained at the door. "What do you know about him?"

"Less then you, I bet." He broke some eggs onto the large griddle. For a big guy, he moved fast and sure in his expertise.

"When did he first come to one of the dinners?" He eyed Frankie.

Cathy seated the young man at a table and sat down across from him. They both gave Ray uncomfortable glances as Cathy apologized for his actions.

"I seen him right after you got back into town. Dash said he introduced y'all. Said y'all had a nice long talk."

He remembered. That put him in town about the same time as the threatening letter.

"Folks come in and go out all the time." Grady spread a layer of butter across the griddle. "Just when you get used to the new ones, somebody'll move on. They're called *transient* for a reason, you know."

Ray was sick of coincidence. But even more sick of suspecting that every detail, every instance was being engineered by all-powerful Sevilla. Playing with them. Toying with the lives of the people Ray cared about so he could enjoy the destruction to the fullest.

And Ray was allowing Sevilla to win his stupid game.

Maybe Cathy was right. The flare was only a cigarette. Not so rare. And Frankie hadn't been actually watching the windows when

Ray encountered him.

His stomach sank. He was either a fool to be taken in by Frankie or a jerk to yell at an innocent kid just for standing on the street. Either way, he needed to apologize.

Guard me, O LORD, from the hands of the wicked;
preserve me from violent men,
who have planned to trip up my feet. ~ Psalm 140:4 ESV

Chapter 17

Cat's whole day slammed into overdrive after Ray's outburst. Though Frankie had taken a seat at a table, he'd leaned as far away from Ray as possible. Even after Ray had apologized, the poor young man hadn't relaxed until Ray left.

Cat didn't blame Frankie. Ray could be formidable. And a little exciting. A spark ignited. He'd run to her rescue. Put himself in virtual danger.

Well, Frankie might have been dangerous. She glanced at the young man, shoveling eggs like they might be snatched from him any moment. She wondered what had driven him to the streets. From the looks of him, neglect had played a part.

But Ray's defense of her budded a glow that remained throughout her supersonic day.

The breakfast rush alone could have matched most of their full-day sales. People she hadn't seen in months decided this was the time to revisit. Probably felt the pinch of visiting Mac's while it still had a McPherson in charge.

Things didn't slow until well after two o'clock.

"Wow. That was some workout." Daisy sagged against the counter as one of the last customers left.

Cathy scanned her friend's face. Paler than normal. "How are you holding up?"

She nodded and sank onto a stool.

The door clunked as Ray arrived.

"I hope you're not planning to eat, 'cause we're about out of everything." Daisy wiped her forehead. She stood and dragged the rolling cart to a table of dirty dishes.

"Not even a burger?"

"I still got a couple." Grady tapped the bell. "Gitcha one right out."

Ray pulled off his gloves and blew on his hands. "Winter decided to revisit."

"Glad Jack Frost didn't come yesterday. We'd have all been popsicles." She hung his heavy coat on a hook next to hers and took in his rugged face. The stitches had been removed, though a slight line still showed where they had been. The scruff of a beard shadowed his strong jawline and curls swept away from his forehead.

He caught her stare and smiled. "What are you looking at?"

"Um ... I noticed you're missing stitches."

"Yeah." He ran his hand lightly over his cheek. "Doc Greer doesn't think there will be much of a scar. I hope not."

She grinned. "Makes you look a little dangerous." Her gaze dropped to the floor.

"Ha. How does that work? The one with all the war wounds?"

"The conquering hero." Her cheeks warmed at her own flirtations. She poured him a coffee and set it on the counter.

His smile fell away. He sipped from the mug. "How are your scratches from last night?" Ray tilted her chin.

206

Electricity danced across her skin at his touch.

He examined them. "Much better. I don't think they'll leave a mark."

"They won't." She wouldn't say a word even if they did. Ray felt bad enough for not tightening the lights as he intended. "And no matter what you think, that wasn't your fault. Sometimes accidents really do happen."

"Yeah, about that ..." He raked his right hand through his windblown hair. "I talked to Dash last night."

"I remember. You and Grady." She sipped her drink. "What did he need?"

"Nothing he needed. Something he noticed. Yesterday afternoon. When we all left to get ready for the party, Dash saw someone up on the rigging messing with the lights."

"What?" Cat shook her head. No. That nightmare was over. "He made a mistake."

Ray blew out a sigh and a crevice appeared between his eyes. "I'd like to believe that, but after that piece fell ..." He wiped his hand over his face. "Dash thought the guy worked for the band until the crash."

"What band? They were just some kids from the high school."

"I know, but Dash didn't. He thought the guy was a roadie." He blew across the surface of his mug and sipped again.

The familiarity of his rough face, the hint of a cleft in his chin, his sensitive chocolate eyes absorbed her.

Distracted her. She blew out her exhale, begging release from her emotional captivity. "So who was this guy?"

"Dash couldn't see him very well. Only his silhouette for the most part." He hesitated. "He mentioned Miguel. Or someone similar in frame and build."

"Miguel?"

"Yeah" Ray shook his head. "That's impossible, though. *If* he saw someone, it was more likely the little guy from this morning."

She squinted. Dash wouldn't lie about something this important. "But he would've recognized Frankie."

"Not necessarily. Up over his head. No lights on."

Hmm. The lot was usually pitch black without lights, even early in the evening. "I'm sure you're right about Miguel, but I'm not convinced he saw Frankie."

"Could have been the other kid that spoke to you after the light fell."

"Skeet. He's pretty shy." Dash must've been wrong. "Using your logic, anyone or anything could have been up there."

"Right." He held her gaze. "Anyone could have been up there. And someone was."

She shook her head. "A bird, a balloon, a plastic bag, a squirrel, even a shadow. I don't believe anyone caused that light to fall. Accidents happen."

Dell entered in his bulky navy jacket. "Wish this cold stuff would stay away for more than a day."

"You'll miss the cool air come August." She pulled out another mug. "Want some coffee?"

"No, thanks. I've got some info to share with you and Ray."

Info? An intense need to stick her fingers in her ears and shut her eyes washed over Cat.

"Because of all that went on the last week, I had Danvers check out the rigging this morning, before the students came over and took the truss down. Also had him look over what was left of the light."

"And?" Ray sounded tons more interested that she felt.

"The thing had no bolts."

Ray swiveled toward the chief. "Of course the light had bolts.

I tightened them myself."

"Nope. Not on the fixture and nowhere on the ground. Whatever you fastened disappeared."

"That's crazy." Cat fisted her hips.

"How could the light stay up there at all?" Ray's brows furrowed.

"Good question. But missing bolts wasn't all he discovered. He got a residue of something. I've sent samples to the lab, but I think it's some sort of acid or a flammable compound."

"Flammable? There wasn't any fire." Fog enveloped Cat's brain.

Dell shifted. "Way I figure, the light was held on by something fairly sturdy, but temporary. Like wax or something that could burn or melt. Some type of flash, an igniter if you will, reduced the temporary rigging at a specific time to disconnect the fixture. A fall was inevitable."

"That's pretty involved, Dell." Ray spoke Cat's thoughts.

What the chief described seemed ridiculously complex. But the place cards at her table bothered her. She'd been assigned exactly beneath that fixture.

Cat tried to push her fears aside. "Don't you think more likely the bolts got lost in the gravel. And as far as the residue: grease, grime, dirt. Take your pick."

Dell strolled toward the exit. "I'll wait for the lab results, but don't be wandering around by yourself, missy." He pointed a finger at her, punctuating his directive, before he left.

A niggling of concern worried the back of her neck. She let her head sag and massaged her temples. *Stop.* She willed the annoying itch to go away.

She raised her head, and her gaze locked with Ray's. "There was someone up there, Cathy. Someone who intended harm. Someone who purposely rigged that light to fall. On you."

Ray hated the way his conclusion darkened Cathy's face. Why couldn't this whole thing be over? What would that take besides Sevilla's success?

Cathy slipped her coat over her shoulders.

"Wait a minute. Dell told you to stay put." He grabbed his own coat and draped it around his sling.

"I know what he said, but I don't live in a cage. I made an appointment with Mr. Heath." She pulled open the door and a gale ruffled the tablecloths. "I'll be back." She sang out and exited without waiting for a reply.

"Heath?" He tracked her outside. "What are you doing with him?"

"Why are you following me?"

"I should think that's obvious."

She blew out an audible exhale and squeezed her eyes shut. When she reopened them, she leveled a soft look on him while the wind tossed her ponytail and bangs. "I'm all right, Ray. I don't need a sitter."

"You do need a bodyguard, and I'm going with you." He shrugged his single shoulder. "Might as well get used to the idea."

She pivoted and marched up Shepherd Street.

"Why are you going to speak to Heath?" He matched her clipped stride.

Her jaw muscle twitched.

"You're going to try to get him to sell you his half?"

Another twitch. "No."

Now that he'd coaxed a single syllable from her, maybe he

could keep her talking. "Then why?"

They neared the man's real estate office.

"You gonna spill?"

"I didn't invite you along, Ray. If you feel you have to come, just stay out of the way."

Ouch. He reached for the door and held it open for her.

She turned to face him. "I'm sorry. I know you're trying to protect me. I need to focus on what's important and not let this ridiculous threat scare me into isolation."

He nodded. *Whatever she's doing, Lord, Your will be done.*

Following her into the office, he shed his jacket right away. The room was stuffy with a heavy rose scent. He coughed.

The receptionist took Cathy's name and apologized. "Mr. Heath has several calls to make. He asked that you wait until he could find time to speak to you."

"Do you have an idea of how long that will be? Should I come back in a half hour?" Cathy's voice stayed calm and kind, despite the annoyance she must have been feeling.

"Oh dear, no. He has a number of appointments this afternoon, and he's quite booked up for the rest of the week. Your best bet is to stay and be ready for him when he has the time for you."

Heath was flexing his muscle. Pure and simple. Ray clamped his molars tight.

"Very well." Cathy flashed her bright smile and took a seat in the corner.

Ray settled in beside her. "You know he's doing this on purpose."

"I can't fault him. I told him off in front of his family."

"Your graciousness amazes me."

Her mouth turned up slightly, and she cut her eyes to the right. She picked up a *Dallas Life Magazine* and began thumbing through it.

Conversation closed. He must have hit a nerve. A little pink showed in her cheeks. Just enough to prove she liked his comment.

Good enough. He picked up a *Modern Home*. Not that he was interested in the market in North Texas or how to stage a home, but she had shut down the communication and wouldn't even look at him.

The pages of the magazine blurred. She might as well have been looking at its reflection in a lake. How was she supposed to keep her mind on convincing Heath to sell his controlling interest when Ray's spicy aftershave and devastating smolder kept numbing her mind?

Ugh. She needed some solitude. Impossible because of Dell's irrational fears. A distraction. Something. Besides Ray and all of the memories of carefree springs and moonlit walks his nearness stirred.

She startled when Heath's door opened. Almost an hour had passed.

"You wanted to see me, young lady?" The sparkle in his eyes resembled a tarsier, only without the cute factor.

She pushed up and averted his gaze. "Yes, thank you." She assumed her most businesslike tone and marched past him as though the office belonged to her.

When he shut the door, she faced him and clasped her hands together in front of her. "I'd like to purchase the two percent of Mac's that you received from my father."

"The part that finally puts me in control of my diner."

His diner? Over her dead body. The thought shocked her. No, over her dad's. Her brain betrayed her with sad, sentimental memories. She unclasped her hands and fingered the fake emerald stud in her right earlobe. "Mr. Heath, Mac's has given you a fine supplemental income for years. There's every reason to believe that it will continue to do so."

"Is that what this is about?" He crossed his arms, palming his skinny biceps. "You don't think I can run Mac's as well as your father and his antiquated ideals. Or better than you, an inexperienced, über-trusting child?

Her irritation festered, but she brushed it aside. "I'm hardly inexperienced, and I'm no child, though I thank you for the compliment." She actually summoned a smile. "This has nothing to do with how well you would run Mac's. Nothing to do with you at all. This is only about me wishing to continue running the diner in which I grew up." She steered clear of using any possessive words.

"My wife has her heart set on creating a tearoom. I've a mind to let her do it."

Her dad's *bleck*-face flashed across her internal screen. "There are any number of buildings around town that can work for such a refined enterprise. And the profit you receive from my payment for your two percent along with the monthly income from Mac's can help you finance such."

He loosened his grip on his upper arms. "How much are we talking?"

She pulled the paper she'd already prepared out of her pocket. "I can write a check for this amount right now." She handed it to him. Surely he would accept. Her figure was three times what the two shares were truly worth.

He glanced at the paper. "Hmph. Nope."

Nope? That was it? "You realize how much the shares are actually worth?"

"A lot less than that, yes. But more than that to me."

She inwardly huffed. Maybe she could get a bank loan? "How

much more?"

"Ha. More than you have. More than you can get. I will not sell my rights away. I will make that diner into my own. What I always wanted and would have had if your mother hadn't destroyed everything."

"I don't understand ..."

"She poisoned your father. The café we would have had ... a vision. A plan before its time. It would never make money, you said. No one wanted a fancy restaurant, you said." He held his finger out toward her.

His eyes had glazed. Cat favored her mom, except her red hair would never have had them mistaken.

"My money was already invested. The agreement already made when you forced Mac to turn his back on me, Emily. How dare you." He raised his voice and took a step toward her.

The door burst open. Ray rushed in.

Cat raised a hand toward him. Heath didn't even flinch. So lost in the bitterness that had festered in his mind, he spewed forth an attack on her mother that he must've conjured for decades.

"I'm not Emily, Mr. Heath. I'm Mac's daughter. I'm Cat. Remember?"

His eyebrow twitched. "I'll prove that my ideas would have worked. Café then, tearoom now. It's all the same." He leaned in close. "So you can take your ridiculous offer along with your parentage and leave *my* place of business."

She lifted her chin and stepped toward the doorway.

Ray's hands fisted. Even through the soreness of his shoulder. He wanted to hit something. Couldn't hit an old man and didn't have a punching bag.

The only thing handy was a brick wall. He resisted and blew out his anger as best he could. "I take it Heath said no."

"You heard him." Cathy kept her head down and pushed through the breeze.

"Doesn't mean Mac's has to end. Maybe the way you know it, but you could open a new place. Call it Cat's."

"It doesn't matter."

"Matters to you. So it's important."

"No. What's important are the people who won't have any food. You think Heath is going to let me keep doing the sunset dinners with the tearoom's leftovers? Like Dash and the others would have them."

The thought of Dash with a tea cup and his pinky extended made his former irritation fade even more. "So let's come up with another way. I heard from Mom that the fundraiser brought in a lot of money."

"More than I thought it would."

"Enough to rent a little space? Maybe have hot plates and crock pots? Open up a little soup kitchen?"

She halted and turned slowly to stare at him. "That's brilliant."

"It wouldn't need much room. Just a fridge to store the food for a day at time."

"I bet we could get some monthly donations of food from some of the stores in town."

"And dishes or paper goods. People will be willing to help if they have a direction."

"Do a paper goods drive. Maybe even have the church's VBS group, or better yet, have the elementary school do a drive." Once the spout opened, possibilities poured out and a sparkle reignited her eyes.

Back at the diner, Ray helped Cathy clean up the dining room and prepare for the sunset dinner. "What do you do when you have no leftovers?"

"Well, now, we usually keep a store of stew in the freezer for cold weather, and we serve sandwiches or salads during the summer heat." She wheeled in the rolling cart and collected the napkin box from the first table. "Walmart's always available if we get in a pinch."

She brushed his arm reaching for a dispenser near him. His skin warmed. "Let me get those for you."

"You don't have to."

He grasped the one she held. "I want to."

Looking into her eyes, he saw openness. Not the veil hiding her emotions like she'd first shown him or the wall her frustration built. But engagement. And she remained close to him, holding his gaze.

His heart swelled. This was the time. The moment he could tell her how he felt. He looked at the metal box and moved his hand to stroke hers. Then again reclaimed her gaze. Her lips separated. He moved to caress her cheek with his finger.

She set the napkins back on the table and laid her hand on his chest. He closed the gap, mesmerized by her tender look. He drew her closer, focused on the kiss he desired.

"Grady thought we should serve chili with this wind kicking up." Daisy rolled a noisy mop bucket into the dining room.

Cathy retreated, chin down and grabbed the napkin holder again. Setting it on the cart, she hurried to the remaining tables. "That sounds fine. Maybe with rice and Fritos?" She pushed the cart into the kitchen.

The blonde eyed them but went about slopping the soapy water over the blue and white tile.

Lousy timing. After they cleaned up from the sunset dinner, though, he tried again. He met Cathy in the kitchen. "Thought I'd take you home. You mind?"

A little smile grew. "Is Daisy still here?"

"I saw her throwing away the garbage, but she didn't come back inside."

Cathy frowned. "I had a feeling she'd bolt. When Grady did the devotion tonight, she fidgeted like a five-year-old." She slipped on her red wool coat and wrapped a dark green scarf around her throat. Between the coat, the scarf, and her brassy hair, she looked like Christmas.

"Does she always leave like that?"

"Not usually. I think the crash last night jarred her. And she's actually been talking about the Lord lately." She pulled green mittens over her hands. "I'll try to talk with her tomorrow. Hey, where is that partner of yours? I thought I'd see him today."

Ray spread out his right arm. "Winging home to San Diego."

"I'm sorry. I know you enjoyed having him here."

His visit had been nice. "Miguel has his own life. Though I'll never forget what he did for me."

Cathy set the lock and joined him at the rear door. He held it for her, enjoying the fragrance of her honeysuckle hair.

The barriers he'd felt growing between them early in the week had dissipated, igniting in him a desire to explore the possibilities of reclaiming the relationship they'd had. Once his heart flew to that prospect, his mind remained fixated.

Climbing into the cab beside her, his nerves heightened. No worries. Not this time. Nothing to stop him from sharing his feelings. Or anything else.

Except the frigid reality his affection might not be returned.

He stuffed the thoughts away and examined the main street before he took the turn. The only vehicles were parked way down the street in front of the police station.

He kept his eyes shifting between the road in front of him and his mirror, offering unimportant responses here and there. Good thing she carried most of the conversation. His tongue proved untrustworthy beyond the occasional *yeah*.

At least no headlights appeared behind him. He relaxed a little. No one could possibly know where they were heading. He'd not said a word.

Maybe he needed to listen to her when she insisted that she was no longer in danger.

"You missed the turn." Cathy pointed to the side road that led to the inn.

How did he explain this? "I thought maybe we could talk a little?"

"Isn't that what we've been doing?" Her voice softened, and she glanced out the side window.

At the next road he paused and took out his phone.

"Who are you calling?"

Warmth crept into his cheeks. "No one." He muted the sound. "I don't want interruptions." He turned right.

"Doesn't this lead to the campground?"

"Yeah, pretty up there." The old Scout camp was turned into a state park before Ray was born. Run down by the time he and Cathy reached high school, the ridge overlooking the lake had been a favorite destination for most of their crowd. A particular visit with her urged a smile.

She turned her head toward him in silence. Her brows arched to meet her curly bangs. The cab of his truck felt stuffy, but he kept his focus forward, wishing he could hold her hand and still drive with his injured arm.

He pulled onto the camp road and proceeded to the moonlit

ridge that stood above Lake Grayson.

A barren landscape and dull gray sky took on color, warmth, and light.

The near miss she'd had with Ray earlier ignited more than a spark. The love for him that she'd tried to forget roared to life at his touch. His caress. His almost …

But the interruptions and the barrage of decisions and common conversations made her fear the moment had passed entirely. Then he zigzagged and brought her to their old stomping grounds. She didn't have the heart to tell him that the sheriff's department patrolled the area so regularly they'd likely get shooed away within five minutes.

He'd probably ask how she knew that. Horrifying. Confessing that she'd been caught up here would be bad enough. But the lame truth was that she could see the ridge from her attic suite across the lake.

When he parked, she could barely make out the windows of that room. "So, what did you want to talk to me about?"

He twisted in his seat and put his good arm on the cushion behind her. His calm brown eyes sought hers, sending sparks of anticipation across her shoulders and along her spine.

"I know when I left, I …" Glancing down, he took a breath. "I didn't mean to hurt you."

She tensed. The memory of his leaving sucked warmth from the cab. "I never understood. I still don't understand why you didn't even tell me. I thought …" She shut her eyes. What she thought didn't matter. Obviously, their relationship had meant little to Ray since he walked away. "My mistake."

"Cathy, I couldn't tell you. The mission team would never have let you go."

She quelled the tide of emotion that threatened but didn't trust her voice to respond.

He shifted. "If I told you about the opportunity—if you didn't like the idea, or even if you simply questioned something—I would have stayed. But I had to go. I knew—I know—God sent me."

"You didn't trust me?" What she'd always believed. "You thought me too spiritually weak to recognize God's leading?"

His jaw twitched. "I never considered that."

She sniffed. "You've always had to be in control, Ray."

"Now wait a minute. I tried to protect you."

"How? By making a decision without discussion, simple information? Even after you'd decided, you refused to relay your plan." Memories of nights full of despair and sobbing enveloped her. "You ran off in the dark, disappearing before I knew anything about your choice. Then you wouldn't answer a letter or e-mail? What part of that protected me?"

"I sent you cards."

"But you never answered any questions."

"I couldn't."

"Why? What possible reason could you have for hiding? You told your mom."

Ray let out a combination of a growl and a heavy sigh. He raked his hair with his fingertips, making his bangs curl over his forehead. "Mom and Dad had to know because they helped to set up the mission on this end. They got the permissions and worked through the state department for the legalities. I couldn't tell anyone else except the Slaughters because Philip and Amy were the forwarding agents."

"Oh, so four other people knew, but not me. I thought you …"

She licked her lips as tears stung her eyes. She could do this. Speak all of the pain. "You had promised to take me with you." The tears knocked again, and she stoned herself against them. She dared not appear a weakling at this point.

"Cathy, the place was too dangerous. The board refuses to let any women in that area. Look what happened to me." He raised his gimpy left arm.

"That's still no reason to stay silent."

He dropped his head. "I couldn't talk to you. If I saw you or even heard your voice, I'd never leave. And once I was there, speaking to you would stir up a need to come home. But I had to stay until the Lord said I was done."

The depth of what he said wrapped her heart in a warm blanket. She turned to him and found his gaze on her.

"My silence didn't have anything to do with you. Only me. I'm the weak one." Moisture glinted in the corner of his eyes. "Can you forgive me?"

"I thought you left me because I'm lousy at talking to people. I mean, I don't have any schooling in that. I figured I'd be a poor partner for you."

"What?" He stretched his hand out again but this time around her shoulder. "With all you do for the homeless and the kids at church, how could you think that?"

"You having a problem with going never occurred to me. I thought something had to be wrong with me."

"Cathy, honey, there is absolutely nothing wrong with you."

She scoffed. "Don't be ridiculous. I'm nowhere near perfect."

He moved closer. His breath, warm across her skin, sent a shimmer of desire through her. "You're perfect for me."

Her attention drifted from his chocolate eyes to his mouth, magnetized to the slight curve. Her lips longed for his touch. She reached to his injured cheek and stroked a strand of hair above his ear. He gave her a gentle smile and lowered his head, lightly brushing her lips with his own.

Brrrrrring. Cat jumped. She caught a view of the caller. Dell. This interruption jeopardized his place on her Christmas list. "I'm a little busy." She answered in a sing-song without saying hello.

Ray stayed close, stroking her hair and kissing her temple.

"Daisy's been hurt. Get out to the hospital, now."

All this time, he had believed Ray's last name was Johnson. How had he missed that little detail?

No wonder his constituent could not locate the man or his home. And his Cathy had been staying there with him as well.

He cringed. Reading people had always been his strong suit. But the innocent performance of Ray and his sweetheart took him in completely.

Luckily, with his stiletto to her throat, the blonde waitress gave up the details of her thin knowledge with little resistance. Unfortunately, Cathy departed with her missionary before he finished with the lovely waitress. But such is the price for a work of art.

Knowing Ray's true identity, now, he had no problem finding his home. Good. No more playing games of hide and seek.

He left his rental on a dirt road some distance from the ranch. He had to duck through barbed wire to get on the property since the drive had a gate. Circling to the back of the house, he found unpopulated darkness inside. That was annoying, but he could wait. He was a patient man. The cold crept through him, reaching into the already icy depths of his soul.

The beams of a truck's headlights delighted him. His task had finally come to an end. The pickup pulled in, coasting to a stop. Ray and Cathy chatted as they emerged, comfortable with one another as lovers should be. They separated. The man collected a heavy looking sack of something from the bed of the truck and walked toward an outbuilding behind the house. The woman pulled several shopping bags from behind the seat before entering through a side door.

He touched the Luger in his pocket. Stealing toward the front, he found a window with blinds raised enough to get a glimpse inside.

Ray re-crossed the lot toward him, his steps crunching on the dry grass of the yard. Ducking and hugging the wall until Ray passed, he watched the man enter the attached garage and lower the automatic door.

Adrenaline pumped as his heartbeat accelerated. He dashed to the next wall. This side gave a view of the kitchen. The delightful figure of a woman appeared, moving around the room. With the thin slats of the blinds pointed down, he had a view of her waist and feet, no doubt purely female. His mouth curled.

A shame really. He'd wanted to play with the kitten before finishing her. Ah, but a chance such as this he dare not let pass.

As the figure crossed the kitchen, he pulled out his gun and dashed past the porch. The bolt rattled and hinges squeaked. A yellow glare shone from the room, flaring down the steps and dissipating into the yard.

Peering past the corner of the house, he watched Cathy cross the space with some sort of wrap around her head and a white plastic bag dangling from her hand. Fumbling with his silencer, he eyed her obvious destination. A pair of trash bins on the other side of the lot in a ring of light from a single gas lamp. If he hurried, he could end this business before the darkness enveloped her.

He took a step and the silencer slipped from his hand. Never mind. He'd been hidden well, though under the moonless sky, he'd have to get close to assure his kill.

He darted forward. With his timing off, he reached her as she stepped into the lamplight. She must have heard his labored breathing. She startled and whirled around, swinging the full bag at his head as the gun went off. Something sharp and jagged plunged into his wrist and pain stabbed him.

The figure went down. Gasping he retreated a few steps before turning and running for his car.

That woman was not the redhead he'd expected to find.

With him is an arm of flesh, but with us is the LORD our God,
to help us and to fight our battles. ~ 2 Chronicles 32:8 ESV

Chapter 18

Cat braced herself in the corner of the truck cab. "Something about Daisy." Cat could explain little about Dell's call as Ray bounced over the back roads toward the regional hospital.

"Get my phone out of my jacket and call Miguel. Ask him to pray."

Cat fumbled but pulled it out and dialed. "You don't suppose she's ... nothing has happened to her."

"Lord, please bless Daisy." Ray's eyes didn't leave the road, but emotion painted his features. "She needs You. Don't let her leave without You."

"Oh, Ray." A tear slid down her nose. The phone kept ringing until a computerized voice started speaking in Spanish. At least the beep was a universal language.

"Miguel, this is Cat. Daisy, you remember the waitress that works for me? She's been hurt. Ray and I are headed to the hospital, but Ray wanted me to call you to pray. Have a safe trip home." She hung up as Ray pulled into the parking lot of Howerton Memorial.

225

Lead embedded Cat's stomach. *Please God, let her be all right.*

She and Ray dashed across the lot to the entrance and found their way to emergency. Dell and Juanita met them in the waiting room.

The woman embraced Cat and held on.

Ray put his arm around her other side and bowed his head. "She needs You, Lord. You've brought her this far for a reason. Don't let her go now."

Dell added, "In Jesus' name."

More tears squeezed from Cat's eyes. "What happened?"

Juanita released Cat and shook her head. "I don't know. Dell and I found her in the alley beside the diner. She'd been stabbed."

"Got'er here soon as I could." He fidgeted with his cowboy hat in his hands.

The woman wrapped her arms around one of his. "You did the best you could. Don't let guilt in."

Cat still reeled over the word *stabbed*. "When? Who?"

"No clue. Danvers is at the scene. Daisy was unconscious." He pressed his hat on his head. "But she had a letter carved into her cheek."

Ray's mouth opened in a silent gasp. He paled.

"What do you mean carved? Like a tattoo?" She wanted to gag.

Ray turned to her, eyes haunted. "No. He means carved. Like cut into a piece of wood." He swallowed.

"That mean something to you, boy?" Dell grabbed Ray's jacket with his free hand.

"Let me guess. An S."

"How did you know that?" Dell stepped closer.

"I've seen the mark before. On some of Sevilla's victims."

No, no, no. Not Sevilla again. But this time, she couldn't fathom another coincidence.

"Can't ignore your danger, Cat. Not now. And I've placed a guard at Daisy's door." Dell straightened.

"Get the facts first, Dell." Juanita rubbed his forearm. "Don't make a decision before you know why."

"Better early than too late."

"Won't be too late." She laid her hand on Cat's shoulder. "You'll stay here, right? Stay here with Ray. You won't go anywhere alone or try to leave?"

Cat's chest tightened. Her questions formed a stranglehold. She nodded. Mute. Submissive. No telling what conspiracies Dell conjured.

"See there?" Juanita's hand returned to the chief's arm. "She'll be fine. Protected. When you collect the data, then you can make a decision."

What decision did he plan? Cat wouldn't ask, but the question melted a hole in the carpet between them.

"All right for now. But I'm looking into this Sevilla thing."

Would Ray never be rid of the man's extended reach? Just when he believed he and Cathy ... His heart swelled with the memory of the moment they shared. He longed to stay there, to relive the exuberance and anticipation.

But, no. His brain didn't work when his heart took over. And with yet another man sent by Sevilla, he had to have his wits on track.

Dad trotted through the doors with the Myersons, their neighbors, on his heels.

"Why are you here?" To Ray's knowledge, Dad hardly knew

Daisy, except for his occasional visits to the diner.

"Raymond." His father puffed and struggled for breath. "I tried to call you."

Ray pulled out his phone. Still on silent. He remedied that and re-pocketed it. "I already know about Daisy. Dell called us."

"No. Your mom. Someone shot ..."

No. Ray needed to hold onto something and found the back of a chair. "Is she ... she's got to be all right."

"Who was shot?" Dell stormed over with Lt. Estrella at his heels.

"Calm down. Let them get the story out." Juanita slowed the chief's progress and silenced him for the moment.

"That's what I'm trying to tell you. The Myerson's and I got her here as fast as possible. She went in there." He pointed through the doors of the trauma unit. "Groggy, but still with us."

"Where? How?" Ray could feel Cathy's warmth next to him. Her hand curled around his elbow.

"The shot went in somewhere in her upper chest or maybe her shoulder. I couldn't tell with all the ..." He took a ragged breath that broke into a stifled sob. "She was taking out the trash."

"Denny, sit down." Mr. Myerson walked around the chairs and eased him into one.

The man's wife put her hand on Ray's slinged shoulder. "Raymond. I believe she's gonna be fine. And I've already called your pastor. He'll be here any minute."

He mustered a smile for the dear woman. "Thanks, Mrs. Myerson."

Ray's already knotted gut tightened further when an ER nurse came into the room with a clipboard full of papers for his dad to fill out. "She's in surgery. I'll let you know whenever I hear any news. You can bring all of this to me when you get the chance."

Mrs. Myerson took the stack of papers. His father stared at the floor.

"God, please take care of Mom." The prayer escaped Ray's lips without intention.

"The doctor said she has a really good chance." Mr. Myerson patted his shoulder.

"A chance?" Ray swayed and sat on the bench behind him. His hand brushed through his hair, trying to sort through the facts and emotions cramming to attain first place in his attention.

Dell pulled out a little pad and a pencil. "What happened?"

Ray's dad took another deep breath. His cheeks showed wet patches. "Violet said some man came at her. She didn't see the gun. She tried to fight him off."

"Any description of the man?"

Dad shook his head. "She didn't get a look at his face. Too dark."

"Did you hear a car? Anything?"

"Nothing except the Myersons, and they came out of their house."

Mr. Myerson nodded. "We heard the shot."

"I can't imagine why anyone would hurt Violet." Dad put his hands over his face.

Ice wrapped around Ray's throat. This was his fault. His mistakes followed him up here and hurt his mom. The hopelessness that edged Dad's eyes convicted him. His dad's normally straight shoulders and proud chin crumpled in front of him.

"Dad, let's pray. For Mom and for ourselves. God'll give us that peace we need right now." Ray bowed his head and clasped Cathy's hand.

"Desperately need." His father's pain uttered the words under his breath.

"Lord, we know You didn't attack Mom. We don't blame You for any of this because evil has no place in You. And we know that You can use even something this horrible ..." His voice betrayed him, and he took a breath to settle down.

Cathy stroked her thumb across the back of his hand.

"You can make good things come out of this. *Please* make good come out of this."

The Myersons had bowed their heads, though Ray knew they didn't particularly care for religion or any *god-foolishness* as they called it. His dad's silence was interrupted by a low moan and Ray looked up sharply. Tears trickled down his old man's cheeks.

Squeezing his eyes shut again, Ray tried to keep his voice steady and continue his prayer.

"Right now, patch up Mom's injury. Replace her blood and repair any damage done. Make sure the doctor does everything correctly to avoid infection or complications."

"And don't let her have too much pain, Lord." Dad's deep baritone wavered. "You know how Violet gets scared when she has pain. She doesn't need to be afraid right now."

Ray tightened his jaw, unable to continue. A tear escaped from his eye. His mom. He'd been so concerned about protecting Cathy that he let his dear mom get attacked. He felt himself spiraling into an abyss of confused hopelessness.

"Amen." His dad's announcement brought him out of the emotional mire like a life ring. He straightened his shoulders, and Ray caught his eye as his glance lifted. "Take courage, son. I honestly believe your mom will get through this. She's strong. And the doctor felt hopeful."

"How long before we know anything?" Ray's question went unanswered as Philip Slaughter and his wife, Amy, came into the room. Ray let the longtime friends talk and pray together while he paced in front of a wide window. Ironic how the glass reflected the gaily lit room, filled with the pain and tragedy behind him.

Dell and Lt. Estrella had moved away, and the chief spoke in hushed tones on his cell phone. After a moment, they mentioned investigating the scene at the ranch then left. Ray sensed Cathy watching him and clamped his molars against his grief.

Why had he ever spoken against that man? Sevilla. Self-appointed ruler of the region. How Ray had scoffed at the man's arrogance. Believing him to be nothing but a self-absorbed ruler in a weak and war-torn element.

He'd had no idea of his far-reaching power. Who could stop him? Even from prison, he had his way. He wielded his weapons, as in charge here in America as he had been in Chiapas.

Ray paced for some time before a white-jacketed doctor caught his attention from the far side of the room.

"Sanderson?"

Cathy rushed toward him. Ray followed.

"I'm Daisy's employer. She doesn't have any family in the area since her parents moved to Florida several years ago." Her forehead wrinkled. She'd been through too much in only a few weeks.

Ray needed to console her. Comfort her. Anything to make up for the plan forming in the interior of his mind.

The doctor nodded. "I see. She lost quite a lot of blood. We've been able to stop the internal bleeding. Of course, there's still some danger of that, but we'll monitor her closely."

"So she'll be all right?"

"There's always risk, but I am guardedly optimistic." He wiped his hands together. "However, the cut to her face is a different issue."

"The mark will scar?" Cathy's eyes widened.

The doctor bowed his head for a moment. "I'm sorry. There's

nothing I can do except sutures. She needs a plastic surgeon. A good one. But even then there are no guarantees." The man shrugged. "The nurse will let you know when she's been moved to a regular room. Maybe an hour or so."

As the man disappeared through the key-entry doors, Ray glanced at his girl.

She brightened. "Daisy's gonna be okay. Just like we prayed." She embraced him, laying her head against his chest. "You'll see, Ray. God will do the same for Vi." Her whispered encouragement sent vines of hopes intertwining with the worry already growing.

After another hour, Dad encouraged the Myersons to return home. "I'll call as soon as I learn anything."

"No matter the time." Mr. Myerson made him promise.

Ray lifted up a prayer that the Spirit moved in the hearts of the couple with this opportunity. *And bless Mom.*

Amy Slaughter left at the same time, giving the Myersons a ride home on her way. Dad and Philip stayed at a table near the doorway, but Ray sat on the corner of a sectional. Cathy approached and settled beside him. She scooted close and draped his right arm about her shoulders. Snuggling, she laid her head against his chest, sharing her silent encouragement and warmth with him.

What felt like a moment later, he opened his eyes. Cathy slept peacefully against him. His dad remained in the chair, head down on his arms across the table. A single snore erupted from the vicinity. Philip had moved to a cushioned seat near the window, his head motionless and relaxed against the top of the pad and his arms crossed over his stomach.

"About time you woke up, amigo." Miguel stood nearby bundled in a bomber jacket.

"What are you doing here? I thought you went home."

"I did. At least I started to. Reached the plane transfer in

Chicago and got Cathy's message. I came straight back."

Ray resettled Cathy on a pillow, stood, and embraced the man. "So good to have you here."

"I have been in prayer for Daisy." His face darkened. "Is she all right?"

"The doctor thinks she will be." Ray pulled out his wallet and moved toward a soda machine. "She's probably in a regular room by now."

The man's dimples pierced his cheeks with his broad smile. "I know you must be relieved. But why are you still here if the news has been so good?"

"My mom was attacked. Shot. About the same time someone stabbed Daisy."

"Daisy was attacked?" The dimples disappeared. "Cathy didn't say anything about that. Only that she was hurt."

"Apparently an S was carved into her cheek."

"What does that mean?"

How could he have worked in Chiapas as long as he had and not know about Sevilla's habit? "The initial was Sevilla's calling card."

"The man is amazing. Even from prison, Señor Sevilla is almighty. Even here in America."

Ray wanted to argue the *almighty* crack but had no grounds. The man had certainly displayed his power over Ray and the people he cared about.

A nurse peeked in. "I thought you'd like to know that your mother is out of surgery."

"I thought a doctor would come and talk to us."

She nodded. "He will. Dr. Kim has another surgery this morning. He needed a few hours of sleep, but he'll find you and your father when he returns."

Ray understood, but it didn't make him feel any better. "She's all right then?"

"For now. He'll need to explain the details, but I'll be monitoring her progress and will let you know when she goes to a room."

"Thanks. I'll tell the others when they wake."

Miguel moved closer. "So what has Daisy said about the attack?"

"She's still unconscious."

"I'd like to see her. Maybe to offer some encouragement. What room is she in?"

Ray took a sip of his Dr Pepper. "I don't know. But Dell mentioned posting a guard, so I doubt they'll let you in." Ray stepped over to a black window, staring out into woods beyond. Only he didn't see forest. He only saw himself. Alone. Trying to stand up to a madman. Taking on an impossible situation.

Stepping back, others came into the picture. Stood in the gap with him. His dad, Cathy, Philip, and even Miguel. He'd never been alone. Not spiritually or literally. And while Sevilla wielded great power, he hadn't been ultimately victorious. Otherwise he wouldn't be sitting in prison.

But Ray still had some work to do.

And the peace of God, which surpasses all understanding,
will guard your hearts and your minds
in Christ Jesus. ~ Philippians 4:7 ESV

Chapter 19

Cat woke with dry mouth. Her neck, having spent a few hours at an unnatural angle, ached. She groaned as she sat up and rotated her head to loosen rigid muscles. Digging through her purse, she found a box of mints and popped a few in her mouth. That woke her up.

Until she could find a Diet Pepsi.

She stood. Ran a comb through her hair as she stretched and pulled up another ponytail. After checking her compact mirror for errant mascara, she declared herself good enough. Draping her purse over her head and shoulder, she scanned the room.

Mr. Alexander rested at the table, and Pastor Slaughter lay against a cushion. The sun barely kissed the gray sky behind him. She glanced around and spotted Ray. He stood leaning against the west-facing window with a cup of coffee in his good hand. He lifted the mug but didn't smile.

How long had he been watching her?

"Miguel got your message. Actually returned to help."

"You're kidding." She looked around. "Where is he?"

"I sent him to get some sleep at his hotel. I'll let him know when Mom and Daisy can have visitors."

She came near and touched his arm. "When do you go see the doctor about your shoulder?"

"Next week. I'll have an MRI. Now that the swelling is down, he can tell the extent of the damage."

That sounded foreboding. "So he doesn't even know all that's wrong?"

"With the dislocation, many tendons and a few muscles might have been displaced. He doesn't know yet if I've strained them or torn them. Though probably a little of both."

"All things that can be repaired though, right?"

"He won't know until he gets a good look at my insides. You mess with the human body too much, and things don't always rebound the way they're supposed to, you know?" He drank from the mug.

Cat felt for him but didn't like his cavalier attitude about what might be a permanent injury. Better than being sorry for himself, though. "Did you hear anything about Vi?"

He swallowed and nodded, staring at the foggy forested area beyond the glass. "She made it through the surgery. They moved her upstairs a little while ago, but she's still out. The doctor should come in after another surgery and tell us what to expect."

"Thank You, Lord." She slipped her hands around his waist and gave him a squeeze. "I knew things would work out." When he didn't respond, she stepped away.

"I'll go check on Daisy." Ray made an innocuous reply. What was with him this morning?

Too early for a volunteer at the information desk, she used the phone marked *visitor inquiries*. The operator, a man, had to be a senior citizen, from the sound of his voice. She requested the room number for Daisy Sanderson.

"I can't give any of that information out before eight o'clock, ma'am. I'm sorry."

"Sir, I've been here all night. I fell asleep in the waiting room, so I missed the nurse's report." She had to make him see.

"I still can't help you."

"I only wanted to check on her." She added a little extra Southern to her voice. Helpless damsel in distress sound.

"Ma'am, these aren't visiting hours. Simple as that."

The line went dead, and Cat's mouth flattened. So much for charm.

She stepped through the doorway to the ER nurses' station and smiled at an older woman with salt and pepper hair. "I'm afraid I fell asleep in the waiting room and missed the report about my friend Daisy Sanderson?"

"Oh, yes." The woman nodded and picked up a clipboard from a rack. "She's been sent upstairs. Doing quite well under the circumstances, but she's under the influence of pretty strong pain relievers."

"Can you tell me the room number? I'd like to check on her before I have to leave." Not that Cat planned on leaving anytime soon.

"Four thirteen. It's not a private room, but she has no roommate at this point."

Eureka. She grinned. "Thanks."

Cat bolted for the elevator before anyone tried to slow her.

The fourth floor still had dim lights in the hallways, but no one stopped her when she stepped off the elevator. She found the room. Danvers sat in a chair at the door. He lifted his head as she approached.

"Shifted you to inside duty, huh?" Her whisper, barely audible, carried easily in the empty halls.

"You're supposed to be downstairs." He stood and propped his hands on his wide tool-belt.

"Wanted to check on Daisy before I head home."

"Home?"

"I thought I'd go for a shower at least before coming back up here." She paused with her hand on the door. "Does Dell have someone at Vi's door, too?"

He nodded to his left. Beyond the almost empty nurse's station, Cat made out another blue-clad shoulder.

"Good. I'd like to check on her, too."

"I guess it's okay." He opened the door for her. "But don't be long. And don't make her talk."

Daisy, half of her face swathed in bandages, lay inclined in the hospital bed nearest to the door. Still asleep, she moved her head and groaned softly.

"You're all right," Cat whispered as she stepped closer. She laid her hand on Daisy's shoulder and prayed softly for her continued healing. "And let her realize how much You love her."

Task completed, she retreated, hoping her prayer hadn't interrupted sleep.

Again in the hallway, Danvers caught her arm. "Violet's not allowed visitors, yet. That's why Ray and Dennis are still downstairs. You should join them."

Danvers wasn't normally so formidable.

"Okay." She'd planned to return to the lobby anyway. Maybe she could speak to Ray again. He sure acted funny before she left. If nothing else, she could lure him into getting some breakfast. He always got impatient and moody when his stomach started growling.

She descended into the waiting room, but Ray no longer stood at the west-facing windows. He sat on the other side, at the table where his dad had been sleeping, and he toyed with his phone. Denny

Alexander thumbed through a section of the Dallas Morning News, his feet propped up on the table in front of him. Philip had disappeared.

"Well, I checked on Daisy. She's sleeping pretty soundly."

Ray stared at his phone. "That's good to hear."

Cat puffed her exhale, ruffling the unruly curls of her bangs. Something bugged him. Maybe he needed more than food? "Ray, why don't you take your dad home to clean up, get a shower and some food while I stick around and wait for word from your mom? Surely there's an hour or more before anyone can see her."

"That's not a bad idea." He glanced out the windows. "But I'll stick around."

She pivoted, facing the corner where windows, finally lit with the dawn, displayed a view of a charming courtyard. "You can go. I'll call if I hear anything, which I doubt."

"This won't work."

She faced him, supporting her slight body onto one leg as she leaned against a sofa. "What are you talking about, Ray? This is a perfect plan. When you two clean up and get a good meal, come back in two cars and I'll take one of them to the inn for my turn."

He still wouldn't look at her, scrolling through some app on his phone. "No."

"I'm not going to keep your car if that's what you're worried about." She chuckled, stepping closer and fingering his curls.

"I'm not worried about the car."

"Well, I'm sure I can get Donna or Ellis to give me a ride, but I'd hate to make one of them come all the way out here."

He sighed. "That won't work either." He glanced up at her then, an odd look on his face. Sort of sheepish, like he'd done something stupid.

"Why not?" Cat couldn't fathom his reticence.

239

He shook his head slightly. "I'm sorry, Cathy."

"You're coming to town with me." Dell's loud voice boomed behind her. Ray lowered his head again, staring at the table in front of him.

"O-kay." She turned to the chief. "I don't care who takes me to the inn, I just thought it might be nicer for Mr. Alexander and Ray to go home now before Vi wakes up."

He turned toward the door, and she followed. At this rate, she'd be back to the hospital in plenty of time before Vi even came out of recovery.

"You're not going to the inn."

Dell's declaration didn't compute. "What do you mean? I want to get there and back before Vi wakes."

"Sorry." His long strides continued to the automatic door that opened as he approached.

She halted several paces behind him. "What's this about, Dell?" He avoided her gaze. Interesting how the same look, almost embarrassment or maybe shame, painted Ray's face.

"Let's get in the cruiser, and I'll explain everything."

Her world felt off-kilter. She straightened and crossed her arms. "You know I trust you, Dell, but you're hiding something. You need to tell me. To believe in me, too."

He took a couple of steps toward her and lowered his voice. "I'm not going to have this conversation in here. I'll tell you when we get in the car."

"I can find another way home." She turned and dug through her purse for her phone.

Dell caught her elbow. "You're not going home. You're going to the jail where I can keep an eye on you."

Cat's stomach knotted. "You're arresting me?" She glanced at Ray. He watched them. Why didn't he step in and help her?

"Not arresting, placing you in protective custody."

She shook her head. "I don't want to go."

"You don't have a choice." His thunder boomed.

Ray stood. "Chief, maybe this wasn't such a good idea."

"You stay outta this, Raymond. You did the right thing. Now, I'm taking this over."

Cat stared at Ray. "What's he talking about?"

Dell tugged at her elbow. "Cathleen, if you don't come with me this minute, I swear I'll slap handcuffs on you and drag you out. Don't think I won't."

"Ray?" Cat watched the man, the one she'd dreamed of during his long absence, turn away from her. Dell pulled her toward the door, and she stopped resisting. The experience of being practically dragged out of the hospital gave her enough humiliation for one day.

Like abandoning her wasn't enough?

Ray's chin sank along with his mood as Dell escorted Cathy outside. Realizing that Sevilla instigated these attacks from the confines of a jail cell confirmed the man's power. Ray couldn't keep Cathy safe. And he'd had little trouble convincing Dell to put her under guard.

If only he had let Dell figure things out on his own. The chief would have drawn the same conclusion. And left Ray out of the decision.

And the guilt.

Cathy would never speak to him after this.

Philip strolled through the automatic door. A large orange-striped sack from Whataburger dangled from his hand, and a puzzled expression wrinkled his forehead. "Was that Cat in the chief's cruiser? I didn't think she would leave until she had the chance to see Violet." He set a small bag in front of Ray.

"She had no choice." Ray didn't have the stomach to explain her protection detail, but Philip deserved to know.

"Jail?" He shook his head. "I'm sorry to hear that. With her need to be among people, that isolation will be doubly hard."

"What do you mean?"

"You know her better than I do, Ray. Has she ever truly wanted to be left alone?"

He was right. She'd only sought isolation when she needed to cry. Like the other night at the hot tub.

"She's an extreme extrovert. No wonder she moved out of her home when Mac died. Being cooped up in that house all by herself would have felt like she died along with him."

And Ray had just thrust her into that same pain. Forced solitary confinement. The despair she must feel. Ray wiped his face. *God even if she never speaks to me again, please comfort her right now.*

The man had stooped over the sack again, his graying dark head bobbing as he extracted breakfast sandwiches and a bag of coffee cups. He glanced up. "Now I didn't say that for you to get a guilt going. This is a serious situation. And Cat's obviously in danger. Don't second-guess yourself, son. You and Dell did the right thing. Doesn't mean I don't hate the idea for Cat's sake."

Philip crossed the room with a bag to coax Dad into eating. What an excellent example of a pastor. He didn't preach the most amazing sermons, but he led his congregation by example. He inspired many into the ministry because they saw his pulpit messages lived out in his daily life.

Transparent.

Part of the holiness that Ray aspired to. He'd never be perfect, but he thought he'd at least reached a place of honesty. Openness.

Until Sevilla started promising to attack the villages where he spoke.

Ray justified his secrecy about the threats. The little towns of his speaking circuit would never have allowed him to preach or even come near if they had known of the warlord's pressure. For the furthering of the Gospel, Ray felt forced to keep the letters and messages under wraps. Otherwise, his ministry ended and his mission failed.

His ministry. *His* mission.

Looking back, he admitted that the deception had nothing to do with the Gospel. He only used that excuse to maintain his position. To continue doing what he knew. And his pride. He wasn't about to limit his work or run from the hollow promises of a defeated warlord.

So instead, he kept the information to himself. Even Miguel hadn't known about the threats until Asmirandu. He'd collected the mail that day and opened the letter before Ray had the chance.

Ray ignored the note. Ignored Miguel's concern. With a haughty spirit he'd set out for his mission and determined to prove to Sevilla and anyone who witnessed that he wasn't afraid and couldn't be chased away.

And people died because he foolishly thought himself smarter and stronger. As though God couldn't use anyone else to harvest His fields in Chiapas.

Same attitude he'd had about Cathy. Like he possessed the power to actually protect her against Sevilla's men. He hadn't even been able to protect himself from the drug lord's marauders.

The air inside the waiting room hung like chains. He needed something fresh and stimulating. He left his meal uneaten and stepped outside, relishing the sting of the wind against his face. On the other side of the parking lot, he found a paved pathway into the woods.

243

Likely some type of rehabilitation course. He followed, hoping to rid himself of guilt and the accusations the evil one hurled at his consciousness.

Did his return to Heath's Point bring the trouble with him? If he left now, could he derail further attacks? The moment he entertained the thought, he dismissed it. He couldn't do anything to stop Sevilla's men at this point. His experience in the conflict at the mission proved that.

Terror from Sunday morning in Asmirandu still haunted his dreams, awakening him with the frightening images. He'd shouted in his sleep more than once but so far hadn't awakened anyone except himself. Thank heaven.

Breathing hard, he realized that he'd accelerated to a jog without intending to. His natural reaction to tension. He slowed his stride and shifted the gears of his mind.

Thoughts of Cathy floated through. Her eyes, the trust they openly disclosed. But he hadn't proved very trustworthy.

In his arrogance, he had felt detached from Sevilla. Thought himself too far away and too American to be touched by the man. His pride had nearly gotten Cathy hurt and almost killed his mom.

Sevilla had made his intentions clear. He planned to destroy Ray by killing the people he loved.

Loved. There. He admitted his feelings for Cathy. He shuddered with a sudden draft. Jogging downhill on the tree-covered sidewalk, he knew his heart belonged to her, whether she ever accepted him again or not.

He'd become a complete failure. He'd lost his mission, and he'd left the only girl he ever loved. All that he had put her through, her loneliness and pain. His silence. He abandoned her.

Never again.

Even if she never spoke to him after this, he couldn't regret calling Dell. Not if sticking her in jail kept her alive.

Marji Laine

*You will keep him in perfect peace whose mind is stayed on You
because he trusts You. ~ Isaiah 26:3 ESV*

Chapter 20

Cat gritted her teeth and willed the threatening tears to stay in hiding. Her gaze swept across the four-by-eight cell, first to the iron bars and the locked door, then to the cinder block wall on the opposite side. A toilet hid behind the wall.

Mrs. Hawkins had taken responsibility upon Cat's arrival. Once Cat's fifth-grade Sunday school teacher, she glared at Dell but said nothing.

At least Cat had an ally, for whatever good that did her. The woman gave her an extra pillow and blanket after leading her to a cell. "The bed in here is one of the newer ones, and the staff keeps things really clean."

"Clean is good." She hugged the pillow and wandered through the barred entrance.

"The chief wants to make sure you're safe, honey. I'll get you something to read, so relax and try not to worry." Mrs. Hawkins gave her a weak smile before leaving.

The lack of prisoners relieved Cat. No one to watch or tease

247

her.

And she did feel safe. No messages would show up on this mirror, actually made out of polished metal. No one could get to her without going through a number of officers outside or a couple of feet of solid concrete.

She sat and curled around the pillow. Her stomach had started cramping in the car. Whether from the tension of her circumstances or from being a woman, she didn't know. She got up after crunching her abdomen for a couple of moments. Forcing herself to stand upright, she paced the eight feet, did an about-face, and marched them off again.

Maybe if she exercised her arms a little? Movement pumped her heart, rushing the pain-killing blood to where she needed relief. Dad taught her that. Wonder how he'd known something so distinctly female?

Stretching out her arms, she swirled her fists in tight circles. Forward and then backward as she retraced her path across the floor. By her third trip, the ache in her middle eased.

"What are you doing?" Dell stood outside her cell with his keys out.

She darted to the bars, leaning her face between two of them. "Are you letting me go?"

"No." He opened the door, and she stepped through. "But since the outer door is closed I didn't see any reason to keep you cooped up."

"Thanks for that, I guess. But shouldn't I call a lawyer or something?"

He shrugged. "I'm letting you have some more space, not unlimited privileges."

She clamped her teeth. She would not cry. But she also wouldn't stay in this horrible isolation without a fight. "How long you been a cop, Dell?"

He cocked a bushy eyebrow at her. "Almost thirty years."

"After thirty years, you forgot to read someone their rights?" She crossed her arms. "That little tidbit can get me out of here, right?"

He leaned toward the opening and crossed one foot over the other. "Could … if you'd been arrested. Which you haven't."

"Then what am I doing here?" Her question sounded far too whiny. Bringing memories of long lines when she visited Dell as her favorite Santa, a part he still played at the yearly Christmas festival. That image ruined, she wondered if she'd ever trust him again.

"I told you, Cat. I aim to keep you safe. I'm not letting you leave here until we've got whoever attacked Daisy and shot Vi."

Truth dawned on her with a shiver down her back. Her shoulders rose without thought. "You still think someone was trying to get to me?"

"Can't know that until I talk to the women. Hope to do that later today."

Wait, his hypothesis didn't make sense. "Daisy's practically a foot taller than I am. No one would confuse us in a pea-soup fog."

"Yeah, but you and Vi could be family except for the pumpkin feathers you have coming out of your head." His teasing didn't strike the fond memories it usually did.

"So how can you think the two issues are connected at all?"

"Simple. They have to be. Otherwise there are two lunatics running around this town trying to kill people. And I don't want to even consider that possibility." He pushed off the bars and shuffled toward the outer doorway. "Mrs. Hawkins is getting you some books and paper and such. And breakfast."

He stepped through. "Sit tight."

She scowled. *Sit tight.* She had half a mind to stand around, if only to disobey his cockamamie instructions. She flounced onto the cot and hugged her knees.

God, please get me out of here?

Was He listening anymore?

I will not leave you comfortless.

Cat always believed that promise. Had been shown its truth when her mom died, and Vi stepped in along with other ladies at the church to help her. And then when Dad died, she'd been surrounded by such love and compassion. Never left alone to wallow. Never to despair.

Until now.

"Here you are Cat, honey. I've brought my Bible and some magazines. Grady's bringing over your favorite. One o' his omelets and some orange jacks to boot." She set the books down on the table next to her. "I know this is a scary time for you, honey. But you're not alone in all of this."

Mrs. Hawkins patted Cat's shoulder and toddled out the main door.

Funny how God's voice could have a sing-song soprano tone and a Texan drawl.

I will not leave you comfortless. No. He wouldn't. Tears stung. He never had. Waiting on Dell's resolution would be hard, but Cat could—would—wait on and trust in the Lord.

Finally, Ray and his dad were ushered into Mom's room on the third floor. Ray shed his frustration over Cathy's jailing and focused on supporting his father. The man had aged at least ten years overnight.

"She's very weak." Dr. Kim tapped the glass of his iPad.

Dad stood near the lifted end of Mom's bed. He absently

stroked her forehead, fluffing the light curls at her hair line.

"The bullet lodged in her right shoulder. Not sure how. The entry wound went through her upper left arm."

"That sounds impossible." Ray tried to picture the path.

"Indeed. And I have no explanation how the bullet missed her heart and lungs."

"Missed them?" Dad glanced down at Mom.

"Entirely. Not even a nick." He closed the lid on the computer. "But she lost a lot of blood. Once we get things into balance, she should heal quickly."

The tension Ray had hidden from his dad escaped with a sharp inhale. "She's gonna be okay?"

Dad looked at the doctor again, hope filling his eyes.

Dr. Kim smiled and paused at the doorway. "She'll be all right, Mr. Alexander."

Ray crossed over to his dad and wrapped his good arm around his father's shoulder, accepting a warm hug in return.

"She's going to be okay." His father's anguished whisper tugged at Ray's heart. He spoke the words again, a little louder, but his voice broke into a cry before he could finish. Ray held him for a few moments while the man who had been the strength in their family all his life wept against his shoulder.

His own tears clouded his eyes. The love his mom and dad shared after all these years, he wanted that. And he wanted that with Cathy. Wanted to stroke her forehead when she was sick. To hold her hand when she worried.

But he'd been a coward. He couldn't face her after calling Dell. She must hate him.

And well she should.

Even in jail, Grady's omelets cheered Cat up. Without her phone, she had no concept of time. She thumbed through one of the fashion magazines Mrs. Hawkins had brought and read the book of Philippians.

She must have slept at some point, because the woman awoke her with lunch from the diner. "Grady told me to tell you everything is fine over there. Donna stepped in to waitress, and Myra's running the cash register."

Pulling the plate off of her meal she eyed the chicken strips. "Doesn't the chief usually order the day's special for prisoners?"

The woman smiled, handing her a napkin and setting a Diet Pepsi on the table. "Grady said you didn't like meatloaf very much so he sent you ... let me see if I can remember his words ... *A more-special special.*"

Cat warmed. Grady had always been there for her. Mrs. Hawkins stayed and chatted a little while Cat ate. Nothing important. Specifically, nothing about the person who attacked Vi or Daisy.

"Has Dell spoken with them yet?"

"Now you know I'm not privy to the investigations that are going on."

Cat knew the opposite. As unofficial lead investigator of the HP Grapevine, she knew and passed on almost every detail of life in Heath's Point. Especially the more interesting aspects of work at the police department. As long as the data didn't compromise a case.

"Did Dell direct you to keep things from me?"

"I think the words he used were, *expressly forbid.*" She chuckled. "I'm sure he'll keep you in the loop whenever facts are confirmed and details are decided."

So he *had* learned something. "Where is he now?"

"I think he went out to the Alexander's place again. Rain's moving in, and he wants to be sure he hasn't missed anything before clues get washed away."

"He found some clues?"

"Footprints and such. And a silencer." Her hand flew to her mouth. "Oh. I wasn't supposed to tell you that."

"A silencer? Like the thing you put on the end of a handgun?"

She nodded. "Dell thinks another hit man was sent. They'd be the type to use such."

With Mrs. Hawkins talking, Cat kept the flow going. "Fingerprints?"

"Nary a one. Not even on the shell casing."

Cat tucked her chin, her brows crimping. "Is that important?"

Mrs. Hawkins smiled. "No fingerprints means the gunman must've had on gloves of some sort, even when he loaded the weapon."

Odd. "And he left his silencer behind? I thought the Meyerson's heard the shot."

"Denny did, too. Everyone came running. Dell thinks he didn't get the silencer to work."

Amateur hit man? "Did Vi recognize the man?"

"Nope. Couldn't see him in the dark except that he was taller than she was. But then who isn't, except maybe you."

Cat smirked. "I have her by at least a half-inch."

"I guess that makes you a suspect then." She tittered.

"What did Daisy say?"

"Nothing yet. She's still struggling." Her mouth formed an O and her eyebrows drew together. "I've said too much. Dell is going to have my hide."

She scurried toward the exit.

"I won't say anything."

The closing door answered Cat. At least she knew as much as Dell did, now. Which was next to nothing.

She mulled over the situation as she finished her lunch. Could there be two different attackers? Maybe they weren't after her at all. Maybe the man sent after her was dead and these two were sent to kill Vi and ... Daisy?

No. Didn't play. Daisy and Ray had never been very close.

But short of stopping every visiting stranger to town, they weren't going to catch this person anytime soon. Cat tried not to let that thought settle.

She put down the barely touched meal and took-in the empty block of holding cells. *Nothing homey about this place.* Smelled of bleach, disinfectant, and metal. The garish lights glared. Bare bars and windowless walls allowed her no concept of time, or weather, or diversion.

And no news from outside that door except what she could finagle from Mrs. Hawkins.

Why hadn't Ray come to visit? Called? Something?

Her heart hurt. "I'm trying to wait on You, Lord." She picked up the pillows at the head of her bed and carried them to the other end. "But am I losing Ray as well as my dad's diner?" She sniffed.

So much had happened. Her fault. She could imagine the highlights on her Facebook page. *This year, I lost the diner that had been my parents' dream. I wound up in a jail cell because some maniac wanted me dead. And the only person I'd ever truly cared for turned his back on me—literally.* A banner month to add to her timeline.

The memory of Ray sitting at the table, refusing to look at her, shattered her confidence. She shut her eyes against the pain, but other thoughts invaded. The death of her precious father. Oh, and her car. Totaled. The news of Vi's shooting. The carving in Daisy's cheek.

The scenes danced around her eyes, spiraling into some macabre parade. She climbed onto the quilt that Mrs. Hawkins had brought her and tucked the two pillows into the corner where the bars met the cinder block. If only she could bring the circling images to a halt. But then she'd been unable to accomplish much of anything.

She'd not even been able to step into her dad's shoes at the diner. Not really. Never able to share herself or her faith with the people who came in needing to hear the Gospel. She'd see the need and try to smile away their pain, but wouldn't give them the hope beyond a trite, *things will get better*. They needed to hear the good news about Jesus.

Especially Daisy. And look where she was. *Oh God, heal Daisy and let her know how much You love her.*

No wonder Ray didn't want Cat with him on his mission. No matter what he claimed, she knew the sad truth of her failure.

Tears welled at the corners of her eyes. The thought had been haunting her since she'd learned of his departure. She hadn't been good enough then, and she wasn't any different now.

The same could be said of how she let down the Lord. He'd entrusted Mac's Diner to her. Not only the diner, but the impact Dad had made. And yet, she'd stayed silent, timid. Why shouldn't He take the place away from her?

She raked her fingers through her hair. This type of thinking did no good. Not for her. Not for solving her problems. And not for her attitude toward anyone—Dell—who might happen to visit.

Whatever is good and … honorable … how did that verse go? *Keep your mind on noble things or something like that.* The *People* magazine next to her didn't exactly fall into that category, but it offered diversion from her dark thoughts.

A few hours later, Dell's raised voice in the outer office yanked her from an article about the British royal family. What was he bellowing about, now? She started when the outer door opened and Myra Stone marched through. Her face was pinched and her neck red.

Cat had rarely seen the woman angry. Good thing she hadn't been on the receiving end of whatever exchange resulted in her new coloring.

Cat stood and ushered her into the cell. Not quite the parlor at the inn, at least she could offer her a seat on the opposite bed. "I heard you helped out at the diner, today. That was so kind of you."

Myra sat, her legs primly crossed at her ankles. "Well, dear, when you didn't come home last night, I got a little worried."

With Myra, *a little worried* looked more like downright frantic. Cat hated that she put her through the distress. She should have called. "I'm so sorry. So much happened."

"Yes, I heard from Amy Slaughter. I've been so concerned about Violet."

Mrs. Hawkins came in with the tray. "I thought y'all might like some tea." She passed out the cups and saucers and set a plate of finger sandwiches on the edge of a TV tray. Such a sweet lady.

"How did you put all of this together in only a couple of minutes?" Myra took a finger sandwich.

"Oh, I already planned to offer some tea to Cat. Just a matter of adding an extra cup. No problem there." With a wave, she left them to their chat.

"You know, I've lived here for over ten years, and I've never been inside this place."

This had been such a great place to play. When she and her friends could persuade Dell to let them. Cat bit into a chicken salad sandwich quarter. She didn't feel like eating anything, but maybe having some food would improve her attitude.

"I suppose the place isn't too uncomfortable. As long as you don't have to share." She sipped the tea. "I'll have to journal about this visit, though."

"Not every day you go to a jail, huh?" At this point, Cat hoped she never saw the place again.

"Exactly. Guess I'll have an interesting topic to share with my quilting buddies next Thursday night."

Cat rolled her eyes. No chance she'd wait that long. News of her jail stay would be passé by the weekend.

Myra lifted her cup from the saucer. "Oh, and Ray asked me to tell you that Vi is going to be fine."

"You spoke to Ray?"

She nodded. "Yes, he called me early this morning. To let me know you were okay and tell me about his mom, though of course, I'd already heard about the attack. Actually, he said the doctor is stymied."

"I'm glad Vi is going to be all right." She lifted a prayer of gratitude. "I knew she'd come through surgery, but that's all. She was still recovering when Dell carted me off."

"I don't understand how he can legally do that." Myra's face clouded over again.

Cat shrugged.

The older lady pinched her lips together again and a deep furrow appeared above her nose. "That man. And after all the nice things I've said about him. I think police chief should be an elected position, and I intend to say as much to the mayor the next time I speak to him."

"He's trying to keep me safe." Wow. Get her. Actually *defending* Dell's choice to toss her in jail. But repeating Mrs. Hawkins's words didn't feel any better than when she'd heard them from the dispatcher. "Though I wish his protection didn't land me in here."

"This hideous place. What a terrible idea." She smoothed her blue jeans. "Ellis was fit to be tied about it. Anyway, I called Grady to offer myself as a replacement for Daisy this morning. Donna was already there when I arrived. She could have handled the job alone.

But I had a good time."

"I can't thank you enough."

She flapped her hand. "Pish." She leaned forward. "You need to snag Donna if she ever stops doing hair. She's quick on her feet."

Cat's gaze hit the floor.

"Oh, dear." She put her hand over her mouth. "I guess that's not necessary after all."

"Not so much." Cat looked up with as bright a smile as she could muster. "I'm supposed to turn over the keys in a few days."

"Will Heath keep Grady and Daisy on?"

She shrugged, wishing the topic to move somewhere else. Anywhere else. "Last I heard, his wife wants to turn the place into a tearoom. I would expect them to change the name."

The truth of that statement carved out a little pit in her stomach, and she set her own plate down, the sandwich still virtually intact.

Myra rose. "Well, I still think Mayor Higgins needs to know how I feel about this jailing situation." She picked up her purse and gave Cat a one-armed hug. "Don't worry, dear. This whole thing will be a distant memory very soon." She walked toward the outer office door.

"Thanks for visiting."

Myra waved and closed the main door behind her. The clank resounded through the pit of her stomach. A tomb couldn't be much worse that this empty room.

She drew the sleeve of her hoodie across her drippy nose.

Would Grady take care of the dinner tonight? The faces of the people who visited drifted through her mind. Mrs. Gutierrez whose husband struggled to regain his health after a serious bout with pneumonia. Mrs. Dupree and her three kids. Rip and Dash who often helped her clean up outside and sometimes even brought new needy people to the meal. And Skeet and Frankie. They'd just started coming to the sunset dinners. Where would they go now?

Of course, *she'd* had nothing to do with bringing either of them to the diner. And she wasn't the one who spoke to Frankie for so long. That had been Ray. Even though he accidentally scared the poor kid.

The revelations only made her feel worse. Everything she'd ever wanted, ever hoped, tumbled into destruction. Worthless and helpless, she curled into a ball and tried to keep the tears at bay.

Marji Laine

For His anger is but for a moment, His favor is for a lifetime;
Weeping may last for the night, But a shout of joy comes in the
morning. ~ Psalm 30:5 NASB

Chapter 21

Ray spent Friday night at the hospital alternating short naps with Dad. They continued the schedule through most of Saturday, but by that night, Dad insisted he return home.

"I'd feel better staying. At least here I can keep my mind on one thing, Mom."

His father shook his head. "Oh no. If you think you're succeeding in keeping your thoughts away from Cat, you're mistaken. I've seen the way you've brooded, boy. Guilt is unmistakable. Especially with your transparent face."

Ray blinked, examining the bare wall beside him.

"Give Cat a little time, Ray. She's a smart girl. She'll understand your actions once this whole thing is over. You'll see." Usually Dad's assurance would convince Ray of anything, but he knew Cathy too well. Honesty and loyalty ranked higher in her values than almost anything else. He'd failed in both areas.

He took his dad's advice, though. Purposely putting his back to the crime scene tape near the trash cans, he clamped his jaw and squeezed his eyes shut. He'd brought this pain down on his mom. He'd almost killed her. As if he'd fired the gun himself.

God forgive me. I should never have thought I could protect anyone. Who could stand before Sevilla's power?

The atmosphere from two days in the hospital returned in his dreams. His father's helpless expression. Sobs from other nearby rooms. The shattered expression on Cathy's face when she called his name that final time. That image appeared even more than the horrors of the raid at Chiapas. Yet another of his disastrous decisions.

After hours of agitated dozing, he gave up. Straightening his sheets, he eyed the box of files on the other side of the room. Maybe he could make up for his duplicity to Cathy by sorting and organizing her dad's information.

He left for the hospital at o-dark-thirty, and the box went with him. He couldn't remember the last Sunday he'd spent away from a church service of some sort. But supporting Mom and Dad and helping Cathy—he knew he'd made the right choice.

He stopped at the nearby Whataburger for another set of breakfast trays, although the thought of food made his lip curl. Maybe with the distraction of the files, he could force some down.

Dawn grayed the sky by the time he reached the medical center. Clouds, heavy and threatening, hung like moss. Cold, clammy air completed the effect.

Ray peeked into his mom's room. Dad slept in the recliner, softly snoring. Careful not to wake him, Ray set down the box of records and stepped away, letting the door close soundlessly.

He handed Officer Phelps a smaller bag. "How long has he been sleeping?"

The squarish man thanked him. "He was out when I came on duty about midnight."

Good for him. *Fully rest him, Lord.* He walked the hall and found Juanita outside Daisy's door. He handed her a small bag and a coffee. "Wasn't sure who might be here, but I figured you'd be hungry and tired."

"Got that right." She smiled.

"Has Daisy awakened yet?" Her prolonged unconsciousness had everyone concerned. Especially Dell.

"She seemed to wake up a few hours ago. Really groggy, though. I'm hoping she'll rebound sometime today."

"May I look in on her?"

She shook her head. "Chief'll holler if I do. Threw a fit to find that Danvers let Cat in. When she wakes up, and I believe she will, the chief needs to be the first person she speaks to. I've been trying to get that through to your friend."

"Miguel's been here?"

"Yep. A few hours ago, right before Daisy woke up. And he'd come by earlier, too. According to Evans. He had the shift before mine."

Sly dog. Cathy was right. Miguel did have feelings for Daisy. Ray would never have believed the man prone to romance. "Well, let me know when Dell does talk to her."

"Now that I can do." She grinned again. "And thanks for the breakfast burrito."

Dad had a worship service from Dallas on the TV when Ray returned to Mom's room. "How'd you sleep?"

Lousy, but he wouldn't tell his dad that. "Better than you, I bet."

He handed him a plate and coffee. "How is she?"

"Steady. Woke up for a bit around midnight." He pointed to Ray's box. "Whatcha got there?"

Ray explained about the drawer full of files that he and Cathy found at her house in town. "She needs to put the events of Mac's death behind her. And now that includes the diner's situation. I thought if I got her files ordered, the issues and grief she's dealing with might fade more easily."

"Good boy. I could use something to work on, too. Think I could help?"

Ray smiled. He'd always loved working alongside his dad, doing projects at the ranch, hauling hay, or repairing some of the tack. He'd missed the times they used to spend together. "You bet."

Even if this was all too close to the office job Dad wanted Ray to take on.

They spent a comfortable several hours making piles around the room. The stacks grew and sometimes combined. By noon much of the large box lay empty. Ray found a receipt, faded and wrinkled, near the bottom. He smoothed the slip of paper out along the window ledge.

"We should probably pack this all up, Ray. Your mom's friends will likely stop by to visit once the church service ends."

"Hang on." He scanned the page once more. "Dad, this is from Alexa Corp." Finding the name of his family's brokerage surprised him.

Dad glanced over his shoulder. "That's the kind of certificate from when I first opened the doors. From 1987 looks like." He pointed to the date, lost to Ray amid several lines of code.

His father started stacking the various papers into folders and returning them to the box.

Ray stared at the slip, recognizing share amounts and purchasing prices. "Is the purchase still good?"

"Well, yes, if Mac never sold the stock. I'd have to check the database to be sure."

Ray's eyes scanned over another section of code. Words here

and there popped out. Then he read one that halted him. Surely he hadn't seen … his gaze found the word again. He shut his eyes then opened them to refocus and make sure he read clearly.

"Dad …" He couldn't take his eyes from the paper. This could change everything.

"Amigo." Miguel spoke low as he edged open the door.

Ray startled. He pocketed the receipt and drew his friend into the hallway while Dad finished packing up the files.

Miguel dimpled. Whatever his news, it was bound to be good. "First, how is your mom?"

"Dad said she woke up around midnight for a few minutes, but I wasn't here."

"Has she said anything about her attacker? Any hint at all."

"No. Made her injury even tougher to take. She caught a movement. No face. She doesn't even know if her attacker was a man or a woman."

He sighed, the shine on his face dimmed. "That is a shame. I had hoped … But what about Daisy. Is there any news?"

Ray shook his head. "They gave her some pretty stout pain medication. She should awaken sometime today, though."

"The police officer outside her door will not let me visit."

"Yeah, I heard you've been asking to see her." He eyed his friend. "Little sparks?"

Miguel's face broke into a broad grin again. "Possibly. She is very beautiful, no?"

Ray nodded, though he preferred the more simplistic beauty of his redhead.

"I thought if I could visit, maybe I could comfort her."

"Ha. Not a chance, my friend. Dell's being careful. Don't hold his protection against him, though." Ray combed his fingers through his hair. "Any number of people could be up here trying to attack. I mean … well, this is Sevilla we're talking about."

"And that is my news, my friend. We are no longer speaking of *Señor* Sevilla."

Ray squinted at him. "What are you saying? We have some other madman trying to kill the people I care about?"

"No, no. But I heard from Pastor Seguirro from Aztippa. He learned from a report on the television today that Sevilla is gone. The man is dead."

Dead? "How? When?"

"I found the story online. He died during a fight in the recreation room of the prison."

Ray grabbed his arm. "He's dead. Does that mean this is over?" Hope welled up. This could mean Cathy's freedom.

"I have been trying to reach a man I knew in Chiapas," Miguel continued. "His brother worked for Sevilla."

"You had a connection to Sevilla?"

"Not that I could contact. Not until this morning. His brother escaped the raids on Sevilla's compound. Said that all of the property and money had been seized."

"How does that affect us?"

"No access to money means the hit man will disappear. He can no longer be paid."

Ray took a sharp breath. "Are you sure about this?"

"As sure as anyone can be with international affairs." The man's left eyebrow arched. "I am happy for you and your Cathy."

Heat skimmed up Ray's jawline. His words doused the excitement that rippled through him. "She's not *my* anything."

"Do not try to fool me, my friend. I have seen the way you look at her."

Ray sighed and leaned against the wall, his flannel shirt making a rubbing noise against the texture. "Yes, but I think she'll view my part in her jailing as a betrayal."

"You had her jailed? How?"

"Her godfather is Dell, the police chief you met. I called him … anyway. She learned that I had a hand in her isolation. And even if she could forgive that action, don't forget that I left her when I went to Chiapas. Cathy's an amazing woman, but she can't forget that abandonment. Who could?"

"I can see your point. You should never have traveled to Chiapas. Never have spoken against Sevilla. Look at all of the trouble he caused for you and the people you love."

Ray hung his head, wanting to argue, but without foundation to support one.

"And yet I do believe you should tell her of your feelings. She might still harbor some affection for you." He put his hand on Ray's shoulder. "As to her imprisonment, I think that was a wise move. But, with Sevilla gone, she can get back to living her life like a normal human being."

Exactly Ray's thoughts. Though she'd still never forgive him.

My kingdom for a shower. Though Cat didn't have a kingdom, a warm shower was part of her future with her release from jail. She didn't look at Dell, who still sat guard in the inn's parking lot after he dropped her off at the porch.

Honestly. When would he stop acting like a mother hen?

She used her key in the front door and stepped into the toasty foyer. Cat took a deep breath, relishing the scent of the lavender spray Myra used, mixed with the smell of Ellis's pipe tobacco. The mixed scent was as much a part of the house as the wing-back chairs in the study. A warm feeling wrapped her shoulders.

"So good to have you home, dear." Myra came from the kitchen and wrapped her arms around Cat's neck.

Ellis followed with a hug of his own. "I thought the police had you in the hoosegow." He took Cat's coat to the hook beside the curved banister of the main stairs.

Hard to explain, but she did her best with what little she knew. "Apparently the guy who threatened my life is dead."

"Is he sure?" Myra stood by the stove and transferred hot cocoa into a deep mug that she handed across the bar. She slid a spoon in the same direction.

Cat stirred the rich smelling liquid. Same color as Ray's sensitive eyes. Those eyes that had turned away from her. She sighed. "Sure enough to let me go. I mean, they know the drug cartel leader is dead. Everything else is supposition, I guess. But you know Dell. If he didn't have some pretty good intel at this point, he'd have never let me out."

Myra patted her shoulder and sat at the butcher block table. "I'm so thankful. But I swear, I don't know about Dell's common sense anymore."

"Don't be too hard on him, hon. I thought about it a long time this morning. What else could he have done?" Ellis pulled open the dishwasher and began extracting plates. "But the whole thing is over now, right?"

"Over is relative. Dell's still sitting guard in the parking lot."

"Hmm." Myra set her cup down. "I have half a mind to go out there and tell him what I think."

"You do and I'll come out and film the event to put up on YouTube." Ellis laughed. "I can see the caption. *Police Chief Shamed into Sitting in Time-Out.*"

"Oh you. He deserves a period in the corner. And I'm not afraid to tell him so."

"Just be glad he's out there, hon. In case he's wrong about the hit man."

Ice raced down Cat's spine. "Oh, he's not wrong." He couldn't be wrong. "You'll see, he'll be frosty for a few nights and realize that he's wasting his time." Her giggle sounded forced, even to her own ears.

She trotted up the steps to the room she had been using. Collecting her necessities, she made for her third-floor suite, finally, feeling somewhat normal again. She put the thoughts of Sevilla and his crazy minions out of her head.

Other things warred for her attention anyway. Reaching the solitude of her bedroom, she made a phone call for which she'd been struggling to find time.

"Mr. Trecoat? This is Cat McPherson, from Heath's Point, Mac's daughter ... Yes, sir, thank you. I miss him, too. But I wonder if you'd be interested in selling or leasing your empty storefront next to the diner?"

Ray climbed out of his truck into the frigid blast of the morning and walked through the inn's rocky lot toward the cruiser. "I've got hot coffee."

Danvers opened the door. "You said the magic word."

Ray pulled the cup from the top of the Thermos and twisted off the lid. Steam rose from the dark contents. "Any trouble last night?"

The man in the uniform squinted at him. "Nothing except a stubborn missionary who wouldn't take no for an answer."

So he'd heard about the exchange. Try as he might, Ray couldn't persuade Myra and Ellis to let him talk to Cathy. She'd gone to bed extra early, they said.

Ray filled the cup with the rich liquid. "Yeah, well, I'll have the chance to talk to her this morning."

Danvers reached for the coffee, but Ray pulled away. "That is, if you'll agree to let me drive her into town."

The cop raised a brow at Ray then glanced at the makeshift mug, its scent filling the air around them. "Okay. But I'll be watching for you in town, so don't take any detours."

Ray handed over the cup and Thermos as Cathy came out of the inn. She hiked toward them.

The lieutenant cradled the Thermos and mug to his cruiser. He pulled out of the lot and down the tar road.

Cathy jogged after him a few steps then stopped and turned toward Ray. She dropped her chin and glanced again at the disappearing bumper.

She hesitated, taking a step toward the inn.

"Rude of him to forget you like that," Ray called out.

She halted. Kept her back to him.

Please turn around. What would he do if she didn't let him speak to her?

She made a slow turn.

"I'll take you." He opened his passenger door.

Her mouth flattened. She glanced toward the house once more.

"You know you don't want to wake them this early."

She took a deep breath that lifted her shoulders and marched toward him. Avoiding his eye contact, she climbed into the seat. "I don't really feel much like talking, Ray."

He started up the engine. "Then you can listen. I have your dad's files behind the seat. Thought you might like to check them."

"I'm sure they're fine." She folded her hands in her lap.

He picked up the stock certificate receipt from the dashboard. "Found a little something I thought you might like to see." He handed the paper out to her, training his eyes on the road beyond the windshield.

He let the silence grow for a few minutes. Though her eyes rested on the slip, she seemed to focus somewhere on the other side of the paper. Obviously, words on the page didn't hold her attention.

About the time he turned onto Shepherd Street, she folded and slipped the note into her dress pocket.

He parked in front of the diner. How could he persuade her to look at the receipt more carefully?

She darted out of the truck. "Thanks for the ride." She unlocked Mac's front door without looking at him.

Hmm. Well, that hadn't gone as he'd hoped. He shifted into reverse and pulled backward several feet.

Wait a minute. Why accept this failure? What did he have to lose if he pushed the conversation? She already showed profound dislike for him. Her feelings couldn't get much worse right?

He shoved the transmission into drive, re-parked and turned off the engine.

Miguel had been right. Cathy deserved the truth, all the truth. The stock shares, his feelings, everything.

The cowbell above the door jangled as Ray pushed into Mac's Diner. Before his determination subsided, he threaded through the chairs and tables and strode into the kitchen. "Cathy, are you in here?"

Silence responded and a quick glance in her office showed its desertion. Where had she gone so quickly?

A scraping sound from the direction of the walk-in freezer caught his attention as the door swung wide.

Cathy appeared, still in her red coat, with clipboard in hand. She squealed and dropped the board, scattering her various papers.

"Ray, what are you doing here?" Her face took on a thunder cloud. "You scared the living snot out of me."

Why could he never make a subtle, smooth entrance? "I really need to talk with you. Please. I have something important I need to share."

Her lips flattened into an I'm-too-busy grimace.

"About that paper I gave you."

"You saw me read the thing. What else do you need to tell me?"

"Yeah, but did you really read through everything on the slip? All of the words?" Especially one of the words. "Do you understand what the receipt means?"

She sighed. "Look, I have to start logging inventory for transferring this place to Heath. I don't have time for games. I'm not trying to be ugly, but please leave me to my work?"

"I think I can help you."

Closing her eyes, she shook her head wearily. "I really don't need any more of your help. Don't take this the wrong way, but ..." She tilted her head and glanced toward the office doorway. "I don't think we should try to be friends anymore."

Was there a right way to take that?

Ray's chest contracted. He'd known, expected her rejection. Especially after his debacle at the hospital. But the actual words scraped his heart.

"I've thought about this a long time." Tears welling in her eyes discounted the mirthless laugh that came out. "I've had two whole days of little more than thinking about this ... you and ... me ... and ..." She bent down and gathered her papers. "I'm not ... what you need. I get that."

Not what he needed? She was everything. "Where did that idea come—?"

"Please. Just go."

Ray should have leveled with Cathy from the beginning. "I'm not leaving until you and I can sit down and have a talk."

"Fine." She sniffed and stood. "Stand there then. I have work to do." She carried the clipboard toward the office. Ray darted to block her.

"What are you doing?"

"I promise to get in your way and make everything you do take twice as long until you sit down and talk to me." If this was the only way to convince her to listen, then he'd play ugly. Might as well.

"Argh. You are so stubborn." She slapped the clipboard against her thigh. She took a deep breath, her jaw muscle tensing. Then she set the board on the counter with a loud exhale. "All right, you have five minutes."

"Ten."

She lifted her hands in resignation. "Okay. You've got until Grady gets here. Then I have to open things up." She marched into the dining room and perched on the edge of a chair.

He sat across from her. "Where's that paper I gave you?"

Her hand slipped into her pocket then emerged with the folded sheet.

He unfolded and spread the receipt on the table, right-side-up for her to see. He pointed to the important word halfway down the page, entangled in a myriad of code.

"Apple." She shrugged and glanced up. Her eyes sought his. "What is this?"

She hadn't discovered his meaning. He paused. The light would pop on any moment.

"Look at the paper, Cathy." Ray watched for revelation. "It's a certificate receipt from Dad's brokerage. From the early days of Alexa Corp. Dad double checked the record last night."

Her eyelids opened wide. "Wait, this is a receipt?" There went the sparkle he sought. "*The* Apple?"

He nodded, a smile spreading. "Your dad bought three hundred shares, and he never sold them."

She rose with a sharp intake of air. "I have shares of Apple?"

Ray stood. "That's right."

Whirling, she threw her arms around his neck. "I have shares of Apple!"

He laughed and clamped his good arm around her, lifting her and spinning around. He set her back on her feet. "That transfer you were speaking of ..."

She sobered and lowered back into her seat. "Won't work. Heath won't sell to me no matter what the price. He wants to prove something."

He sat as well, but beside her and scooted his chair close. "Prove what?"

"I don't know. That he can run the diner as well as my dad." She traced the words on the receipt. "That he's a better man than my dad."

"Then he's gonna fail."

A slight smile curved, and she glanced up at him. "But I took your advice yesterday. About serving the dinners from a small storefront. At least for the time being, I've leased the one next door. It's bigger than we need, but I thought it would work for a little while until we find the perfect place. And the people already know where to find us."

"You realize with this stock, you can buy the whole building." He pocketed the receipt.

"I could open up a soup kitchen?"

He chuckled. "You could do a lot more than that."

Her whole face took on sunshine. "Oh Ray, do you really think so?" She grabbed hold of his shirt front, and moved closer. Her emerald eyes, full of hope, captivated his with their pleading.

Resisting the urge to kiss her right then, he answered her question instead. "Yeah. I think, with an investment like that, you could open a whole food pantry or even more. Help people get back on their feet."

"I'm still losing Mac's." A slight pucker formed between her eyebrows.

"But look at what you might be gaining. You've always made a difference, just like Mac. Now you can continue his work."

She spun out of her chair. "You're right. Dad cared about the people, not the counters or the salt shakers. Heath can have this place." Her orange ponytail bobbed. Her features softened. "How can I ever thank you for this?"

"How 'bout you make me a partner in your new venture. Let me stick around more often." Ray gazed down at her sweet face, hoping she'd like the idea.

Her eyelashes lowered, but a smile crept onto her face. "Partner. That sounds rather nice."

Rise up, O judge of the earth;
repay to the proud what they deserve! ~ Psalm 94:2 ESV

Chapter 22

Opportunity for Cat to dance over her new knowledge swiftly fled. Grady's arrival brought along several regulars, who arrived earlier than normal, probably wanting to miss the promised icy blast.

"Again?" This winter had broken a number of records already, at both ends of the thermometer.

Grady winked. "That's what they're tellin'. 'Course you can never count on ..."

"Weathermen or the stock market. Yes, I've heard that before." Cat laughed. "But I'm not believing the stock market part." She leaned over and whispered her news to the dear man.

His eyebrows shot up. "What are you going to do with all that money?"

She grinned. "I've got a few ideas."

Grady set down the metal spatula and raised both hands. "Thank You, Lord. Shore am happy for you, my girl." He swallowed her in a big hug. "And you, too, preacher-man." He moved toward

Ray.

Cat misted. Ray had done so much for her. Even the jail thing, she could forgive. He hadn't wanted her there, but was willing to risk having her as a friend in order to ensure her safety. Sounded twisted, even in her head, but her heart swelled. So grateful.

No. Grateful didn't begin to describe all she felt.

The cowbell called her out of her revelry, though. She whirled and grabbed her apron and an order pad.

"I'm not doing anything today, and you need help." Ray caressed her shoulder. "Why don't you let me do the cashiering and table cleaning?"

"I can't make you be a busboy." She owed him everything. How could she reduce him to such a state?

"You forget. I'll also be head cashier." He brushed a bit of hair behind her ear. "That partner thing can start right now if you let me. And you're not making me. I want to." He leaned toward her ear and lowered his voice. "I bet you can figure out a way to thank me later."

His whisper shot electric volts all the way to her toes. Her cheeks warmed and a smile crept over her face as he preceded her into the dining room.

With an armful of menus, he began seating the early arrivers. Good thing. She'd not done any of her normal prep work beyond turning on the grill.

"A day like today deserves something really special." Grady rummaged through the pantry and came out with two large bottles. "I been waiting for the chance to try a new recipe."

"Bourbon? Where did you get bourbon?" And how did Cat know nothing about the bottles?

"Was a gift some years back. This stuff's too rich to make on any regular day."

Cat shrugged. "You better not let me smell any on your

breath."

He laughed hard and loud. "No chance o' that. I'd rather eat this stuff than drink it any ole' day."

As the icy weather ebbed and stayed to the north, customers flowed throughout the morning. News of Grady's dish spread down Shepherd Street. During what was normally the lull between breakfast and lunch, every table was taken. People wanted to try Grady's breakfast concoction. And no wonder. Heavenly smells drifted through the diner.

Cat had to congratulate him. "Everyone loves your French toast."

"Ain't nothing French about my cookin'. Pure-D Creole's what it is. From my mama's side the family."

"Wish we could have Creole Toast on the menu all the time."

"Too bad the bourbon's so expensive. Just ain't the same without the extra flavor." He measured out a portion from the first bottle, still rather full, and replaced the container on the shelf above the grill.

"Well, whatever you call the stuff, make sure you save a serving for me." The cowbell caught her attention, though Ray had been seating as many people as she had.

Darrell Heath came inside. "What do you think your trying to pull, little girl."

His outburst quieted the laughter and chatter. This man had a talent for sucking all of the joy out of a room. What did he want now?

Dell followed him into the room. "Now calm your boots, Darrell. What's all this about?"

"You've made a grave error, child."

Cat was the one with the job to do. She ground her molars. "Mr. Heath. I warned you that I'd get a restraining order if you continued to bother my customers."

Dell took the cue. "She's right, Darrell. This is a place of business. If you're not going to eat …"

He sidestepped and plopped onto a stool at the counter. "Coffee. Black."

Murmuring stirred around the room. The diners couldn't seem to decide if they wanted to chat among themselves or eavesdrop on Cat's conversation.

Ugh. She filled a mug and slid it across to him.

"I wasn't joking about the error." He had lowered his volume slightly, but Dell settled into seats at the table behind him and watched. Ray wasn't nearly as subtle. He laid his right hand on his hip and stood to the side of Heath like a sentinel.

Heath sniffed at the coffee. "You've wasted your money already."

Fine. She'd bite if it meant getting rid of him quicker. "How?"

"Renting the space next door. I know all about it." His lips pressed together in the semblance of a baby's smile or gas pain. "What you obviously don't know is that your father and I had an agreement drawn up with Trecoat when we first leased this part of the building from him."

Agreement? The man fairly burst to spew it out. She silently wiped down the counter without asking, if only to prick his impatience a bit.

The old man wriggled on the rotating cushion. "We have an exclusivity clause. Any business that rents the space next door can't sell any food whatsoever."

His delight put on the final straw. She faked surprise, widening her eyes. "You mean I can't open another diner?"

Ray blew an exhale in a quiet scoff.

"You can't sell so much as a candy bar." Heath burst into a single laugh.

Cat crossed her arms and narrowed her gaze. "I already know about the exclusive retail food rights that Mac's holds here."

He lifted his chin and regarded her through half lids.

"And I have no intentions of selling food next door. I plan to give it away."

"Give it away?" He tilted his head forward and to the side like a bird trying to identify a foe.

Ray nodded. "A food pantry, maybe a soup kitchen."

"Puh." The old man's sharp exhale carried as much concern as confidence.

"We're definitely continuing the sunset dinners, but I might also offer a lunch or a breakfast."

The man squirmed. "Next door. Homeless ragamuffins running around all day?"

A few chuckles erupted around the room.

"Like the idea, Cat." The owner of the lumberyard sat in the back corner with a few of his workers. "Count me in to help you when you're ready to set it up."

Several others chimed in with encouragement.

"I won't stand for it." Heath leaped to his feet and leaned close to point a finger in Cat's face. "You can't rezone the area on a whim." Darrell stood and Ray laid a hand on the old man's arm.

"No need to rezone." She smiled. "Check your contract with Trecoat."

Dell put a hand on Heath's shoulder. "Maybe this wasn't such a good idea, Mr. Heath."

Cat took his mug away. "Coffee's on the house. Have a nice day."

Heath reddened. "You're a fool, Cat. This place is still going to be mine next week and your little annoyance can only last as long as your inheritance. What was Mac worth, Cat? A month's rent or

281

two?"

Cat clamped her molars, but Dell had the matter in hand. "We're done here." He fisted the old man's coat at his shoulders and practically dragged him out the door. Heath should've known better than to slight the chief's best friend.

Dell returned after the forced eviction. "I'll probably get a reprimand from the mayor over that." Red-faced, he accepted a fresh cup of coffee from Cat.

"Saw the whole thing, Chief. Clearly disturbing the peace." The lumberyard owner toasted his mug toward the front of the room and several others followed suit, echoing his reply.

"Thank you both for standing with me. But he still wins. He gets Mac's."

"Is that the win?" Ray lifted eyes full of worry to hers.

"It is to him. I don't see the justice in it all. He gets his way. Wins my father's diner and succeeds in destroying everything Dad did for this town."

He shook his head. "Except the most important part. Heath doesn't get the impact Mac made. He doesn't understand it, can't duplicate it, and will never remove it. And the help you hope to continue offering to the homeless will prolong that legacy for years."

"Longer, I hope." She laid her hand on his. "If you'll help me?"

Ray wanted nothing more than to help Cathy with her new enterprise. But her old one required immediate attention. He barely had time to nod before the room began filling up with people again.

Mac's renowned lunch rush was bigger than he'd ever seen. With no open tables, or stools, a few latecomers even shared a table.

And more than one patron served himself coffee or tea refills. At one point, Amy Slaughter filled a pot and made the rounds.

Miguel came in about the time the final few tables emptied. "I am glad to have caught you both. Your area is lovely, but I miss the warm breezes of home."

"You have a flight?" Ray touched his friend's shoulder. "You need a ride into Dallas?"

"Yes. And no. I have a flight in a few hours and will take back the car I rented. But I thank you for the offer. I am delighted that your trouble is at an end, dear Cathy. I wish you good luck in your endeavors."

"What will you do in San Diego?" Cathy gave him a brief hug.

"My father runs a business there. I will join him at present."

"Not the ministry?" Ray had thought that was the man's dream.

"No, amigo. Mission work is not for me. For you, perhaps. But I like comfort too much."

Ray mustered a half-smile that he didn't feel. "I'm sorry to hear that. And I'll miss you."

Miguel took his offered hand. "I am sure we will meet again, my friend."

Cathy closed the door behind him, shoving it against the breeze that kicked dirt into the room. "Don't look like that, Ray. He's still a good man. He just isn't the perfect missionary you thought him to be."

He shook his head. "You know, I don't really know that much about him. But I owed him so much. I thought he was serious about God's work."

"He probably is. But in his own way." She straightened his collar.

He shot her a sidelong look. "So you're saying a person

doesn't have to be a minister or a missionary to have a ministry and make a difference for the Lord?"

Revelation dawned on her face. "Did you rig Miguel's exit to trap me or only take advantage of his words?"

She'd figured it out. He took a step closer. "I simply recognized the truth of what you said. And you're right."

She fixated on the collar of his shirt, a slight smile spread. "The important thing is you're serious about God's work."

Grady bellowed from the kitchen. "Well, somebody better be serious about *our* work. That ugly cloud y'all are seeing out there s'posed to unload on us right about sunset."

Cat glanced out the window. He was right. The overcast had a green tinge in the distance. Never a good sign. Wind from the north carried an intense chill, and thunder rumbled. She glanced at the black clock.

"Looks like we're in for it." Grady turned on his little radio and tuned-in on a news and weather station from Dallas.

The national weather service has issued ...

"Great." While Cat loved rainy nights, she had never been fond of the instantaneous weather changes in North Texas and sure didn't cotton to the stormy appearance outside. "This is going to make for a soggy dinner."

"Let's bring them inside." Ray joined her at the glass.

Grady wiped down the largest section of the grill, already cooled. "Oh, Mac tried that once. Had half of the silverware gone the next day." He squirted water across the top and sopped it up with a clean towel. "Only takes one thief with deep pockets."

"I think we have to take this chance. We can still use the

plastic ware and Styrofoam bowls we always do. Nothing to steal with that."

"What about Dash and them others 'at don't like to come inside?" Grady punctuated his question with his fists on his hips.

Cat glanced outside again. Lightning flashed.

"They'll come inside tonight." Ray pulled the flat of water bottles out from under the counter.

She knew better. "No they won't. At least Dash won't. But he'll be okay under the awning of the empty building next door."

Grady grumbled something and headed into the kitchen.

Thunder rolled past, covering the older man's complaint. Cat tore her eyes from the west-facing windows and turned to find Ray staring at her. The intense expression on his face caused her heart to flip.

"We need to talk."

Marji Laine

He rescued me from my strong enemy, from those who hated me,
for they were too mighty for me. ~ 2 Samuel 22:18 ESV

Chapter 23

Ray watched Cathy wipe down a perfectly clean table. She buffed the edge for a solid minute before he laid his hand on hers, insisting on its stillness.

She turned her beautiful green eyes toward him. In them, he witnessed a blend of hope and fear.

He reached for her, cupping her face in his palm. "You're my hero."

The hope he'd seen faded. Her chin dropped. "Your what?"

"My hero. I mean it. I love how you've embraced the ministry God laid out for you. You don't even realize what He's doing in your life. The people that come to the meals know you care."

He moved in to kiss her, but she tilted her head downward, forcing his hand away. "I'm no hero, Ray. You're the one who stopped that drug cartel. I just stayed here doing what I've always done."

The memories flooded through his thoughts, burying the romance he longed to rekindle. Pain gripped his chest with the images. "I didn't stop anyone." His voice had a sharper edge than he'd intended.

He took a deep breath to quell his emotions. Before he went further, she deserved to know what a complete failure he was. "If I'd been focused on the work God had for me, those people at my mission would never have died."

"I knew the mission was attacked. What happened there?"

"I'd been warned for weeks to get out of the country. Then the threats started, including the places where I spoke." He gritted his teeth as a tear formed. "I didn't tell anyone. Thought I could talk my way out of anything. I was wrong."

Silence lingered. His gaze drifted out the window where the wind blew dust and trash down the street. He swallowed. "Hooded men came into the mission in Asmirandu. They didn't want to talk *or* listen. They started swinging their knives." He took a sharp breath as he saw Matteo and heard his voice again in his mind.

"I don't even know who survived. I just ran."

She moved toward him, but he turned. He had to finish. Had to show his complete fraud. "If I'd left Sevilla alone. Not tried to be a hero. None of those people would have been hurt. Nothing would have changed."

He felt her eyes on him. Her fingertips found his back. "You'd never have come home."

Startled, he turned his head and locked eyes with her. The truth of her words gored a hole straight through.

God brought him here. Led him to this place. Reconnected him to Cathy. "You're right." He cupped her cheek.

Her breath warmed his face as she accepted the light brush of his lips. She laid her cheek against his chest with her hands on either side. He wished to hug her properly.

At the risk of breaking the moment, he leaned back, unlatched the sling that trapped his left arm. Still sore, the pain seemed worth the effort if he could properly hold her again.

Thankfully, she waited in silence then settled again into his arms, both of them this time. His heart beat faster as he took in her scent. The honeysuckle of her hair, the citrus perfume she wore. Slowly, her hands drifted to encircle his neck and he drank in her nearness. His lips found her temple. Traveling downward across her cheekbone, he pressed another kiss beneath her eye.

They brushed lower, gently caressing her mouth. She didn't draw away. He kissed her again and felt her response. With a sigh of surrender, his mouth fell upon hers. Hungry to dispel her doubts. Desperate for his own to fall away.

Her head tilted as she melted into him, returning the passion he'd been denying for weeks. Her fingers curled where his hair had grown over his collar.   ·

The kiss cooled and Ray took a deep breath before he opened his eyes. Cathy's were still closed, her fringe of long, tinted lashes lying like lace against her creamy skin. He strengthened his hold on her, burying his chin in the warm curve of her neck.

"Ray, I've missed you so much." Her breathy confession in his ear ignited a fire in his heart. One that had never fully burned out through those long years sprang into a charged inferno with her gentle words.

He breathed in her scent. "I don't ever want to leave you again."

She released him like he burned her, her eyes wide and her chin hanging. "Do you mean that?" She gave a slight shake of her head. "Do you really mean that?"

Closing the gap she'd made, he rested his hands on her waist. "I want so badly to believe you."

He'd not let her down. Not this time. "Cathy, I love you." His

289

own whisper almost escaped his hearing. "I've always loved you." His voice strengthened as he continued. "I don't know how I survived in the field without you. To go on without you now would be like living with only half of me.

A precious smile crept across her face as a tear spilled over her eyelashes and down her cheek. He pulled her into another embrace. "I want you always in my arms. You fit here."

She lifted her face and locked her eyes with his once more. "We fit together." Her lips pressed against his. Combined with her words, the kiss sent his mind whirling into forever thoughts.

"'Bout time you two worked stuff out." Grady's laugh startled them both, but the clunk of the front door ended their revelry.

Cat felt tingly down to her toes. Even after Dash opened the front door, she had to steady herself.

"Mister Ray. Something done happened to Frankie. You better come."

Dash actually stepped through the door to give his announcement. Cat gasped. Something bad had altered his behavior.

The big man glanced up and stiffened. He eyed the entrance and caught the door as it closed. Stepping back outside, he shoved his foot over the facing to hold it open.

Grady hustled in from the kitchen as lightning flashed outside. "Cat, stir the stew and turn the grill back on."

"Will do."

He probably didn't even hear her. He and Ray followed Dash out the door at the moment the sky opened. She lost sight of them in the washing machine effect of a hard, westerly wind.

Wouldn't do any good to stand there staring. She shut her

eyes. "God, bless Frankie in whatever trouble he's in. And keep Dash and Grady and Ray safe. Oh, Lord, keep my Ray safe."

She said the last with open eyes as she crossed to the kitchen. Thunder rumbled again, closer and louder. She carried pans of leftover cornbread and cobbler from the cooler and laid them out on the counter. The stew was in a pickle bin. Her stomach growled as she hoisted it onto the side of the grill. And no wonder. She'd had nothing since the bite of Grady's special breakfast. She slipped opened the fridge and pulled out a plastic bag of lunch meat. A bit of the cornbread would make a good sandwich.

She reached to flick on the grill, but the sound of a nearby click caught her attention. Cat spun, dropping the handful of deli meat to the floor.

Miguel stood inside the kitchen entrance. The glint of a stiletto winked at her. But the broad smile on his face and the mean look to his eyes caught her breath. "Well now, my dear Cathy. Did your friends finally let you out of your playpen?"

"What are you doing here? I thought you were catching a plane."

"To fly to San Diego? No my dear. I live, quite freely I might add, in my kingdom in Chiapas. Your missionary did not succeed. I will have my country under my control again in a matter of days." His dimples didn't look nearly as cheerful with his hard black eyes boring holes in her.

She gasped. "You're Sevilla?"

He nodded with a brief bow.

"But you can't be. You're the one who saved Ray's life."

"And he trusts me entirely, does he not?" He took a step into the room. "My intention has never been to kill Ray. Not until after I destroy him. Then when he begs me to end his life and his torment, I will consider the matter." He spoke through gritted teeth. "But first, I will remove everything he loves."

In a nanosecond, the rage passed over his face replaced by a tender smile. "And whether you believe or not, my sweet Cathy, he loves you."

"Why would you do all of this?"

"I am only doing to him what he has done to me. That is scripture, no?"

She shook her head. "No. You're supposed to treat others the way you *want* them to treat you."

His eyes became slits. "An eye for an eye. And a tooth for a tooth."

She glanced down, her gaze landing on the large knives that pierced a block of wood on the other side of the island, but they were out of her reach. "Is that why you want to hurt me?"

"I do not wish to hurt you. I wish to kill you. As my dear wife and my precious ..." His voice broke.

"Ray wouldn't. He didn't kill anyone."

"Oh no. He could not do such a despicable thing." He lifted his arms and pivoted. "The heralded *informante de la policía.*"

Cat watched for an opportunity to reach for a knife, but he didn't turn away from her.

He leaned on the wooden island. "A glor-i-fied tat-tle-tale." He pronounced each syllable carefully.

He took a step toward her, and she retreated. She'd never reach the knives at this point. In her periphery she caught sight of pots and pans on nearby shelves and hanging from a rack.

"*He* started the raids. He sent those killers to my house. He might as well have pulled the trigger himself." The man's voice shook with rage. "And murdered my son. My son." He took a step toward her.

She flinched, breathing deep. "But why Daisy? Why Violet?"

Maybe if she kept him talking, the others would return.

He made a soft growl. "Impatience is my greatest weakness. Daisy finally confided to me where I could find you at Ray's house. I would like to say I attacked his mother on purpose, but that was simply a misidentification." He chuckled. "Not a situation that will be recreated here."

Before she could think, he rushed at her. She grabbed the closest weapon, a cast-iron skillet. She pulled it from the shelf in mid-swing, catching him above his ear. The man's scream reverberated with the dull tone of metal hitting bone.

Pain seared through her arm and across her chest as his stiletto pierced her. Shoving away, she slipped on the meat she'd dropped, falling to her knees.

The man stumbled through the entrance cursing her.

She crawled across the floor, between the island and the sink. Putting the firm wooden structure between them, she reached to turn the knife block toward her. "Why are you doing this?"

Her question only brought more curses but bought her the time she needed to grab her best knife. Much larger than his, she had an advantage. But the pain from her left side told her she wouldn't have energy for much longer.

She listened for movement, but the hard rain and rumbling thunder disguised nearby sounds. Maybe he'd gone? She grasped the edge of the island and peered over the surface.

What was he doing?

A crash of thunder and the flickering of the lights startled her. She felt her adrenaline subsiding, her arm already covered in blood. He poured something all over the aprons hanging in the doorway. Why?

Too late she realized that the liquid was Grady's bourbon. At the moment of revelation, the material, the boxes stacked on the shelves, and the door facing lit up with a roaring sound. Cat peeked around the island and found her only exit to be an inferno. As she watched, he turned over a table to effectively block the doorway. Even if she moved the heavy piece, she couldn't act quickly enough to escape from getting severely burned.

She grabbed at a hand towel on the edge of the counter and covered her nose and mouth. Standing she eyed the serving window. Thankfully, she never turned the grill on.

Crawling through there had been a game when she was little, but not for the last ten years. Could she still fit?

Ray's shirt adhered to him the moment he left the shop. The rain almost swallowed the big man, but he kept Dash in sight and Grady stayed by his side.

They tracked down an alleyway and found Frankie struggling to sit up. A large lump had risen on his head.

"What happened?" Ray's alarms shifted into high gear.

Frankie mumbled in Spanish, but Ray understood that someone had hit him from behind. Frankie leaned hard to his right, and Dash supported him, practically lifting him to his feet.

"Let's get him to the diner and get some ice on that mountain." Grady shouted over another nearby lightning strike and its accompanying sonic boom. He and Dash supported him while Ray darted ahead to prepare a place for him inside Mac's.

The rain subsided somewhat as he rounded the corner from the alley. A man flung out of the diner, falling against Ray's truck.

"What's going …?" Ray hesitated a moment. The man wore a hooded coat, and he staggered like he was drunk. He seemed to catch his balance and darted down Shepherd Street.

Ray made a beeline for the diner. An eerie glow flickered through the windows as he burst through the front door.

Flames licked at him from the kitchen entrance. He reached for the extinguisher next to the counter and directed the spray. If the flame retardant made a difference, he couldn't tell. Yellow fingers slapped at the ceiling and set off a steady roar that grew louder. They spread to the booth situated next to the opening and the paper goods at the counter.

"Cathy!" She had to be there. Ignoring the ache in his shoulder, he slipped off his jacket and started beating at the flames.

"I'm here." She climbed slowly onto the counter and slipped over into the dining room side. "I climbed through the window." She slid to the floor.

"That's real good, honey." He tried to lift her, but with his weakened arm, he only shoved her a few feet closer to the door.

He hadn't missed the bloody sleeve of her uniform. And with the smoke filling the room, they had to get out. Now.

Dash burst in. "Miss Cat."

"I've got her over here. I can't lift her."

He came toward them. "I got her. You hold the door."

Ray stumbled toward the exit with Dash at his heels.

He pulled the door open and found Miguel leering at him. Blood coursed down his face. "Miguel, are you all right?"

He caught sight of the man's knife.

"She is dead. Your Cathy. As I promised."

Truth dawned with a blinding flash. The resounding crash thundered through his body. "Sevilla?"

"You are a fool, Raymond Alexander. To think you could stop me? To think you could beat me?"

Blood oozed from a wound and tracked down the right side of his face. He kept that eye closed. If only Cathy and Dash would stay in the man's blind spot.

"May I add that your sweet Cathy died a grueling, painful death."

"Not without a fight, I see." Ray pointed to the man's head.

The man growled. "And I'll let you pay for her violence and failure."

Though they plan evil against you, though they devise mischief,
they will not succeed. ~ Psalm 21:11 ESV

Chapter 24

Cat eyed the picture of her parents as Dash carried her to the door. "Wait." She couldn't leave that precious memento behind to burn. He set her on the floor, which tilted a bit before she got her bearings. "I can't leave this. She pulled the photo from on the wall. The heavy frame weighed her down, making her droop, but she struggled to lift it with her good arm.

A voice halted her. Miguel's voice. No, Sevilla's.

Ray hesitated outside the door and responded to him. Sevilla's stiletto appeared beyond the facing of the door. Ray leaned away and said something else.

Cat struggled to raise the picture above her head. She brought it down on the hand as the man jabbed the knife. With a sick, cracking noise, Sevilla screamed and tumbled forward.

She tried to lift the picture to strike another blow, but the frame slipped from her grasp.

Dash stood next to her, ducking under the ceiling. He rushed forward, grabbed the picture, and slammed it down on the man's head.

Glass crashed. Wood splintered. Sevilla went down as the photo ripped. Chunks of frame and dangerous slivers littered the sidewalk.

Cat fell as well, in a heap next to the man.

Ray kicked the knife out of Sevilla's lifeless hand. He knelt beside Cathy and snatched his phone from his pocket, dialing 9-1-1.

Dash hovered, shaking. "Need to get that bleeding stopped."

Grady hollered from the porch area in front of the other store, "What's happened?"

Dash scooped her up again and joined the other men under cover.

Ray glanced at Miguel, no Sevilla. The man hated him so much. He felt for a pulse in his neck.

Dell pulled his cruiser to a stop in front of him. Flashing lights illuminated the area in red and blue.

"This is Sevilla." He pressed his neck again. "Though I'm not convinced he's still with us." Ray stood and left Dell to deal with the man. He joined Dash on his knees next to Cathy.

The big guy had used a handkerchief, surprisingly clean, as a bandage against Cathy's shoulder. She winced, but he kept on the pressure. "Lemme have your jacket, Mr. Ray. We don't need her going into shock or nothing."

"Where'd you learn about first aid, Dash?" Ray slipped off the jacket and bunched it up.

Grady lifted her, and Ray smoothed the pad under Cathy's shoulders.

"Army. I's a medic in Afghanistan. Ts'how I got my name. All those tight little buildings. I always went in for the soldiers, but I's the quickest out for shore."

Claustrophobia. No wonder he preferred the outdoors. Ray leaned over Cathy and kissed her forehead.

"I'm okay." With her eyes closed and face pale, the words calmed him.

Alarms from the volunteer fire department took over for the subsiding thunder. The engine pulled close to Mac's, blocking off part of the street and drawing onlookers from drivers and shop owners all over downtown.

Danvers arrived at a run with an EMT to look over Sevilla.

Dell crossed toward Ray. He started trotting, his cheeks awkwardly pale. "Need some help over here." He knelt on the wide step next to them. "Is she gonna be okay?"

"I'm fine, Dell." Her voice sounded strong, though Ray wondered if she'd faked the volume.

"Well, your friend over there has head trauma. A lot of it. And a broken wrist from the looks of things."

Ray glared at the man he'd believed in. He couldn't see his wounds, but his eyes remained closed. His face almost innocent, though Ray knew better. "No friend of mine."

"I wasn't trying to kill him er nothing." Dash breathed heavy. "He had a knife."

Ray turned his attention to someone who deserved it. "Easy, big guy."

Dell lifted a calming hand. "You're not in any trouble. I only want to know what happened." He kept his voice low.

Ray patted Dash's shoulder. "Dash did the head banging. But that broken wrist was all Cathy. And here we thought she needed protection."

Grady waved at one of the EMTs. "What she needs is a doctor."

Ray moved out of the way and let the men work. Another

tended to Frankie, flashing a light in his eyes and icing the knot at the back of his head. "I don't think he has a concussion." He spoke to Frankie in decent Spanish. "Says he doesn't like hospitals."

"I'll take care o' him." Dash helped him stand, and they started across the street.

"Hey, Dash." Ray caught up, extending his hand.

The big man took it.

"Thanks for what you did in there."

"We's all gots jobs we do. Y'all's is inside. Mine's out here. Protecting these folks best I can. Helping them get on. Like Cat and her daddy." He shook his head. "With God's help, wouldn't let nothing happen to her."

Ray grinned and tightened his grip for a final shake.

By the time he returned to the diner's side of the street, the fire was out. Paramedics loaded Cathy onto a gurney and lifted her into an ambulance.

"You think I could go with her?" he asked the one who latched the door.

"Family only."

"She doesn't have any family. I'm her ..." Business partner? Boyfriend?

"Sorry, mister. If you're not married or engaged to the lady, you can't ride with her."

He grimaced as the man climbed into the cab and pulled away.

That issue would need a quick remedy.

Dell clamped a hand on his shoulder. "Why don't you and me go for a little ride?"

Ignoring the pain in his shoulder, Ray braced himself as Dell drove steady, but fast. Every turn stabbed him, but not more than he deserved.

How could he not have recognized Sevilla? True, the man had

a heavy beard and sideburns in all of the pictures he'd seen. But that fact didn't make him feel any better.

"You didn't do this, Ray." Dell read his mind.

"I should have known he was Sevilla."

"Not if you'd never met him before. Never heard his voice. Why do you think he gained your trust down at the mission?"

"He wanted me to welcome him here. To get close enough to Cathy so he could cause me the most pain."

"Exactly." He turned into the emergency lane at the hospital. "And he failed. Don't forget that. There's no such thing as absolute power. Not on this earth, anyway."

He climbed out. "Looks like she just arrived."

"Are either of you gentlemen family?" The nurse at the desk stopped Dell from advancing closer to her gurney.

"I'm her godfather. She doesn't have any other family."

She handed Dell a clipboard full of papers.

"Not yet, anyway." Ray spoke more to himself than to the nurse, but Dell heard him and turned to stare.

Ray matched his look. "What? I'm ready to finish what I started."

Dell's face thundered over. "You better be careful with her heart this time. Hear me, boy?"

"Yes, sir." He nodded, meaning every bit of his promise.

The chief relaxed his glare and eyed his shoulder. Without the sling, his arm dangled at an odd angle.

"Miss, I think my friend here needs a doctor as well. He has a severe dislocation to his shoulder."

The nurse handed him another set of papers on a clipboard.

"Oh goody." Dell moved to the waiting area.

"Friend, eh?" Ray followed.

"I figure I should get on your good side early if I'm wanting an invite to the wedding."

He had to smile at the thought.

Philip Slaughter rushed in through the visitor doors. "Ray, are you all right? Dash told me that someone attacked you and Cat."

Dell stood and calmed the man. "Both are fine. Cat has been on the wicked end of a blade, but she's getting stitched up. She'll be okay."

"Thank heaven."

"Indeed." Ray couldn't agree more.

"And I have good news for you." Philip took a seat opposite. "Your mother is stronger. Your dad wants you to come up as soon as you can, but he doesn't want to leave Violet alone."

As much as he wanted to check on Mom, he couldn't leave Cathy. Not now. *Not ever.*

"Now, your dad is the one who should fill out all of your paperwork, boy." Dell stood. "I'll just take this right up there to him. And I can sit with your mom for a few minutes to let him come down."

Ray thanked the man. God reminded him again that he wasn't alone. Not in facing Sevilla. Not in taking care of his mom. Not even in dealing with his feelings for Cathy. How odd that God had used that madman to give him the courage to restore their relationship.

Philip glowed. "But that's not the best part. Your information was completely wrong, Ray. I heard from Pastor Hernandez in Chiapas. Your mission in Asmirandu recovered fully from the attack and is going strong."

Ray's eyes widened. Of course Sevilla lied about the mission's destruction. Anything to hurt Ray. His mouth hung open. "I have no words."

"That's a first." His eyes twinkled. "He told me to tell you that your young student, Matteo, is doing a fine job of sharing the gospel and preaching."

"I thought he was dead."

Philip shook his head. "No, son. None of the people there died. Matteo had a bad gash across his shoulder and several others were injured, but the only person who died was one of the marauders that the congregation killed by accident. Several of the members picked up the stumps they were sitting on and threw them at the man."

His mouth hung open. In God's mercy, his error in judgment hadn't cost the lives of those dear people after all. And Matteo preaching? He'd always believed the man had that ability in him. The mission would be in good hands.

"Ray?" Dad rounded the corner from the main entrance. "What's this I hear about Cat?" Wrinkles formed around his eyes.

"She's going to be okay, Dad." He gave him a one-armed hug.

"You've gotten the doctor report already?"

"No, no. I just know." He recounted as much as he could about the attack on Cathy.

"Your friend was your enemy." He shook his head. "How did none of us see that?"

Ray had no answer.

"But the good news is, he's done. He has no power that we don't give him." Dad's words struck a nerve. He had to make sure that Sevilla had no chance to escape this time.

One of the EMTs walked into the waiting room and Ray met him. "You brought in the man with the head injury, right?"

"Got him outside. You family?"

"No. I'm the one he tried to kill. You do have police with you right?"

"Yeah. Lieutenant Danvers rode back there, but there was no need."

"People can fake being unconscious. And this guy's a master at deception."

"Maybe. But they can't fake dead." The EMT continued through the security doors.

Danvers entered, scratching in his notepad with a short pencil. He glanced up. "Ray. Need to talk to Dell."

"He's upstairs in my mom's room, but …" He caught the policeman's arm as he started in the direction of the elevator. "The EMT said Miguel, I mean Sevilla, is dead."

"Yeah." He nodded. A smirk appeared. "Both of them."

Ray didn't enjoy the death of anyone, but this man's demise put a final ending to Cathy's danger. "You're sure."

"Flatlined. Cat's no longer in danger."

Many waters cannot quench love,
Nor will rivers overflow it; ~ Song of Solomon 8:7 NASB

Epilogue

A light texture of gray washed over the April sky and Cat shrugged on a jacket over her sweats and T-shirt. Returning to her parent's historic Victorian in town had been rough. Back to the place where she and her dad had been so happy. But she needed to stop running away from her sadness. Facing the feelings, the grief, helped her overcome and hopefully put that chapter of her life behind her.

She passed the picture of her parents that had saved Ray's life. Freshly repaired by an expert in Dallas and rehung in a less weighty frame. At least that had been saved. She touched the faces gently and wished they were here.

Zipping up her mint warm-up jacket, she trotted down the steps and out onto the street. Her left hand felt empty without Ray's diamond adorning it. She glanced down at the mild tan line left behind when she returned the ring to him almost a week ago. Shouldn't the mark be gone by now?

Jogging down a few blocks and around the corner, the sight of her beloved, burned-out diner came into view.

Thank You, God, for that fire. What a crazy thought. But the complications and financial burden required for the repairs finally convinced Heath to sell. And not just his controlling interest, but the entire fifty-one percent. He planned to sit back and watch her business crumble into bankruptcy.

Maybe so. Maybe not. Being so close to losing the place gave her more of an acceptance should that be the case, someday. And if her failure was Heath's only pleasure, she felt nothing but sorry for the man.

She slowed as she neared the building. Most of the charring on the walls had disappeared, the front half of the dining room gutted and cleaned along with the kitchen and the office. Reinforced beams in the roof hid under a bright blue tarp. Her windows, though covered with soot, remained intact. They needed a lot of elbow grease to get transparent again.

Running the block, she crossed into the other side of the downtown area before reversing her course. She took the last bit at a sprint. Raising her hands above her head, she walked a ways, passing the diner completely and standing in front of the empty storefront next door. The new sign looked great.

Sunset Mission.

She'd scheduled the official opening in a few weeks, but the ministry had received pledges and donations to stay open for a year or more. Office cube walls gave some privacy. Already a couple of men had spent a few nights there while they found new footing, jobs, and places to live. Hot plates, crockpots, and a couple of George Foreman grills weren't ideal, but they worked for any hot meals they needed until the diner reopened in the fall.

Cat had even learned how to speak freely about her faith. Starting with Daisy as soon as she woke up. Her new sister in Christ had such a hunger for the truth.

Dad would be so pleased. A wave of loneliness washed over her. Unwilling to let despair have any influence on her, she turned in the direction of the McPherson homestead and returned the way she'd come at a slow walk.

She rounded a corner and spied Donna sitting on her steps. Daisy lounged in a chair on her porch, the scarred initial still visible on her cheek, but not affecting the joy and hope that filled her face. She claimed the S stood for *saved, sanctified, and standing before the throne.*

"There you are. Myra has called three times."

Donna stood next to her. "I can't believe you took off like that."

"I always jog on Saturdays."

"I told you she'd forget." Daisy stood and leaned across the railing. Her hair, cut short and back to its natural dark color, blew across her forehead. Her eyes danced.

"I didn't forget anything." Cat snatched up the towel that Donna held out and trotted to the shower with her friends at her heels.

She'd only barely gotten under the water when Donna pounded on the door. "You'd better hurry, or you'll miss your hair appointment.

"Ha, fat chance." Cat knew better. Her stylist was also her chauffeur.

"I'll take care of the bags." Daisy called up the stairs after Cat turned off the water. Funny how their friendship had grown. Daisy still had her moments, but she always smiled with a genuine glow and spoke of how Christ saved her—first her life and then her soul.

Cat slipped on some jeans and a t-shirt and wrapped her hair up into a towel.

Donna shoved a green sweater into her tote. "Am I really going to need this?"

"You can bet your gonna be cold in the mountains." The bob of her head shook the black curls.

Cat let her friends spoil her. A delicious breakfast at a restaurant on the freeway. Manicure, makeover, and hairstyling at Betty's Beauty Salon. Letting Donna drive, Cat rode in her sleek new burgundy Sonata across town, feeling primped and pampered.

Myra met her at the door of Shepherd Street Baptist Church and whisked her into the large sitting room outside the ladies' bathroom. Floor length mirrors took three corners and the scent of roses hung heavy.

"Everything's ready, and I brought you some homemade butter cookies to snack on." She gave Cat a brief hug and dashed out of the room.

"Don't eat too many of those." Donna teased her and pressed a comb into the crown of her hair.

After more primping and cookie-snacking, the trio made their way down the hall to the foyer. Cat stared in the mirrored wall behind the guest desk. Nothing like she expected. She actually appeared … elegant.

The sheer material on her shoulders and down her arms accented the lace-covered bodice that broke into a silk skirt with lace insets at the waist. No kudzu. No kewpie-doll waddle.

Her veil, thin as smoke, gave a halo effect. White was usually an awful color on her, but the sweetheart neckline of the dress camouflaged her pale skin and completely covered the scar of the night Ray saved her.

Ray. He waited at the end of the aisle. Waited to return that diamond, and the cluster that went with it, to her finger.

She glanced at her two friends, wearing unmatched light-blue dresses, as they stepped down the aisle. She fingered her bouquet. Each of the fragrant, white roses as perfect as the silk bluebonnets nestled between them.

Dell joined her and tucked her hand into his elbow. He gave her an encouraging grin, but the tear in his eye revealed his grief for the man he replaced.

As much as she adored her dad, he wasn't the man of her dreams. She stepped to the doorway and caught a glimpse of that man. Her hero. Her gaze locked with Ray's in hope of forever. She grasped the soft skirt and took her first step into a new life.

Discussion and Bible Study Questions

1. COUNTER POINT deals with power. What can a young woman do when exalted power wants her dead? That's the premise of the story, but it's also an answerable question. Check out David's answers in the Psalms, chapters 3, 7, 52, 54, and 59. All of these Psalms have the answer in common, but not the circumstances. What is going on in David's life as he creates these songs?

2. The story begins with what seems to be the ending of Sevilla's drug cartel, but instead it opens a wound that nothing but blood and death would heal. While Sevilla isn't a likable character, at least I don't think so, how is his vendetta against "the missionary" justified, within his own mind if nothing else?

3. Psalm 20:7 provides a foundation for this book. It's obvious to see how Sevilla leans to the wrong side of this verse. It's probably easy to view the same tendencies in others you might know. But have you ever placed your faith in something besides the Lord? Maybe friends, reputation, prestige, talent, money? When is a time that you found yourself sideswiped when something or someone you depended on didn't stand up to pressure? (Do I sound like I'm speaking from experience? Oh, yeah. I've been there.)

4. In Chapter 3, Cat asks God, "How much more can I lose, Lord?" At that moment, she'd lost her car, the man she cared about, and her father – in fact all of her family. Every element of her life was being peeled away. She has a ping of conscience with her lack of gratitude, but is it wrong to ask God questions? Where does it seem that she's placing her faith at this point?

5. Cat's struggle to maintain a good attitude and kind behavior toward Williora and Lila Heath make an impact on Daisy. And Cat's continued compassion, even toward rude or unkind people, serves to turn Daisy's heart. Everyone has seen the effects that poor reactions have on people. Have you ever witnessed effects from positive, godly reactions? Have you ever been the one under pressure to display the fruits of the Spirit toward someone who doesn't deserve your kindness? (Galatians 5:22-23)

6. Psalm 1 cautions the reader against walking in the way of the wicked, standing in the path of sinners, and sitting in the seat of scoffers. Looking around at the world, it's easy to see how this progression works. The verse that opens Chapter 7 is about the haughty, arrogant man. The character for whom the verse has been chosen is apparent, but who else in this chapter could benefit from remembering this verse?

7. In Chapter 7, Mrs. Heath fusses about the owner of the hardware store because he's unwilling to close his shop in order to make deliveries to her. In today's world, there's a growing atmosphere of entitlement. People believe they deserve things that were considered privileges in other eras. What does the Bible say about what we, as human beings, deserve? What do we, as Christians deserve? If there's a difference, why?

8. In Chapter 10, Mrs. Dupree speaks to Ray about her kids, Micah and Melody. Particularly, she mentions how her young people, in seeking freedom, go about searching for it all wrong, being moody and striving after the wind. 2 Peter 2:13-19 speaks about the "freedom" that the world offers. Contrast that with the freedom described in Galatians 5.

9. In Chapter 13, Ray's dad pressures him to work for Alexa

Corp, the family brokerage. Ray resists, but this isn't the first time his father had tried to coerce him to give up his passion and work for him. Have you ever given in to pressure such as this, doing what someone else wants you to do even though you have no leading in that area? Have you ever been guilty of acting on your own personal agenda trying to influence or persuade another to do as you wish? How does Joshua 24:15 apply to this situation?

10. Is there a character from this story with whom you particularly identified? Who? And what do you feel you have in common with that character?

Other Books by Marji Laine

Working as a crime scene cleaner is perfect for neat-nick Dani Foster, who has recently been relocated by her witness security contact. But she can't hide the investigative reactions drilled into her by her detective father. Even though her discoveries, and the explorations they instigate, often put her into funny, uncomfortable, and sometimes dangerous positions.

GRIME BEAT, Book 1, is available at Amazon for free. Also available are GRIME WAVE, Book 2, GRIME SPREE, Book 3, and GRIME FAMILY, Book 4.

About the Author

Schooled by experts such as Perry Mason, Jessica Fletcher, and Dr. Mark Sloan, Marji Laine writes the mysteries she craves with a touch of romance and a thread of faith. Her series are made up of stand-alone stories with satisfying endings where justice prevails. She sets most of her books in and around the Dallas area, where she has lived all of her life, or in the small towns of East Texas that she adores.

A homeschooling mom of four, she loves to discuss possible book scenarios with her daughters. Their conversations have even been known to alarm waiters and store clerks. At which point, one of her girls will roll her eyes and say, "My mom's an author." That pretty much explains the way her mind works.

Catch up with Marji at her website, MarjiLaine.com, on Amazon, Facebook, Twitter, and at WriteIntegrity.com website.

From the Author

Dear Reader,

My sweet mom asked me if time and money were no issue what would I be doing? Back then, I had a thriving scrap booking business and spent every spare moment working on my next class or planning my next retreat. So when I answered, "Write," without hesitation, I actually surprised myself.

I hadn't realized the passion that the Lord had given me for writing. I'd been trying to follow His leading but finding myself more and more frustrated and stressed. The revelation of my passion brought about a new question: Why wasn't I writing?

He'd given me story ideas, so procrastinating was, in reality, me refusing to follow where He was leading. I'm so thankful to the Lord for giving me this passion and helping me use it to His glory. And patiently coaxing me onto this path. What a blessing to indulge in a "job" that gives me so much joy!

Some wonderful people came alongside me with this first published novel, both challenging and encouraging. I so appreciate my critique friends from the Dallas Chapter of the American Christian Fiction Writers for teaching me so much about writing and publishing. Special thanks also goes to Jennifer Slattery and Carol Towriss for their revision expertise.

I'm so grateful to Tracy Ruckman, Fay Lamb, and the group at Write Integrity Press for believing in a brand new writer and giving me the support I needed to keep honing my craft and putting out more books. I also appreciate my three clutch players – friends, prayer warriors, and proofreaders: Angela Maddox, Julie Hausmann, and Fran Williams, for their help and expertise in making

COUNTER POINT as polished as possible.

I especially thank my family. My dear boy and adored daughter-in-love who cheer me on. My precious girls who help me work through scenes and refuse to let me get down or give up. And my sweet hubby who takes care of so many details, so I can indulge in my passion and give this career the attention it deserves.

And I thank you, dear reader, for taking this journey with me. May the story inspire you as you walk your own path with the Lord, and ignite the fire of your "first love" within your heart.

In His Spirit,

Latest romantic suspense release by Write Integrity Press

Grieving, threatened, running for her life.

Abra Carmichael's husband, Beau, has been murdered. She begins to realize that the man she loved was never who he seemed. Beau's secrets endanger Abra, their twin sons, and everyone who loved him. When Abra's life and the lives of their boys are threatened, she flees to Amazing Grace, North Carolina, and to Beau's family-- people she never knew existed until the day of Beau's funeral.

The walls have ears ... and voices.
Voices that threaten ...

**Thank you
for reading our books!**

**Look for other books
published by**

Write Integrity Press
www.WriteIntegrity.com